KILLIAN

WHISPERS FROM A HIDDEN WORLD

BOOK ONE

TN TARRANT

KILLIAN

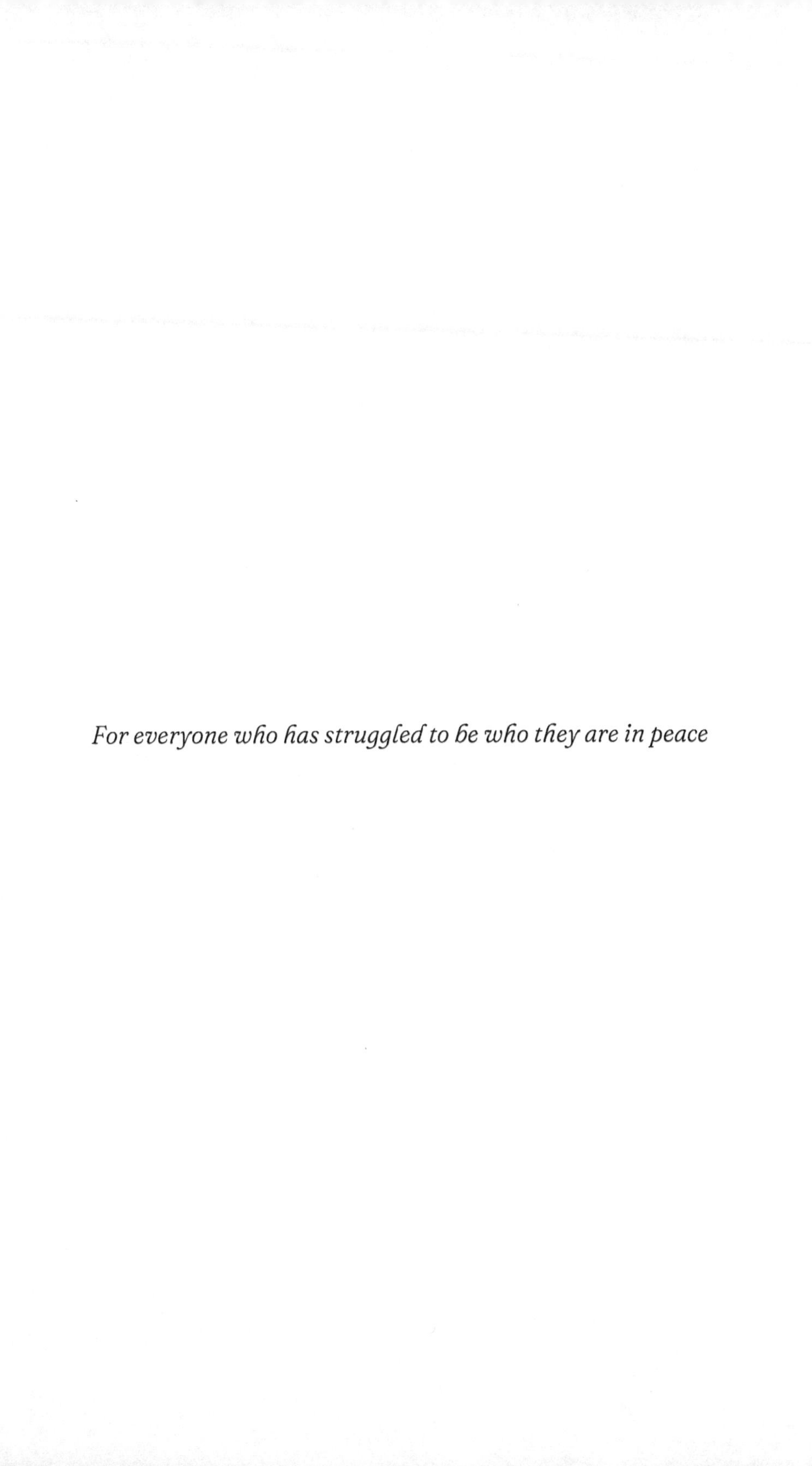

For everyone who has struggled to be who they are in peace

Acknowledgments

To Lisa Arhart and the What Writers, thank you for listening to me go on and on about my aliens and their issues, and your support for my work. Hopefully, there's enough setting in here for you, Lisa!

GLOSSARY

Artris: Matriarch, Clan Leader. Usually a woman, but title, or formal address of "Lady" does not change if holder of the rank is male.

Senki: Mother. Variations: *Seƀki, Secki*

Senka: Father. Variations: *Seƀka, Secka*

Masenki: Grandmother

Masenka: Grandfather

Mysen: Beloved child

Mysena: Beloved grandchild

Myseni: term of affection or comfort for a small child

Ausen: aunt, *Auseni-* friend of family type aunt

Usen: uncle, *Useni-* friend of family type uncle

Sennrojai: Rare type of *Tii-su*, with far more diverse psionic abilities, a kind of Guardian of Rimalia and its culture and citizens. Often work to protect Rimalians from humans, but also to protect humans from Rimalians when needed. Facilitate communication, and even travel through telekinetic abilities.

Miisen: Pronounced (me-ee-sin). Lifemate. A psionic bond so powerful that that those who experience it will die together. It cannot be mindblocked, or prevented, and attempts to reject the bonding can be devastating, even fatal. The bond supersedes all others, and is not subject to rules and agreements concerning marriage, or any other relationship. Is usually only between two people, without regard to gender or sexual orientation, but is known to occur in three, or more rarely, four people.

Verification: procedure by which the memories/knowledge of a person or persons is psionically examined by qualified *Tii-su* and, oftentimes, members of the *Artris* Council, or the entire Council. On occasion, the participants of this procedure may be limited. In rare cases, after a special vote which must be unanimous, a Verification may be forced, although there can be severe consequences to such a decision.

Tii-su (tee-ee-su) Healer: Title earned by all practitioners of the medical arts. Applies equally to nurses, physicians, counselors, surgeons, etc. An earned rank, without bias toward male or female, although some *Tii-su* earn the rank through the need to protect their own well-being, not out of a wish to go into medicine. All *Tii-su* are very strong telepaths and/or empaths, and are expected to act for the health and safety of their patients, and others in general.

Nameless: those who have been disowned by their Clans, or that have disowned their Clans. Usually male, but females are among them as well. Most likely to have the most unwanted duties within a community and most likely to be abused, due to their lack of family ties and rank.

Rimalians: humanoid alien species almost indistinguishable from humans, due in part to small genetic adaptions upon arrival, evolution, and some interbreeding. Rimalians are psionic in nature, with varied levels of sensitivity, are generally stronger than humans, have a distinct size difference / sexual dimorphism (females being larger than males), and exhibit a skin color range in both "human" tones, as well as their original colorings of deep shades of purple, red, green, black. Rimalians that display such coloring and/or the iridescent shimmer of their evolutionary past are called Ancient-skinned or throwbacks, and in recent centuries, as prejudice against darker skin became more prevalent, have been hidden away in protected enclaves in Africa or on the Island.

Rimalia Island: the large island the Rimalians colonized initially when they arrived on Earth and named after the planet they came from. While Rimalian enclaves exist all over the world, Rimalia remains the center of their culture and government. Every Clan has a House there. The Council Building, the Medical Complex -- which includes the Asylum and Baths -- and the Archives were built on a large plain not too far from a very large natural harbor. The island has been continuously occupied since arrival, and despite having no standing army or navy, has never been conquered. The Island of Rimalia is located in the Atlantic Ocean, not far off the coast of Africa. Basically, a micro-continent formed much like Iceland, near the Romanche Trench area of the mid-ocean ridge, but is considerably older, and thus not as active geologically. The channel between the island and the Necropolis territory on the African continent claimed by the Rimalians upon arrival is less than one hundred miles at its widest point.

FOREWORD

What if humanity wasn't the only sentient humanoid species on the planet? What if they hadn't been for over thirty thousand years? And what if this other species came from the stars ...?

The second of two species that had evolved separately on the same planet, Rimalians were all that remained of Rimalia, a planet long since consumed by its dying sun. Forced to land due to dwindling supplies and deteriorating spaceships, they made Earth their new home, their new hope for the future. With them, they brought the last children of the Ancients and what little science they found useful.

A matriarchal society, Rimalians had learned from the errors of the Ancients. They would not despoil this new planet, or themselves, through war and ever-escalating technology. Instead, they would be an agrarian people, caretakers of this gift Deity had given them.

Remaining completely separated from the evolving humans, they thrived, partially because Rimalians were physically and mentally mature after fourteen Terran years, and partially due to the things they had brought with them from their doomed home world. In time, the last children of the Ancients died—some having lived over four or five millennia—content in the fact that those few they had trained would continue to guard and guide the Rimalian people.

These *Sennrojai*, especially strong psychics whose normally recessive Ancient genes were dominant, and incredibly important to the safety of the Rimalians, could be born of any Rimalian family, although generally a larger number of Ancient ancestors meant a stronger likelihood of a *Sennrojai* birth. The fact a *Sennrojai* usually lived more than a millennium, combined with the decisions they were often called upon to make, and the violent fear their abilities sometimes evoked from the other Rimalians, led the *Sennrojai* to retreat from the general Rimalian populace for their own protection. After all, watching those you love die, year after year, while you remained healthy and young, would break the strongest of hearts. Eventually, it came to pass that a Rimalian could live their entire life without ever seeing one of these fabled beings.

Over time, humanity spread across the globe, and a hard decision needed to be made. Rimalians would either have to live side-by-side with humans, close but separate, outwardly adapting while remaining true to themselves ... or stay immured on their island, which could not support their growing population and so was unfeasible. Thankfully, human societies of the time considered a child to be an adult by the time they reached their early teens, and were still primarily agrarian in culture, making integration easier. Rimalians adapted by living mostly in Rimalian-only towns and villages, called enclaves, and life went on.

By the twenty-first century, as humans reckoned it, human children were no longer considered adults so young. Now, eighteen was considered the threshold of maturity. Had Rimalians matured at the same rate, this would not be any trouble. However, the Rimalian homeworld had a shorter year, about ten months, instead of twelve. It meant that the equivalent of eighteen Rimalian years was only fourteen Terran years. As long as Rimalians stuck to their own, this was not a problem. However, thanks to Social Security numbers, or other identifying numbers, a governmental policing system, and an interconnected computer system, issues with humans arose. Most of these problems were circumvented by home schooling and self-policing, even with the rapid growth of Rimalian young. A Rimalian of fourteen looked like an eighteen-year-old human and had adult responsibilities, which could lead to some conflict when a human learned of this.

Still much the same as they had been when they first arrived on this planet so long ago, the Rimalian people lived, laughed, and loved, hidden in the midst of a younger, more volatile species. As humans became more technologically capable, Rimalians prayed to Deity for their human "neighbors" to outgrow their more violent inclinations before they, like the Ancients, destroyed their planet of origin. Earth.

PROLOGUE

THIRTEEN-YEAR-OLD Killian Larrestes limped down the hall to his mother's study, followed by his little sister and little brother, as well as his father. He was bleeding from his cheek, shoulder, and groin, and his knee was twisted, but he still had his virtue, at least. His mother would not allow this insult to go unpunished. How dare Anan touch him without his consent!

He knocked on the door, ignoring the rest of his family as they asked what had happened. He looked at his father, and then glanced at his younger siblings and shook his head. His father caught on and shooed the younglings off. Whatever had happened wasn't for young ears. Killian promised them he was okay, and he'd talk to them later. His mother finally answered the knock, telling him to come in. His father followed him, for which he was glad. This way he'd only have to say it once. He felt shaky as it was.

His mother, Janet Larrestes, stood up behind her desk, with a surprised look on her face, when he and his father came in. "Killian, what happened? Were you attacked?"

He nodded grimly. "Yes, *Senki*, I have been, but I fought back well enough to escape Anan."

"Anan?" Janet's expression was puzzled. She shook her head. "I don't understand. Are you saying Anan attacked you?"

Killian nodded again as his father put a comforting hand on his shoulder. "Yes, *Senki*, Anan attacked me. She attempted to rape me, *Senki*."

"Surely there must be some mistake, Killian. Anan is your fiancée. This marriage has been arranged for a year now. I thought the two of you liked each other." Janet sat down again, not even bothering to ask how bad his injuries were.

"I thought so, too, *Senki*. I mean, I liked her. She has always acted properly, even if I haven't always liked the way she treats me. But this is different. This isn't a misunderstanding of two people needing to learn how to deal with each other. She tried to rape me. I had to walk home from the park in the square because I wasn't getting back into that car. Who knows what she would have done then? I had to slash her face with my dagger to get her off of me long enough to get away." His knee really hurt, but his mother had not given him leave to sit. His father had taken the first aid kit out and busily began to clean Killian's face, carefully removing Killian's shirt to look at his shoulder.

"Janet, this wound on his shoulder needs stitching," David Larrestes told his wife softly, as he gently checked the wound. Killian hissed and barely managed not to say every cuss word he knew.

"That can wait until we settle this." She picked up the phone. "I'm calling Anan here. We're going to sort this out."

"Can I at least take the boy to get him cleaned up and dressed properly?" David asked, silently warning his son to be silent. Killian obeyed, giving his mother a respectful look. She was a good woman, but a bit of a martinet.

Janet held her hand up for silence. She spoke briefly on the phone, ordering Anan and her mother to come to the house to sort out this obvious misunderstanding. A cold chill went through Killian as he listened to those words. Surely, his mother believed him, didn't she?

Janet hung the phone up and looked at her husband and son. "Anan is getting her face stitched up. Apparently, you've done some damage to your fiancée." She spoke sourly.

"Good, maybe she'll learn that no means no," Killian said. "There's no misunderstanding, *Senki*. On my honor, I promise you. She attempted to rape me. I ran as soon as I was able to get away, and the only way I could make her let me go was to use my dagger."

"Go get cleaned up. David, see to his shoulder and get him back down here in two hours. That's when Anan and her mother will be here. We'll deal with this then," Janet ordered.

Killian opened his mouth to protest, but David gave him a quick pinch, warning his son to hold his tongue.

"Of course, Janet, two hours," David agreed.

Killian bowed his head. "Yes, *Senki*."

David gently led his son out of the study and helped him up the stairs. Taking his son to his own bathroom, he gently sat the boy on the side of the tub, helping him strip out of the torn and bloody pants. When the boy was nude, David saw bloody scratches on the boy's groin, including what looked like scratch marks on the boy's penis. Killian was beginning to shake. Wrapping a thick towel around his son, David hugged Killian, and then knelt in front of him.

"Look at me, Killian." He waited for his son to focus on him. "Janet isn't likely to accept your version of this incident." Killian started to protest, but David gently covered his mouth with his fingertips. "I believe you." He closed his eyes. "But she won't. Your mother just has no use for males, other than marriage fodder and to keep her comfortable."

For the first time, Killian realized there was no love in his parents' marriage—just vows honored to bitterness. He wanted to say something, but he had no idea what.

David had more to say. "Listen to me carefully. Males have rights your mother's not taught you, as she should have. But my *Senki* taught me, and now I'm telling you. Any male has the right to ask any woman of age to speak for him, if no one in his family will. I hope I am wrong about your mother, but I don't think I will be. Your sister isn't old enough. Normally, you could ask

Anan, as your fiancée, but you are accusing her of attempted rape. You can't ask her, and her mother is unlikely to agree to. Do you understand me?"

"Speak for me how?" Killian asked, confused.

"Speak on your behalf to the Magistrate or the Council, or an *Artris*. Actually, you can speak to the Magistrate on your own in this case. You've been assaulted. This should be brought to the Magistrate. I don't think that your mother will do it. Get in the tub." David had started the water running as he spoke.

"Isn't this washing away evidence?" Killian asked without moving.

"The *Tii-su* can look into our minds, Killian. If it is brought to Magistrate, you'll be your own witness. So will Anan. Get in, my boy."

Killian obeyed this time, with his father's assistance. His knee hurt like a bitch and it was badly swollen.

David whistled. "You walked home on that? From the square?"

"Marabel Solentai offered to give me a ride, but..." Killian didn't finish. His father didn't need him to; he understood that Killian wouldn't want another female to touch him.

"That was very good of Marabel," David said neutrally.

Killian reassured him. "I was polite to her, told her I'd be okay, that I'd rather walk. She just followed me in her car until I got to the house."

David nodded. He wouldn't be surprised if Marabel's husband Lyle had some questions for him the next day. Marabel wasn't an idiot. The whole village knew that tonight was the first unchaperoned date between Anan and Killian. At twenty, Anan was older than David would have liked for his sensitive son, but Janet hadn't asked his opinion. When he'd tried to give it to her anyway, she'd reminded him of his place with the back of her hand. He quickly planned on how best to help his son, just in case. While his older son was in the tub, washing, almost scrubbing himself raw, David quickly went to the nursery room. His younger son Jaden was almost too old for the nursery, but his daughter Araminta would be there for another year. He gathered them close and hugged them.

"Come, be quiet, and come give your brother a hug and tell him good night. Tell him you love him. He's had a bad night."

"Will Killian be okay?" Jaden, asked, holding Araminta's hand.

David nodded, hoping he wasn't lying to his children. Never had he been as glad as tonight that Janet was as psi-blind as he; otherwise, she might know of his efforts to help his son. He suspected that his wife would try to enforce the marriage contract, and he knew his son well enough to know Killian would refuse to marry a woman who would try to rape him. Moreover, Janet might just disown him for it. He prayed to Deity he was wrong as he sent the children to their brother. He opened the bottom drawer in the antique changing table his mother had given him when Killian was born. The first time Janet hit him, after his mother's funeral five years ago, he began secreting money into the false bottom of it, carefully hoarding his pin money, without being obvious. Then Marabel's husband would deposit it for him, in an account his mother had set up for him before her death, that Janet was unaware of. Tomorrow was when he and Lyle normally had lunch, but he didn't think Lyle would be making that deposit tomorrow.

He quickly took the money out and counted it. A few hundred. It wasn't much, but hopefully it would be enough to keep the boy safe awhile. Sticking the money into his pocket, he quickly fixed everything and went back to his bathroom. Killian was carefully leaning over the side of the tub so the younglings couldn't see his groin. Araminta was staring at his shoulder. As David watched, she reached out and touched the slice on Killian's shoulder very lightly. It stopped bleeding. Then she touched it again, and it visibly healed even further. Araminta dropped to her knees, and Killian caught her awkwardly.

David jumped forward and took Araminta in his arms. Killian stared at him, then at his shoulder, and then back at Araminta.

"Better now, Kil?" she asked with a tired smile.

"Yeah, Araminta. I'm better now," Killian answered, giving her a smile, and touching her gently. As Killian touched her, he got a buzz of her tiredness, and that her shoulder ached now. While David held her, he gently pushed aside the shoulder of her nightgown, enough to see her shoulder. It wasn't marked, so he wondered if he misinterpreted her feelings.

Without a word, David took her to bed, praising her and Jaden for helping their older brother feel better.

A few minutes later, David was back, and Killian finally felt clean. David held up some antibiotic ointment and indicated Killian's groin and the scratches there. "I'd better do this, okay?"

Killian nodded, flushing. He tried to focus on something else. "What about Araminta?"

"Do not tell your mother. I'll have to think on this. The best thing is for a *Tii-su* to discover her, but it has to be done carefully. I have to figure out how to make sure Jaden says nothing, as well." David finished anointing the scratches, and then handed Killian his robe. "I'll get you some clothes. You're very cold right now, so I'll bring you two of everything."

Killian gave him a confused look but nodded. What was his father so worried about? He hoped Araminta came to a *Tii-su*'s attention soon. It was important to train *Tii-su* from a young age, and she was already four, almost five.

His father came back with clothes for him, warm leggings to wear under clean jeans, and a T-shirt, as well as a heavier shirt and a sweater. Two pairs of socks and his heavy winter boots. What in all the worlds? Then it hit him. His father was dressing him well, in case his mother threw him out.

"She wouldn't." Killian looked at the sad, resigned look on his father's face. "Would she?"

"Deity, I hope not. I hope I'm wrong, that I'm bundling you for nothing. But for your sake, I can't take that chance. There's an estate fifty miles from here, south, held by the Jonai. The Jonai have a reputation for taking in people when they need help. If need be, get there. You'll be safe there."

David finished giving Killian exact instructions and made him repeat them. Their two hours would be up in thirty minutes.

"If that's what happens, that's what you do, Killian. There's money and jewelry in your leggings."

Killian had wondered what the flattened lump was.

"It'll get you a cab, lodging, food, whatever you need for a few weeks if you're careful with it. Just don't let any humans you come in contact with realize that you are underage, even by our standards."

Killian listened carefully, his throat swelling with the effort not to cry. He hadn't broken down when Anan attacked him, or when Janet seemed not to believe him, but his father preparing him to be thrown out was threatening his control. He looked at his father and saw he was having the same difficulty. Killian threw himself into his father's arms.

David began to cry. "I'm sorry, Killian. I don't know what else to do. I have to take care of your siblings, too..."

Killian cried, too. He understood. His father was torn between the child old enough to fight back, and the ones that weren't. He made sure he put his dagger in easy reach. Never had he been so glad before tonight that David had quietly taught him a few tricks about using a dagger. They held each other tight, saying their goodbyes, just in case.

Two hours later, Janet physically dragged her disowned son out of the house, threw him down the front steps, and slammed the door. He began walking south; following the instructions his father had given him. He tried not to think about anything, just put one foot in front of the other, with one goal in mind: the Jonai estate. He had no name. He was nothing. He was just another Nameless male.

1

WHEN KILLIAN FINALLY ARRIVED at the Jonai estate, after three days walking, and ill from infection of his injuries, he found the *Artris* himself in residence. Richard Jonai, one of the few male *Artris*, was surprised when one of the tenants brought an unkempt, injured, exhausted, and scared thirteen-year-old to him. Some of his bruises had been freshly given, because he'd flipped out when one of the farmers who greeted him was a woman. Without thought, she had reached out to support an obviously hurt and tired young man, and he'd lost it. She'd called for her husband and her eldest son to come help her, as she restrained him, trying to keep him from hurting either himself or her. Her menfolk hurried over to help calm him, and she went and got the horse and cart. As soon as they'd calmed him a little, they got him in the cart and brought him up to the manor, her boy sitting in the cart with Killian. The tenant had called ahead on her cell, so Richard and his young granddaughter, Janara, who was training as a *Tii-su*, were waiting.

Richard had carefully picked Killian up and taken him inside, followed by the tenant's son, as well as Janara. Janara reached out and snagged Richard's wrist and sent him the psionic suggestion to call Georges, a male *Tii-su* with a talent with children and young adults. He nodded in agreement and left the room to do so. The tenant's son, William, stayed and sat next to Killian, holding Killian's hand.

"It's okay. Lady Janara won't hurt you, and Lady Richard won't either," the boy told him, rubbing his knuckles.

Janara nodded. "That's right, Masenka will take care of you. So will I. What's your name?"

Killian's face burned with shame. "I have no name, my Lady." He couldn't look her in the eye.

Her eyebrow arched. "You were disowned?"

He managed to nod, closing his eyes. The boy holding his hand gripped tighter when he tried to take his hand back, curling in on himself. The pain in his chest was far worse than the pain in his knee, feet, or more private places. He felt a gentle touch on his knee and then his feet. The pain lessened a little—a feather light touch over his forehead, even a feather-light touch near his groin, and it suddenly seemed easier to breathe. He still hurt, but it seemed just a little easier to bear. He opened his eyes to see Janara leaning over William to touch him. She smiled.

"What was your given name?"

"Killian, my Lady," he managed, still unable to look her or William in the eye.

"Do you wish to keep that given name?"

He thought about it. He didn't know. It had been the only name he knew. Should he choose something else? Janara patted the hand William continued to hold.

"It's okay, Killian, you don't have to decide right now. We'll call you Killian for now. It's better than 'Hey you, what's yer face.'"

Killian couldn't help it. He laughed weakly at the sudden mental vision of going through life, answering to "Hey you, what's yer face." William and Janara both smiled gently.

"We need to clean you up, get that knee elevated," Janara said briskly. "I'll go get some warm, soapy water and some clean clothes."

William gave her a startled look. "I'll go get them, my lady," he said quickly.

She patted him on the shoulder, shaking her head. "No, you stay here with our new friend, William. I need to see when Georges will arrive. Killian's knee needs serious attention, but I don't know enough to say what he needs for it."

Killian looked at her, confused. "What do you mean?"

She gave him a serious look. "You may need surgery to repair your knee, or you just may need to stay off of it for a week or two. I'm in training, and I don't have enough experience to advise you properly as to what you should do about the injury. Speaking of advising, how old are you?"

"Thirteen, my lady."

"Okay, so we need to find someone to speak on your behalf, as well. Okay." She came back to the bed, took his free hand gently. "Who disowned you?"

"*Artris* Janet Larrestes."

"All right. You relax. We'll take care of you. William, stay with him."

Georges later arrived and examined him, deciding the knee would need an X-ray, and the injuries to his groin would need a specialist's care. Georges then asked Killian's permission for he and Janara to examine him psionically, which Killian allowed. Something about Georges made him feel safe and warm. They learned of everything that had happened, including the incident with Araminta. They assured him that the matter would be brought before the Magistrate, and that they would see to Araminta as well.

The next day, the Magistrate arrived and questioned everyone, including young William. Then she called Anan before the *Artris* Council, including Janet. Janet protested the proceeding, stating it was just a hysterical male's ramblings. Lady Jonai pointed out that the "hysterical boy" was the son she disowned four days previously.

The trial had proceeded quickly, held two days after Killian arrived at the Jonai estate, and based on their own memories, Anan was convicted of attempted rape. She was sentenced to be publicly flogged and to pay reparations to

Killian, for three quarters of her inheritance. Janet was castigated for her treatment of her son and her refusal to protect him.

When Janet returned home that night, she caught David trying to leave with the children. Both Jaden and Araminta witnessed their mother murder their father, and Araminta's mental screams attracted the attention of every sensitive in the area, including a *Sennrojai.*

Lucretia, the *Sennrojai* in question, followed the mental signature of the child's screams to appear in the hall, stopping Janet before she could further harm either of the children. Within seconds of her arrival, Lucretia sequestered Janet in the Jonai estate's holding cell; the only place in the area designed to safely hold any accused criminal.

Lucretia gently gave both Araminta and Jaden the relief of unconsciousness. Quickly assessing the children, as well as looking at their memories of what happened, she learned Janet had flown into a rage that David was leaving, taking Araminta with her. David had told Janet he had a responsibility to protect his children, even from their mother, if need be. He informed her he was leaving, and he would have someone contact her about the divorce he was going to request. Janet had attacked, attempting to get to Araminta, and David had fought back, which led to Janet literally beating him to death. Poor Jaden and Araminta had been frozen with fear, never having seen such behavior from either of their parents.

After grabbing Janara from her bed to look after the children, giving her quick instructions, Lucretia then took herself to the Jonai manor and began pulling in the entire Council of *Artris.* When questioned, she explained to Lady Milossa Jarvai, the Head of the Council, what had happened. Lady Jonai's phones began ringing, both his cell and the phones in the house. Several cars and horse-drawn carts began arriving and people got out, demanding to know what the highest-ranking *Artris* in the area was doing to find the terrified child they'd heard in their minds. Richard sent them all into the house, telling them to make themselves comfortable.

It took the Council an hour to get organized, including calming Killian, who was frantic about his siblings. He, too, had heard the cries, but he'd been sleeping, unsure if it was nightmare or reality.

Lucretia, and Lady K'Arith as *Sennrojai*, took the Council through Janet's memories of the incident. Janet had refused to give permission, and the Council, with Kelia K'Arith abstaining, voted unanimously to order the two *Sennrojai* to do it anyway. Only later would Killian learn the risk that vote entailed. And only later did he learn how unusual it had been for the Council to conduct justice at the "scene of the crime" as were as well, but with a *Sennrojai* having had to intervene, it wasn't unheard of. All those who came to the estate, looking for answers and to help the child whose cries disturbed them, were seated outside, having dragged every blanket in the house out for everyone to huddle under, to watch the proceedings. There just wasn't a room big enough in the house for everyone.

The Council Head called for any objection to the unanimous vote, and the people were silent. *Artris* Larrestes had to answer the accusation, whether she wanted to or not. What they found was a pattern of quiet abuse that began after David's mother's death, five years previously. Lyle Solentai stepped forward, telling the Council of David's efforts to plan the escape of himself and his children, of the money he'd slowly and carefully saved, which Lyle had faithfully deposited into an account secretly opened in David's name.

Janet defended herself by stating that a woman had the right to kill a husband who displeased her, especially one kidnapping her heir. Milossa replied that that may have been true a thousand years before, but it was no longer acceptable behavior. David hadn't been trying to harm her, or the children. He, therefore, had done nothing that would excuse Janet's actions. She had no grounds to kill him.

The Council deliberated for another hour, this time with Kelia's participation. The Council convicted Janet of the murder of her husband, and she was sentenced to death. Then Killian was called forward. William, who had been asked to stay with

Killian until he felt a little safer and could get around on his own, helped him to stand in front of the Council.

A chair was brought to Killian, and Milossa indicated he should sit. He swallowed nervously. He'd never seen a Council gathering before Anan's trial, and now he was facing another one in the space of a day. His mother had never taken either her husband or son to the quarterly gatherings on Rimalia.

"Killian, you are the disowned son of Janet Larrestes, are you not?" Milossa asked formally.

"I am, my Lady."

"This Council knows of the events that led to that unjust punishment. The Larrestes name is proud and honorable, the actions of Janet notwithstanding. The circumstances here are unusual enough for the Council to make a few out-of-the-ordinary decisions. First, have you anything to say on Janet's behalf?" Milossa asked.

"No, my Lady. Until a few days ago, I would never have believed that my mother had no sense of true honor."

Many of the Council nodded in understanding. Milossa continued. "Second, the Council unanimously offers to restore your name."

"You can't do that! I am *Artris* of the Larrestes! You cannot override my decree of disownment!" Janet burst out.

"You, Janet, are no longer *Artris*. You have shamed your house and Clan, and you sully this body. You are not fit to be *Artris*, and you are sentenced to death. A sentence to be carried out shortly, but we can do it sooner, if you like," Milossa responded coldly. She waited for Janet to respond. Then she looked at the crowd that had grown even larger. "Is there anyone here, woman or man, who would plead clemency for Janet?"

The Council watched carefully, waiting a full ten minutes for anyone to speak. No one did. Killian was surprised Anan's mother said nothing on Janet's behalf—they were thick as thieves.

Finally, Milossa nodded. "So be it. Does anyone here, woman or man object to young Killian being restored to his name?"

Now Anan's mother Sienna did speak. "A woman has the right to disown a male that dishonors his family, bringing shame to them. That is what that little male did. It is wrong to overrule that decision."

Lucretia spoke before Milossa could. "The only ones who brought shame and dishonor to their families in this incident are you, Anan, and Janet. Killian Larrestes acted with honor, both to preserve his virtue and his house's honor. The female who should have been the first to defend him, instead, attacked him. The woman who should then have defended him, and called out his attacker, tried to sweep the incident under the rug because doing the right thing by a male was too inconvenient for her. It was easier to get rid of the boy who refused to marry one that would rape him, and offer up her younger son instead, despite his youth. The young male acted honorably at every turn."

Milossa gave Lucretia a short nod. "Quite true, which is why the Council has taken this unusual step." She looked around. "Does anyone not involved in that shameful attack have any objections?" Again, the Council waited for ten minutes for anyone to speak. Milossa nodded again. "So be it. Killian Larrestes, you are restored to your name and the responsibilities and privileges of your house and station. As you are still underage, and it will be ten years before your sister Araminta is of age to assume her rightful place as *Artris*, the Council will appoint a caretaker for you and your siblings.

"You will attend Council meetings, and Araminta will join you upon her seventh birthday. You will learn to manage your estates, and you will teach both Araminta and Jaden. I understand Araminta has been identified to have a *Tii-su's* touch. When she is of age, you will see to it that she is properly trained. Have you any questions?"

Killian stared for a moment. "Has the Council decided on a caretaker?"

"Lady Jonai made a suggestion that the Council has accepted on your behalf. Mistress JoAnne M'Ilvith is an estate manager of considerable experience and competence. He says that she also has a gift for teaching estate management. In two years, we will convene again, to see if you are capable of holding the regency of your clan until your sister can assume her duties. Upon regency, you will have the responsibility, privilege, and title of *Artris* Regent. Until then, Lady Natalya Nedai has offered to speak on the behalf of the Larrestes in Council, or any other proceeding wherein the Larrestes may be called upon to act."

"She'll live in the house, my Lady?" Killian asked, a little nervously. He wondered if he could deal with that.

"She cannot look after you and your siblings from the garden, Killian. We all understand your concern, but you are perfectly safe with JoAnne. She's allowed me to tell you that she is a rape survivor and understands your caution," Richard, Lady Jonai, told him gently. "She is very good at her job, and any estate I have put in her charge has prospered. She will be leaving her home to spend until your fourteenth birthday in your household. After that, she will return to her home in Sailida and visit you every few weeks, unless you need her help otherwise."

Killian nodded. It was all a lot to take in.

Janet had been held tightly in Lucretia's grasp throughout this exchange, and sensing that her justice was about to be dispensed, she struggled.

Milossa reiterated the charge against Janet, and that she was convicted on the evidence provided by the memories of both Janet and her younger children, recovered within minutes of the incident. Milossa called one more time for objections or requests for clemency, but, again, the crowd was silent. She nodded grimly, and, in a swift movement, Lucretia broke Janet's neck. Two women from the crowd, as well as Kelia and Milossa, stepped forward and verified her death.

Lady Nedai quickly organized several women to go and deal with David's body and to clean the hall where the murder occurred. Janara had charge of the children and had kept them asleep, as well as kept their nightmares at bay. Georges would be asked to counsel all three siblings. By the time the two younger children were allowed to awaken the next day, as much evidence of violence as possible had been removed, although the carpeting in the hallway hadn't yet been replaced. At least the children wouldn't have to walk over the bloodstains.

2

EIGHTEEN-YEAR-OLD KILLIAN walked into what had been his mother's study to check on his siblings, thinking back to five years before. He had only been gone from the house for a week before he returned, with a caretaker, to look after them.

"Killian? Killian!" The irritated tone and the smack on his arm drew Killian from his memories of that awful week. He looked at his sister. "Do I really have to go?"

Killian sighed. Araminta really didn't want to leave for training as a *Tii-su*, but Killian certainly understood why she didn't have a choice about it. Her untrained use of her abilities was occasionally painful, in a variety of ways. He hugged her.

"Yes, you do. You are of age to begin training, and, believe me, you need it. You don't have to be an active *Tii-su*, once you're trained, but you have to learn to control your abilities. It's one thing to mindblock a child who can't control themselves, but to leave those blocks in place as an adult isn't a good idea. You're old enough to start learning, and you will, Araminta." He looked her in the eye, brooking no argument. His sister was a good-natured child, generally, but she did have a stubborn streak.

Finally, the girl nodded, sighing. "I just don't want to leave home," she said softly.

Killian nodded back, understanding. He hugged her again. "Council is in six weeks. I'll bring Jaden with me, and we'll visit you. Now go finish packing."

Ten-year-old Jaden smiled from the desk where he was working on his homework. Killian smiled back. He knelt down beside his brother to check his progress. It had taken time, and there were still bad periods when Killian called Georges, for himself, or his siblings, but they had all recovered. Jaden and Araminta both knew what happened, even though they didn't quite understand why. Killian didn't know what to tell them because he didn't understand either. He often felt like the mother he'd grown up believing in had never existed. When JoAnne, Killian, and Lady Nedai had gone through the books, they found Janet had run the estate nearly into bankruptcy. After discussions of what happened, Lyle, Killian, and Lady Nedai had gone to the bank, armed with David's death certificate, and had closed the account out, finding David had squirreled away an impressive ten thousand dollars in American funds—and then some—over the years.

Lady Jonai and Lady Nedai both discussed the matter, deciding it was one thing if Janet had lost the estate, but it wasn't fair to the Larrestes children, particularly since they were all underage. Therefore, they decided to make a loan to the Larrestes, at a minimal one-percent interest, giving the necessary funds to get the estate in the black and keep it there while Killian learned the ropes. The reparations from Anan were divided by Killian after getting advice from Lady Nedai, with one half being put into the family coffers, and the other being placed in a savings account for himself.

Killian was happily getting into Jaden's math homework when there was a pounding on the door. He frowned. It couldn't be any of the few hundred tenants he had, as they knew they could just come in during the day, although he preferred they knock and wait from early evening on, for family time. It was barely three-thirty in the afternoon. Jaden gave him a puzzled look. Killian shrugged and went to the front door.

He opened the door and found a stunning young man on his doorstep, a stranger. The stranger stared at him, looking frightened.

"Please, may I speak with the lady of the house, sir?"

"I am the Lady of this house. What can I do for you?" Killian replied calmly. He gestured the man inside; however, the man didn't move.

"I seek Sanctuary, my lord," he answered.

Killian chose not to correct the man about his title, no point in embarrassing a frightened male when he obviously hadn't meant any insult. "Why?"

"My *Senka* insists I marry a woman I do not want to touch me. It isn't a peace arrangement, nor a command from Council. He cannot get his inheritance from my mother until the arrangement she made with my fiancée's mother is honored."

"He doesn't get the money until you get married?" Killian asked, wanting to make sure.

"Yes, sir. Please, sir, I haven't much time. If I cannot find Sanctuary here, where might I go? A tenant farmer sent me to this house." The man truly was frightened, and his accent was odd. He sounded American. Why in the world was he in Europe?

As Killian briefly considered, he saw a car drive up in a rush, and the woman who got out of it made his blood go cold. He looked at the young man. "You seek Sanctuary from her?"

The male glanced over his shoulder and crowded against the door, without crossing the threshold. "Yes, my lord."

Killian stepped back. "I grant you Sanctuary, of my home, for as long as you need." He grabbed the man by the shirtfront before he could even process what Killian had said, pulling him into the house and behind him. Killian watched as the woman from the car stalked up the steps. He had his dagger at the ready.

"Hello, Killian," Anan said with a sneer. She pointed her own dagger at the man hiding behind him. "That's mine."

3

K ILLIAN STOOD HIS GROUND and even managed a polite smile he did not feel. "I'm sure there must be some *misunderstanding.*"

Anan's eyes glittered as she studied him. She looked much the same: tall, dark skin, very pretty face until you looked into brown eyes that seemed soulless. The scar on her face had faded away. He had witnessed her seventy-lash flogging for attempted rape, as had the entire village. Her torso must be terribly scarred from the flogging, and he was fiercely glad of it. Floggings were rarely handed out as punishment, public ones even more so, but it was the lightest possible sentence for attempted rape. Some on the Council had felt she was young enough to learn a vital lesson, and others had felt the scars she'd gained from Killian's escape from her would be a punishment in and of itself. So Anan had escaped the death penalty, with the warning the Council would not be so lenient should there be any repeat of such behavior.

"No misunderstanding, Killian—"

"You will address me properly, Anan Nyirej," Killian said calmly. He was Regent *Artris*, and she knew it. "You have no leave to address me so familiarly." Wits would win this battle, not anger.

Anan scowled. Killian watched her consider her options. "Lady Larrestes, the male hiding behind you is my fiancé. We were supposed to marry several hours ago, but the male chose to run away during the ceremony. It is an understandable fit of nerves from a sheltered male, but enough is enough." Again, she indicated the man still hiding behind him. "Send him out here so we may be about our business, and there'll be no trouble."

"I have given this man Sanctuary, Anan Nyirej," Killian replied, aware that both Araminta and Jaden had come into the hall. Knowing them, they also had their daggers in hand. Thanks to Lady Nedai, all three of them now had more than adequate knife skills. "He stays here, and there will be no problems. I will contact the Magistrate to mediate this dispute." He raised a taunting eyebrow at Anan, then smiled coldly. "Unless it is agreeable to you that I mediate?"

"Of course not, you—"

Standing at Killian's shoulder, Jaden interrupted. "I'd be careful about calling Lady Larrestes names." The derision in Jaden's tone caused Anan to glare at him. "Male Artris, Regents, or otherwise, don't have to find a woman to act for them. They can take care of it themselves."

Anan scowled angrily, but there was nothing she could legally do. If she tried to take the man, Killian could defend him however he deemed fit—up to and including killing her for breaking Sanctuary. "I'll call the Magistrate myself," she said.

"You're welcome to do so, but don't do it on my property. I ban you from my houses and from my fields, Anan Nyirej, and I ban those that would act on your behalf, except by the Magistrate's or Council's order. Leave now, or you will be ... assisted to leave." Killian was not a scared thirteen-year-old anymore.

For a minute, Killian thought Anan would try her luck, but she did not. She stormed back to her car and drove off recklessly.

Killian turned in time to catch the man as he fainted with sheer relief. Killian picked the young man up, feeling a strange tingle throughout his body as he held the man close. He turned to Jaden to tell him to call Lady Nedai, but his brother already had his cell phone out, making the call. Araminta followed him and their guest to an upstairs bedroom.

At Killian's request, she ducked into a bathroom to get some clean cloths dampened with hot water. Killian carefully laid the man down on the bed in the largest guest room, wondering why he had come to Europe for Sanctuary instead of seeking it in his homeland. Unable to stray too far away from the stranger, Killian sat on the bed.

"My girls, my girls," the man moaned quietly as he came to awareness.

Touching him gently to get his attention, Killian asked, "You have children?" He took the chance to study his guest, who seemed to be about Killian's age. He had darker toned skin, like milky coffee, and in the afternoon light, faint iridescence in a streak here and there on his face and hands, his only exposed skin. Most Rimalians had duller skin these days, since Earth was so temperate a planet. And very oddly, he wasn't dressed like a young man about to marry, more like a male in mourning. The man's eyes opened, leaving Killian speechless. How had he not noticed earlier how stunning those eyes were? Green, like a spring meadow.

"Children? I don't have children ..."

"You were fussing about your 'girls' ..." Killian said, taking the cloth Araminta handed him and washing the man's face.

"I own dogs. Three Boxers. They're my girls." The man suddenly curled up on his side, moaning. "My father's probably already killed them. What was I doing?"

"What do you mean?" Araminta asked softly. She sat on the other side of the bed, patting the stranger's shoulder.

Killian carefully pushed tendrils of the man's black hair out of his face.

"My girls came with us. *Senka* didn't want them, and Anan said I could keep them, especially after she found out that breeding them can make good money. But three days ago, after I told my father I was still having serious doubts about marrying Anan, that she gave me the creeps, I woke up to find them gone.

Senka said I could have them back after I married Anan. If I didn't, he would have them put down." Pain came off the man in such waves that Killian could feel it even though he wasn't touching the man. Strange, his empathy usually only worked with skin-to-skin contact.

Concerned, Killian glanced at Araminta, who was far more sensitive. Tears ran down her face, but she seemed to be in control.

Killian touched the man's cheek, marveling at how soft his skin was. "What's your name?"

"Sh-Shiloh Zahirris," he said as he visibly struggled not to cry. Surprisingly, he curled closer into Killian's touch.

Killian gave up trying to keep some distance between them and pulled Shiloh onto his lap, holding him carefully. Clearly the other man needed the comfort. Shiloh pressed close, as if he wanted to crawl into Killian's skin. Killian was shocked at his body's response to that wriggling, and he hoped Shiloh didn't notice. Either Shiloh was too distraught to notice, too scared, or just too polite to say anything. Whatever the reason, Killian was grateful, and he tried to focus on Shiloh's situation, not his body's unheard-of reaction.

As Killian held a crying Shiloh, Jaden brought Lady Nedai into the room. She must have been nearby to arrive so quickly. Killian didn't worry about greeting her properly. One of the first things she had taught him was that there was a time for formality, and a time to ignore it. This seemed like the time to ignore it.

Lady Nedai sat down in the chair in the corner -- Killian assumed it was to seem less imposing since she was taller than everyone else in the room -- and motioned for Araminta to come to her. Natalya Nedai often acted as a maternal figure for Jaden and Araminta, having no trouble giving them affection. Araminta ran to her and crawled into her lap. Being *Tii-su* born, Araminta occasionally needed extra coddling.

Continuing to hold Shiloh, Killian told Natalya what had happened and what they'd learned from Shiloh. She held Araminta and listened quietly.

"You did the right thing, Killian. I would have given him Sanctuary as well."

Killian felt a curious pride that someone he respected had given him her approval. He didn't really need it, but it was nice to have. "I have to call the Magistrate, right? And she'll mediate the dispute?"

She nodded. "That's right. In the meantime, Shiloh stays with you, under your protection." She studied the small man in Killian's lap. No longer sobbing, he seemed to have calmed a little. "Shiloh, I am Lady Nedai, what is your mother's name?"

"Zahirris, my Lady. Elizabeth Zahirris was my mother."

"She died, what, three years ago?" Natalya asked gently.

"Yes, my Lady. My father is Ewan Zahirris." Shiloh tried to sit up, almost falling off the bed altogether. "None of my Clan have taken over as *Artris*."

Having helped Shiloh onto the bed, Killian's arms felt strangely empty. He pushed the thought aside to consider later.

"Shiloh, where did you run here from?" Natalya asked, still rubbing Araminta's back.

"Pavia, my Lady. We came three weeks ago, rented a small house." Shiloh shuddered. "When the priest asked me to say my vows, I couldn't do it. I just bolted. I forgot about everything but getting away. I even forgot my girls." Tears began to slide down his face again. Shiloh covered his face with his hands, shivering. "How could I forget my girls?"

Killian patted his back, trying to offer comfort. "Natalya, can we do anything about finding Shiloh's dogs?"

Natalya chivvied Araminta from her lap and stood. "I'll go to Pavia and see what I can find. The logical place is any kennels there." She walked over and held her hand out to Shiloh. Slowly he took it. "Does your father have a cell phone?" He nodded and gave her the number. "Very well, I'll call him and see if a little gentle intimidation gets the information."

"You can bring them here, if you find them," Killian told her.

She nodded. "I'll take Araminta with me, if that's all right? Show her a few tricks of the trade, so to speak."

Killian glanced at Araminta, who looked hopefully at him, so he smiled and nodded. She hugged him, patted Shiloh's hand, and then ran out of the room. Natalya followed with a more dignified, but hurried pace

Killian looked at Jaden. "Go see if we have any clothes that will fit him, please."

"Stand up, will you?" Jaden asked Shiloh. Killian was proud of his brother for not arguing the chore.

Shiloh stood. Even in his shoes, he was about five-foot-five, and his slenderness didn't help him seem any taller.

"Killian, all we've got are your clothes, and they're going to hang on him."

Killian shrugged. Jaden was right, but it couldn't be helped. Killian was four inches taller, and stockier, taking after his paternal grandfather. Unlike many Rimalian males, their grandfather had been tall, broad-shouldered, and heavily muscled. And helping to run the biggest farm estate in the enclave gave Killian a regular workout.

"They're clean, and will do until we take him shopping. See if you can find something with a drawstring, okay?" Jaden nodded and zipped out. Killian turned back to Shiloh. "You're safe here, you understand?"

Shiloh nodded. "Thank you." He looked down shyly. "I'm sorry, my Lady."

Killian tilted his head, confused. "Why?"

"I insulted you, and yet you still gave me Sanctuary."

"By calling me 'lord?'" Killian guessed.

"Yes, my Lady. I didn't realize you really were the Lady of the estate. I thought you were like my father, widowed," Shiloh explained, still looking at the floor.

"It's all right, Shiloh. I understood you meant no offense." Killian reached out and lifted Shiloh's chin to see his eyes. They really were the most stunning green Killian had ever seen, and he found himself drawing Shiloh into his arms again and tucking him close. There was something oddly peaceful about holding the young man. Shiloh slowly, tentatively, wound his arms around Killian's waist. Killian could feel the small tremors in Shiloh's body as he tried not to fall apart again.

"It's okay if you still need to cry, Shiloh. You've had a rough time of it the last few days." As if he'd been waiting for permission, Shiloh began to sob again, burying his face against Killian's chest.

Jaden slipped into the room, carrying a pair of Killian's sweatpants and a T-shirt. He put the clothes on the bed and then left, shutting the door quietly behind him.

Eventually, Shiloh cried himself out.

"Come on then, let's put you to bed. You need to sleep a while." Killian helped Shiloh back into the bed, reluctant to lose touch with the man, then helped him remove what little jewelry he wore, setting it on the nightstand. Killian pointed to the end suite. "That's the bathroom. When you're done sleeping, come down and join us. Don't worry about dinner. If you sleep through it, I'll fix you something when you do get up. My bedroom is across the hall from yours. When you get up, we'll talk about whatever you may need besides clothes. This will be your room as long as you stay with us." Tucking Shiloh in, clothes and all, he left Shiloh to sleep after a final pat on the shoulder.

. . .

Shiloh watched Killian leave, feeling oddly bereft. Never had he felt so safe as when Killian had held him. Taller than him, Killian was really broad-shouldered, with thick, muscled arms, black hair that fell to his hips in a thick braid, and deep blue eyes, like sapphires, they were so blue. His skin was pale, but tanned deeply, almost as if sunburned. He smelled wonderful, too, and Shiloh's touchsense said he was a kind man.

He shuddered as he thought about touching Anan. The few times he had, he'd almost been sick. Thanks to his touch-sensitivity, he could feel how she felt about him, and she didn't care about him at all. A possession to acquire for her comfort, he was just a means to an end, a way to raise enough money to buy her birthright estate back.

Oh! That's why Killian seemed so familiar! He'd gotten flashes of Killian's face from Anan's memories. Had he instinctively made his way to Killian's house because of that? After all, the Jonai estate had been closer, and the Jonai had a reputation for helping out wherever needed. Then he remembered something else: how much Anan hated Killian. Killian had to know.

Determined, he crawled back out of the warm, soft bed, even though he wanted nothing more than to sleep for three days.

He stumbled down the stairs. "My Lady?" he called.

Killian stepped out into the hall from another room, a concerned look on his face. "What's the matter?"

Shiloh grabbed Killian's arm, careful out of habit not to touch skin. "Please, you must understand something important, my Lady."

"Come sit in the study and talk to me, then." Killian led Shiloh to the study and helped him down into a seat. "What's the matter?"

"I'm a very strong touch-sensitive, my Lady." Although the ability was almost universally common among Rimalians, in varying degrees, Shiloh was at the higher end of the spectrum.

Killian nodded and gestured for him to continue.

"I usually avoid touching anyone, I just don't want to know what they're thinking or feeling." That, too, was normal among Rimalians. A psionic society, they learned ways to respect each other's privacy early in life. "I've touched Anan a number of times, a few times by accident, and once deliberately. Sometimes I pick up things I don't realize at the time; it's like my mind just files it away unless something triggers the memory. Anyway, I just remembered why you seemed familiar when we've never met. I've seen your face in Anan's memories. She hates you, my Lady. You have to watch yourself with her. I'm just a means to an end, of no importance, but she absolutely despises you."

"Firstly, Shiloh, you are important. Don't ever let anyone make you feel any different. Do you understand me?" Killian waited until Shiloh nodded. "Secondly, I know Anan hates me, probably as much as I've hated her." He sighed, apparently thinking. "Have you seen Anan's scars?"

"Scars?" What scars?

"She was given seventy lashes, and fined seventy-five percent of her inheritance, for attempted rape." Killian was quiet for a moment. "Of me."

Stunned, Shiloh sat there, unable to say a word. And his mother had arranged for him to marry such a woman?!

Killian seemed to know what he was thinking. "Perhaps we should give your mother the benefit of the doubt? You grew up in the States, yes?"

Shiloh nodded, still too shocked to speak.

"Then it's possible that your mother never knew of the incident. I understand Lady Zahirris was ill for several years. I don't recall seeing her at the trial. And I'll be the first to admit Anan can be quite charming when she wants to be. Until our first unchaperoned date, I had no qualms about marrying her upon reaching my majority."

Shiloh found his voice. "That's when ...?"

Killian nodded.

"How old?"

"I was still a few months shy of adulthood. Jaden was five and Araminta, four." Shiloh listened, rapt, as Killian quickly told him about his past. "How old are you, Shiloh?"

"Seventeen Terran years, my Lady."

"There's no need to be so formal all the time. You can call me Killian." Killian grinned at him. "Besides, I'm not much older than you. It's a little silly to answer to 'my Lady' all the time." Killian's smile was breathtaking.

Shiloh smiled back shyly.

Killian stood up. "You need to go back to bed; you're almost out on your feet. Those adrenaline rushes can take it out of you."

Killian took his arm gently, respecting the tacit social rule of not touching a strong touch-sensitive's bare skin, leading him back upstairs. Anan had never respected him like this. Shiloh relaxed a little more. Maybe coming here had been the right choice after all.

"By the way, the Magistrate will be here tomorrow to speak with you."

"What about a *Tii-su* to Verify my story?"

Killian chuckled. "Lady K'Arith's name was drawn from the Magistrate hat this duty period. She's a *Tii-su* already, as well as an *Artris*. No need for another *Tii-su* to come along. Have you ever met her?"

Shiloh shook his head. When would he have come in contact with a *Sennrojai* so strong?

"Well, I'll warn you, she is one scary female, but she's a good woman, too. You really do have nothing to fear from her."

Exhausted, Shiloh sighed in relief when they got back to his room. Killian helped him back under the covers again, tucking him in and smoothing the covers down. Shiloh felt a little embarrassed when Killian gently tucked a lock of Shiloh's hair back behind his ear. He must look a fright, his hair coming loose, and Deity only knew how puffy his face was from crying.

"Don't worry so much, Shiloh. It will all work out fine. Just sleep now, all right?" Killian brushed his knuckles lightly over Shiloh's cheek, letting Shiloh feel the truth of his words.

Since he didn't seem to mind the connection, Shiloh held Killian's hand to his face for a moment, enjoying the touch-sense of the man. Something peaceful about Killian eased Shiloh's stressed mind.

His eyes closed, sleep finally taking over. The last thing he felt was Killian marveling at how soft his skin was.

4

H IS GIRLS WERE READY to go out, Shiloh thought as they jumped on the bed, licking his face. He'd take them out, then he'd come back to bed. He was so tired. Shiloh opened his eyes just as one of his girls slobbered all over his face again.

Then he remembered the past few days and sat up, grabbing his girls, hugging them, looking each Boxer over carefully. He ignored the chuckles from the doorway in favor of hugging his babies. They walked around on the bed, sniffing and wiggling, and barking happily now that he was awake, licking his face and everything else in reach.

He gave them a few more minutes of playtime, and then pointed to the floor. "Sit." All three of his girls jumped off the bed and sat in a row, watching him intently. "Good girls," he praised.

They were well-behaved. They thumped their little stubby tails, but didn't move from their spots.

"Impressive," Killian said from the doorway. He grinned. "They didn't obey me that well."

"How long?"

"Have they been here? Natalya returned about midnight last night. It's eleven in the morning. We brought them up, but you slept right through them sniffing you," Killian said.

Jaden and Araminta both came in and petted the dogs.

"You should have seen them, though. They're very smart dogs. They were quiet, no jumping on the bed, just checked you out, licked you a few times, and settled on the floor to sleep. It was like they knew you needed sleep more than you needed to be woken up by slobber-pusses."

Shiloh flushed at the approval he heard in Killian's tone. He had worked hard to train his girls. First thing in the morning was when they got to play and mess around. They woke him up every morning when they needed to go out, jumping on his bed, licking him. After that first walk though, he expected them to behave, and they knew it. "I need to take them out."

"Oh, we already did that," Jaden told him. "It was fun. They had to sniff everything." Both children laughed. The dogs looked at them, thumping their tails some more, but they still didn't move from their spots.

"Killian figured we'd see if you were ready to get up yet," Araminta told him.

"They must have thought you were, because they zipped straight up the stairs and onto the bed," Killian added, grinning.

Well okay, since he didn't need to get dressed without them underfoot—they'd already been out—he would let them up. He looked at his girls, who looked right back at him. "Visit."

The dogs stood, but with some dignity this time. They took turns sniffing everything, and getting pets from the other three. He watched the Larrestes handle his Boxers. He had two browns and a brindle. Sweet-tempered dogs, they were all from the same litter of eight, their mother having abandoned them at just two weeks old. He and his friend Larry had taken charge of the pups, four each, but two hadn't survived. The vet said that it was impressive they managed to save so many of the litter. The two they lost were small and not as healthy as the others were, so even if the litter hadn't been abandoned, they probably still would have died.

Killian eyed Shiloh for a minute, then straightened up from the crouch he'd taken to pet the brindle, Jenny. The other two were Fancy and Rosie.

"We'll let you get dressed. It's just about time to eat," Killian said softly. The two children got off the floor where they'd been playing and left the room. He indicated the dogs. "You want me to leave them here, or should I take them with me?"

Shiloh shook his head. "No, I'd rather they stayed with me."

Killian nodded sympathetically. "I can understand that. They are quite protective of you, you know. All three met me at the door when I came to check on you before going back to bed." Killian sounded pleased.

Shiloh looked at him closely, checking for tooth marks. "They didn't bite you, did they?"

Killian shook his head, smiling. "Oh no, they just growled for a minute. They settled down once they figured out I wasn't here to hurt you, or them. Same thing this morning when I got up at seven to take them outside, only a little quicker. Apparently holding leashes and 'outside' is the correct password."

Shiloh laughed. "I'm surprised you didn't get dragged to death. The first walk of the day is part of their playtime. That's when I let Fancy, Jenny and Rosie just do their thing: sniff, wrestle, run. Boxers are energetic dogs; they need structure and playtime."

"I believe it," Killian said with a laugh. "Get cleaned up and dressed. When you are ready to leave the room, tell the dogs to find the kitchen; they've been there already. Natalya and I completely forgot to get dog food, so that is one of the things you and I need to do today."

"What did you feed them?" Shiloh asked, a little worried.

"Some of her tenants have dogs. She brought over a couple of meals for them. When we go into the village to get you some clothes, we'll get food for the dogs, as well. Do they need toys?"

"Well, they are still puppies and like to chew on things, and they love to play tugga."

"Tugga?"

"Tug-of-war," Shiloh clarified.

Killian grinned. "Got it, tugga. What works for that?"

"Well, most stores that sell dog stuff have rope toys. That's what I get them. I also give them rawhide bones to chew for clean teeth, and treats for training and rewards." Shiloh climbed out of bed, and then stretched to work out the kinks of a long sleep. His cheeks heated under Killian's watchful gaze.

Killian quickly looked away, a slight blush on his face, as well. "I'll-I'll let you—" He waved his hand vaguely towards the bathroom before he disappeared down the hall, supposedly toward the kitchen.

Shiloh considered Killian as he stepped into the bathroom, carrying the borrowed clothes. He resisted the temptation to bury his face in them, to smell Killian's scent. He'd just get dried dog slobber on them.

He looked around the bathroom, noting it was decorated simply in creams and blues. The tub was large, plenty of room for a soak, and the showerhead had several settings. The water felt great as he stepped under the spray, and he lingered there to think some more about Killian. He wasn't surprised when his cock decided to add its opinion about Killian, becoming hard and leaking. He had the feeling, though, that Killian was clueless about what to do about his attraction to Shiloh.

After washing quickly, he took care of his arousal, letting his mind conjure all kinds of nice fantasies about what Killian would look like, naked and wet with him in the shower.

But as he dried off, he sternly reminded himself that Killian was Regent *Artris*. The man could do better than some worthless male from the States. Especially one engaged to the same woman who had tried to rape Killian five years ago. Even though he'd been willing to offer Shiloh Sanctuary, Killian probably wouldn't thank him for bringing Anan back into his life.

Depressed by his thoughts, Shiloh sighed as he put on the borrowed clothing. Jaden had been right about Shiloh swimming in it, but he didn't mind. There were worse problems in front of him.

Giving his girls the command to lead him to the kitchen, he followed them.

Araminta and Jaden were setting the table. They paused to pet the dogs, and giggle at Shiloh in his oversized clothing.

Standing at the stove, Killian grinned when he saw Shiloh. "You look like a little boy playing in Daddy's clothes."

"Want to be my Daddy?" Shiloh asked before he realized it. Shocked, he slapped his hand over his mouth.

Killian blushed as he got the meaning of Shiloh's question, while Araminta snorted.

"Killian's not old enough to adopt you, silly."

Shiloh smiled at her. "You're exactly right. I'm not awake yet."

Turning back to the stove, Killian said nothing, and Shiloh didn't ask for a response. He still couldn't believe what he'd said. Killian turned from the stove, bringing a large pan of soup over to the table, carefully pouring it into the bowls as Shiloh held them, in turn. Once the soup had been poured and the empty pot placed in the sink to soak, Killian sat down at the table, as well. The dogs sat attentively at the children's feet, sensing the children were more likely to sneak them a bite. Looking under the table at the trio, Shiloh raised an eyebrow and pointed to a spot over by the wall. All three dogs slunk over and lay down, giving all at the table wistful puppy eyes.

Killian tried not to laugh. "They're very good at begging without begging, aren't they?"

Shiloh nodded, rolling his eyes. "They're spoiled rotten."

"Nah, they're just sweet babies and they know it. What do you do with them at home?"

"If they behave, most of the time I let them lick the dishes, if there's enough for them to share."

Killian nodded. "Well, if you're okay with it, I don't have a problem with it."

In between bites of cream of chicken soup with soda crackers, the children asked all sorts of questions about the dogs. It was the most enjoyable meal Shiloh had eaten in a very long time.

After lunch, Killian asked Araminta and Jaden to clean up the kitchen while he and Shiloh visited Lady Nedai's. Assuring them he would be only a couple of hours and back in time to make meat loaf for dinner, he asked the pair to take the dogs for a walk, and then check in with the tenants and find out if there were any problems they needed taken care of. Both children assured him they would, and asked if they could go into the village after that. Killian paused for a minute, and then nodded. "Since you're going, find out if any of the tenants need you to pick up anything for them. Be home by six."

Killian hugged each of them, telling them he loved them, and getting the same in return. Shiloh's throat got tight watching them. He couldn't remember the last time he'd gotten such affection; wasn't even sure if he'd ever gotten such affection. He swallowed against the jealousy he felt. It wasn't right to feel that way.

Following Killian out to the garage, Shiloh got into the small car inside.

"It's a twenty-minute drive to Natalya's. Kelia is staying there while she adjudicates this." Killian peered at Shiloh, concern on his face. "You okay?"

Shiloh nodded politely. It was a lie; he was scared beyond words. But he trusted Killian, and that would have to be enough for now.

•   •   •

Almost an hour later, Killian and Natalya sat at her kitchen table drinking tea while Kelia questioned Shiloh. Natalya's husband was out shopping, and her children were at school, so it was the perfect time to talk to her about Shiloh and his confusing reactions to the man. His dreams last night had all involved Shiloh, and calling them X-rated would be an understatement. After five years as his mentor, Natalya knew him pretty well; maybe she could help sort him out.

"What's bothering you, Killian?" she asked after watching him scarf down another shortbread cookie. He tended to crave sweets when he was upset.

"I'm not sure how to answer that," he replied. "It's Shiloh, or rather, uh ... um ..." He covered his heated face, embarrassed beyond belief. "I had these dreams ..."

Natalya smiled. "Ah, I see. You're attracted to him."

"I am?" Killian asked, startled. She didn't usually joke around, but ...

"Maybe so. These dreams, were they sexual?" she asked gently, giving him a steady look.

Her calm response relaxed him. He could do this. He nodded. "Very. And every one about Shiloh. I've never had such dreams."

"Never?" Now she did sound surprised. "Those sorts of dreams are quite common in adolescence and early adulthood, both in humans and Rimalians. You're still young enough that these should be normal for you." She reached over and patted his hand where it rested on the table, concern on her face.

"I either dream about working in the fields or cleaning the house, or I have nightmares about the assault and my father's death. I don't ever dream about anything else," Killian told her matter-of-factly.

Natalya's eyebrows furrowed in puzzlement. She was silent for a long moment. "Killian, may I ask some very personal questions?"

"It's a pretty personal subject I brought up already."

Natalya nodded in agreement. She thought about how to address it delicately, and then decided there probably wasn't any way to do so. So she spit it out. "Before the assault, were you attracted to Anan?"

"How do you know if you're attracted to someone?" Killian asked, obviously confused.

"Well, I suppose I can only tell you from my own experience. When I met Ignacio, I felt kind of fluttery, and my skin felt hot," she said. "I got aroused when I spent time with him, and that part I can tell you was also true for him. Some of the dreams I had would have made porn stars blush." She paused when she saw Killian's expression change from curiosity back to confusion.

"Porn stars?"

Natalya felt her eyebrows try to get past her hairline. "Pornographic film stars?"

"What's that?"

As she stared at him, Natalya had a sneaking suspicion. "Killian, what did your parents teach you about sex?"

"That it was something that happened after marriage; that I shouldn't worry about it, and that Anan would teach me what I needed to know after we married. *Senka* told me that if someone touched my privates without me saying they could, it was rape," Killian told her, wondering what she was getting at.

Natalya tilted her head in thought. "That definition of rape is actually a little broad, Killian. David should have told you more. There are circumstances wherein a person might touch someone's privates without permission, without it being rape, or even inappropriate, such as a medical situation."

"What do you mean?" he asked, hugging himself in distress.

Natalya had seen this reaction before. Killian had mostly recovered from his trauma, but he was still uncomfortable discussing it.

"Did I falsely accuse Anan after all?"

Natalya shook her head as she got up. "No, you didn't. Hang on a sec; I'll grab a blanket for you." Ducking into the laundry room off the kitchen, she came back with a blanket that she shook out quickly and offered to him. "It's a little dusty."

"That's okay. I can still pretend it'll help me get warm," Killian told her with a tight smile.

"Now remember, I was there for Anan's trial. I saw your memories of the incident, and hers, both viewpoints. Her actions through your eyes and hers. You didn't falsely accuse her. And if it truly had been a misunderstanding—as Janet, Anan, and Sienna insisted—Anan would not have been punished. She might have been chastised, but that would be all. You told her repeatedly that you didn't want her to touch you, and yet she continued, even to the point of using force. You raised your hand in violence towards a female—didn't you ever wonder why no one reprimanded you?"

"I thought that was why Janet disowned me," Killian mumbled.

Natalya sighed. "I'm sorry, Killian. I should have had this conversation with you a long time ago. I thought your parents had taught you about these things, and I'll bet the *Tii-su* did, too." She paused to take a deep breath. "Okay, basics. Do you know exactly what sex entails?"

"It's the marital act. That's all I was told."

"Okay. You've seen a stallion cover a mare, right?"

"Of course, I have a working farm, I know how animals mate," Killian said, rolling his eyes. The light clicked on in his mind. "Oh, it's the same with us."

"Yeah, pretty much, although the emotional aspects are a lot more involved. I don't think animals really care who they mate with, as long as it's the same species. Dogs with dogs, cats with cats." She grinned. "Humans and Rimalians, on the other hand, are more difficult species. Our emotions affect our sexuality, which is why you felt violated by Anan. If that weren't true, either you would have just fucked her or you would have been completely indifferent."

Killian thought about it for a few minutes. "Okay, I see what you mean. My emotions were part of what made it an assault."

"Exactly! Her actions mostly, but a small part was your reaction." Natalya smiled and went on. "Now, before that, did you ever want Anan to touch you? Anywhere?" She reached over and took his hand. "For instance, like this, just holding your hand?"

Killian thought about it for a few moments. "I don't know. I don't think so, but I can't really say either way." He looked at their clasped hands. "How is this supposed to feel?"

"How does it make you feel?"

He thought about that. "I like it, I guess. I mean, I like you. You're my friend. You've looked out for us a long time, and you've taught me a lot. It's ... comforting."

"Okay, that covers emotionally. What about physically?"

Unsure what Natalya meant, he shook his head.

She nodded, as if she expected that sort of answer. "Okay, sit here for a minute. I need to go get my laptop." Natalya rushed away, leaving Killian to sit and think. He tightened his grip on the blanket she'd wrapped around his shoulders. How did questions about Shiloh turn into questions about me, he wondered.

She came back and sat down again, booting up her laptop. A few minutes later, after typing something, she motioned him closer. "Come look at this."

On the screen was a nude woman, lying on a bed, her legs spread so that he could see the grown-up version of things he'd only seen changing Araminta's diapers when she was an infant. He drew back, staring at the laptop. "Why ...?"

Natalya gestured to the screen. "This is a pornographic picture, off a site my husband likes." She grinned. "Actually, I don't mind looking sometimes myself, but that's another conversation. Anyway, what do you think of her?"

"Natalya, is this supposed to be attractive?" Killian asked her, bluntly. "I mean, am I supposed to feel something?"

"Well, most men would feel she had a certain attraction, but don't fuss. Give me a minute. Let me pull up something from another site, one I like to frequent for some 'eye candy,' as my husband puts it." A moment later, she gestured to the screen again. This time it was a nude man.

Unaware he was doing so, Killian leaned closer to the screen, letting go of the blanket in the process. The man was slender, with short black hair falling loose over his shoulders. Killian felt an odd twitch in his groin.

Natalya watched Killian as he stared, nodding to herself. It looked like her young friend was gay but had never realized it. The *Tii-su* would never have asked who he found attractive, and from his reactions and questions, it seemed her young friend had never found anyone, male or female, attractive before.

"Is he more interesting to look at?" Natalya asked quietly.

Killian nodded. "That makes me feel funny, if that's what you wanted it to do."

"There's not a genteel way to ask, but does looking at him make your jeans tight?" she asked, carefully not smiling as he shifted in his chair. She noticed he had let go of the blanket.

But was this picture a fair test, though? She had, after all, picked a man with a passing resemblance to Shiloh. Quickly looking for something else, Natalya found a lovely, heavily muscular blond man, also nude and aroused. "Is this one better?"

"Actually, I liked the other one more. He's very handsome, but ..." Killian said, looking back at his mentor. "What are you trying to figure out?"

"Well, I'm trying to help you figure out what you're attracted to. I think Anan left you with an aversion to anything sexual. Once you emotionally recovered, you had little to no time or energy to explore anything sexual. Add to that you're an unmarried male, with two children to raise. I think what's happened here is that Shiloh blindsided you."

Killian opened his mouth to object, and she raised her hand to hold him off.

"Not on purpose, mind you. Maybe you are just finally ready for some romance in your life, and Shiloh is the first person you've found attractive enough to truly gain your attention."

Stunned, Killian sat back and thought for a few minutes. Satisfied with the answers, he found himself unreasonably curious about something else. "Natalya, why do you let your husband look at pictures of other women naked?"

Natalya laughed. She reached over and poked his shoulder. "Because it gets him all hot and bothered and I get to play with him."

At Killian's blank look, she clarified, "It arouses him, and we make love. Maybe we should table this part of the discussion for a while, okay? Let's just say, I don't mind him looking, as long as he doesn't try to touch. He feels the same way about me. He doesn't get upset about me looking at other naked men, as long as I don't try to touch them.

"Now, about Shiloh, do you still have questions, or did the 'show and tell' help?"

"I think it helped a little. You're saying that Anan's assault first made me not interested in sex?" At her nod, he thought back to those nightmarish weeks. "You know, I think maybe Georges said something about that."

"I'd be surprised if he hadn't. I understand it's a very common reaction in sexual assault victims. A perfectly normal response," she told him, keeping her voice calm and encouraging.

"And then I've been too busy?" Frustrated, Killian looked at her. "That, I don't understand. You're just as busy as I am, maybe more, because you have more estates to see to, on top of helping me with mine, but you obviously find time for sex."

"Well, that's where I think circumstances have worked against you. Sex tends to be a little more readily available when one is married, or in a committed companionship. You have no wife, and no companion, and apparently, no sex drive either, so I'm guessing it didn't bother you. The lack of sex drive probably originated in your assault, but probably became habit." Having closed the laptop, Natalya patted his shoulder gently.

"And Shiloh kicked me out of a rut?"

"That's my take on it, yes. To be honest, Killian, I don't think you need to worry about any of it much. Your reaction to Shiloh is perfectly natural, if a little embarrassing. There will be some issues you may have to deal with if a romantic relationship develops between you and Shiloh. Issues that wouldn't exist, say if you dated a female, but that is something to talk about later, if need be," she told him. "There's also the fact that right now, he is under your protection, and cannot be approached on such a level, especially not by you."

"Why him? I've given Sanctuary before, and to another frightened male." Killian thought about that incident, a year before.

A local boy had been the subject of a traditional marriage Hunt. It had taken a few days to sort everything out, the woman mortified when she realized she had scared her intended by her fixated pursuit, and the young man had been embarrassed at overreacting. Killian and their parents had sat down with them, after giving them both a couple of days to calm down, and they had helped the two young people sort themselves out. After counseling, the young man agreed to accept his capture, and Killian fully expected to be attending their wedding in another two years. Once they had learned to pay better attention to each other, they got along fabulously.

"Maybe you just weren't ready yet," Natalya said, breaking his train of thought. "Apparently you're ready now. Even though nothing may come of it with Shiloh, your mind is apparently telling your body that you're ready to explore romance." She smiled. "This isn't a bad thing. Think on it for a while, and do a little research at home, online."

"How? What kind of research?"

Natalya grinned ruefully. "I can't believe I'm saying this to an innocent young man, but I think it might be the best thing for you. When you go home and have some time alone, I would strongly suggest that you do this in your room, on your laptop: type in 'free porn' and just look around at anything that interests you. Don't pay for any of it, there's plenty of freebies that can give you a good idea of what's interesting to you. There's straight porn, gay porn, bi porn ... Look at them all. Then, if you want, you can come over tomorrow and Ignacio and I will sit down with you and answer questions, alright? There are also instructional videos that can be found. Ask a *Tii-su* for them, if you wish. After all, porn's great for fun, but not always the best educational source."

Killian nodded obediently, but then thought about something else that had been bothering him since last night. "Natalya, can I ask something else about Shiloh?"

"Of course."

"I hugged him a few times."

"Yes, that's understandable, he was very upset. We all need a hug sometimes. Are you wondering if you stepped out of bounds?"

"No, I don't think so ... I was just wondering why ... Well, it's like my arms are empty, not holding him." He blushed as he said it.

Natalya studied him for a moment, and then smiled gently. It sounded like Killian may have fallen in love at first sight. She wasn't going to tell him, though—better to let him find out if it was real or just a crush. She hugged him, kissing his forehead with maternal affection. "Well, I think the answer to that will come in time."

5

KILLIAN SIGHED IN RELIEF as he closed his bedroom door behind him. Shiloh had been quiet as they drove home, seeming to have curled in on himself. Not knowing what else to do, Killian had simply not mentioned it, and carried on. Occasionally he gave in to the urge to pat Shiloh's shoulder, trying to comfort him a little, but Shiloh had remained quiet and withdrawn.

The children had given him a list of remarks from the tenants, and when he went to his study to deal with the list, he'd invited Shiloh to come with him, and told his siblings they could go watch TV in his room for a little bit. Fancy and Rosie had followed the children upstairs, but Jenny had followed Shiloh into the study. Shiloh chose to sit on the small couch, Jenny sat at his feet, with her chin on his leg, and he sat there, staring out of the window, petting her head.

It took Killian two hours to sort out the tenants' remarks, including a misunderstanding caused by the children's misinterpretation of what one of them needed. Then he went and sat on the couch next to Shiloh and held up his arm, offering to let Shiloh snuggle under it. Shiloh scooted under, and laid his head in the crook of Killian's shoulder, but remained silent. Killian had rubbed Shiloh's arm gently, and asked if there was anything he could do to help, which only got him a headshake and tears. He'd held Shiloh until the younger man had fallen asleep, and then picked him up carefully and, calling Jenny to follow, took him upstairs to the guest room and tucked Shiloh into his bed. Jenny jumped up onto the bed, quickly followed by the other two coming in, and they settled down with their master.

It took Killian another hour to get Araminta and Jaden bathed and into bed, and settled down to sleep, and then he let the dogs out one more time. Shiloh had still been sleeping.

Now he had some time to himself, time to think about his discussion with Natalya, and Shiloh's impact on his life. Kelia had spoken with him briefly after questioning Shiloh. When Natalya had taken Shiloh outside to get some air, Kelia had told him to treat Shiloh gently, and that she still had to question Shiloh's father and Anan.

Killian sat down at the small writing desk in his room, what had used to be his father's side of the *Artris'* suite, and booted up his laptop, glad he'd gotten the wireless router. He quickly checked his email, and then typed "free porn" into the search engine. Amazed, he stared at his screen: there were thousands of links. Clicking one at random, Killian looked through the thumbnails, stunned at the pictures. He clicked one of the thumbnails, a man and a woman having sex on a patio table in broad daylight. He watched until the clip ended, and then went back to the preceding page. Killian typed "straight porn" in the search bar and got more of the same thumbnails that he'd already looked at. So he tried "gay porn."

The thumbnails showed men—sometimes by themselves, most often in pairs, but occasionally groups of three or more. He clicked on random thumbnails, and watched, finding his body reacted to these more quickly and more urgently than it had to the scenes with women involved. He found himself rubbing his erection through his jeans, startled at how good it felt.

Seeing a thumbnail of a slender, black-haired man—like Shiloh—naked on a bed, he clicked on it. As he watched the clip, the man in it fondled himself, stroking his cock, and cupping his balls. Killian stroked his own dick almost in rhythm with the man in the clip. His body felt like it was on fire. Liquid shot out of his erection in spurts, soaking his jeans, and he held himself tightly as his body shook so hard he almost fell out of his chair. He barely managed to hold in the shout that wanted to leave his throat. Opening his eyes, Killian saw the man in the clip climax, his dick shooting streams of creamy looking liquid all over his stomach and chest. The man swiped some of the ejaculate up with a finger, and sucked that finger into his mouth. Curious, Killian unzipped his jeans, and swiped his finger into his underwear, gathering some of the cooling liquid. He tasted it, finding it salty and tangy at the same time, with a slightly bitter aftertaste.

Feeling strangely lethargic, Killian cleared his browsing history—just in case one of the kids used his laptop—then shut it down. His groin began to feel sticky, so he stumbled into the bathroom and started the shower.

Killian felt curiously good, if tired, as he soaped himself. His body tingled as he cleaned his groin, and the sudden image of Shiloh in his bed, stroking himself like the man in the clip had done, popped into Killian's mind. In his fantasy, he touched Shiloh as Shiloh stroked himself, and when Shiloh came, Killian licked the cum off Shiloh's body. His body exploded again, and he sank down the wall of the shower as he realized he'd been fondling himself again. Sitting there, waiting to catch his breath before trying to move again, he had a vague memory of something like this and he thought hard about it. Finally, Killian remembered being caught doing this by his father, who had told him it was a shameful, sinful, dirty thing, and he had better never do it again or Janet would be informed. He'd been ten at the time, and his father had scared him about it so bad that, except when he'd had to at the *Tii-su*'s, he had never done it again until tonight.

Now he had conflicting feelings. How could something that felt so good be as bad as his father had said? And why didn't it feel this good when he used to have to do this at the *Tii-su*'s?

He decided the best thing would be to talk to Natalya and Ignacio. Maybe they could explain the matter to him. He stood carefully, his legs still feeling shaky, rinsed, and shut off the water. He quickly dried off and pulled on his pajamas, just a pair of soft sweats and a T-shirt. Killian opened his door a little, and listened in the hall for a moment. All was quiet, so, leaving the door ajar, he crawled into bed, falling asleep before his head hit the pillow.

·   ·   ·

Shiloh woke up in the middle of the night, his heart racing until he recognized the bedroom Killian had given him. His girls all lifted their heads to look at him, snuffling gently at him. Petting them all, he quietly told them to go back to sleep. Even so, they watched as he carefully got out of bed; he stopped them from following him as he stepped into the hall. He noticed the children's bedroom doors were ajar, and he walked down the hall, looking in on each of them. As he turned from Araminta's bedroom door, he found Killian standing nearby, watching. Scared at first, he held a hand to his chest until his heartbeat calmed a little.

"You okay?" Killian asked softly.

Shiloh nodded. "Just startled. Did I wake you?"

Killian nodded. "It's okay. I'm a light sleeper, in case they need me." He waved to indicate his siblings. "Something wrong?"

"Just a nightmare."

Killian crooked a finger at him. "Come on, let's go to the kitchen. I'll make you some hot chocolate."

Shiloh followed Killian downstairs and back to the kitchen, sitting at the table as Killian put a pot of water to heat on the stove. Still feeling disoriented and out of sorts from the dream, Shiloh shivered. He didn't notice as Killian left the kitchen, and then came back with a blanket. He started again when Killian gently wrapped the blanket around him. When did Killian get a blanket? Killian gave Shiloh's shoulders a quick, comforting squeeze and then left him, to finish making the hot chocolate. Eventually, he turned to Shiloh, holding both mugs.

"Come on," Killian said. "Let go sit on the couch in the den. You can drink your hot chocolate and tell me about it if you want."

Shiloh nodded as he stood and clasped the blanket to him. He followed Killian to the den, and sat down on a soft, cushy, overstuffed couch. Killian handed him his mug and sat next to him. For a few minutes, they just drank their chocolate, and looked out the floor-to-ceiling windows the couch faced.

"She knew," Shiloh said dully.

"What?"

Shiloh turned to look at Killian a moment before turning back to the windows. "She knew, *Senka* knows, they both knew about Anan."

"How do you know that?"

"I asked Lady K'Arith if it were possible that *Senki* made the arrangement without knowing about Anan's past. She looked at me like she wanted to lie, but she didn't. She told me that she herself had told my mother about the whole incident, because Kelia'd held my mother's Proxy when she was too sick to attend that particular Council Assembly. Kelia told me it was part of her duty as Proxy to report everything to my mother." Shiloh shuddered, not quite able to absorb the horrible truth about his mother. "How could she do this to me?"

Killian set his mug down on the side table. Reaching out, he gently took Shiloh's and set it down, as well. Then he pulled Shiloh close. "Maybe Anan convinced her that she'd learned her lesson?" He squeezed gently. "With Elizabeth dead, we'll probably never know. Can you tell me what else Kelia said?"

"That she might need to bring the matter before the Council, because nothing I knew of showed any deception on Anan's part, other than the fact she didn't tell me what she'd done five years ago. Because my parents knew, and still made the arrangement, as far as she can tell, the betrothal is valid. My father's behavior is suspect, though, she said. *Senki's* will complicates the matter, too." He settled his head in the crook of Killian's shoulder, one hand in his lap, the other resting on Killian's stomach, taking comfort in the closeness.

"Well, if I know Kelia, she'll not only question Ewan and Anan, but she'll look at your mother's will and she'll talk to anyone else she thinks will have useful information. If she takes this to the Council, she'll give them every single detail she can lay her hands on, so they can make a decision based on all the facts, big and small," Killian told him softly.

"And what do I do if they say I have to honor the agreement, even though I never wanted anything to do with her in the first place?" Shiloh shuddered at the thought, a reaction shared by Killian.

"You can appeal the Council's decision if need be. You have that right. If it comes to that, I will speak on your behalf."

"But you're a male."

"I am Regent *Artris* Larrestes as well. I have the rank to speak on anyone's behalf that I deem sufficient," Killian reminded him quietly.

"You would do that for a stranger you've known for twenty-four hours?" Shiloh asked, surprised.

Killian nodded. "I would. I admit it's partly because I feel sorry for any male bound to Anan, but also because I like you. You deserve better treatment than you've gotten. As you said, this isn't a peace marriage, or a Council command."

They fell silent, but Shiloh didn't seem to want to move, and Killian had no inclination to let him go. Gradually, Shiloh slid until his head was pillowed on Killian's leg, and he curled up on his side, falling asleep quickly. Killian adjusted the blanket, so it covered Shiloh as much as possible. There was a faint click-clack of nails on the floor, then the brindle, Jenny—if Killian remembered correctly—came into the den. She snuffled quietly at Killian's feet; then, giving him a look, she jumped up onto the couch, settling in the space created between Shiloh's legs and the back of the couch. She laid her head on Shiloh's knees and, with a whuffling sigh, she settled down to sleep. Killian reached over and patted her head, and then resumed stroking his hand over Shiloh's soft, thick hair.

They were still like that, Killian awake and watching over Shiloh, when the kids got up later that morning.

6

FOR TWO WEEKS, Killian looked after Shiloh, who was deeply wounded by his parents' betrayal. Killian understood. He would have felt the same way, in Shiloh's shoes. He did call Kelia and asked her to recommend a *Tii-su* when Shiloh still seemed lost in a silent daze after a week. Kelia would have been his choice to treat Shiloh, but as Magistrate, she could not treat someone involved in a dispute before her, unless it was life threatening. She suggested Celie K'Arith, an older kinswoman. Killian called the woman, and paid for her travel, offering her a guest room in his house. When she politely refused, stating that it might make Shiloh uncomfortable, he asked Natalya, who was happy to accommodate the lady. Kelia was also pleased, as it meant she got to spend some time with a beloved kinswoman. Killian also paid for travel arrangements for Celie's assistant.

Part of Killian's concern was that Shiloh's nightmares continued to drive him to the couch in the den every night. Killian followed him downstairs each time, making hot chocolate and sitting with Shiloh, holding him close. Shiloh usually fell asleep with his head pillowed on Killian's leg, and

Jenny's head pillowed on Shiloh's knees. The dogs never left Shiloh alone, even following him to the bathroom, although at night they seemed torn between staying with Shiloh and traipsing after Jaden.

Araminta had gone to the Island of Rimalia two days after Shiloh's arrival. She called every evening, and spoke with everyone, even Shiloh. Natalya reported to Killian that she also called the Nedai frequently. Killian wasn't surprised; after all, Natalya was as close to a mother as his siblings had.

After realizing Shiloh was terrified to be alone, Killian took him with him out into the fields, into the village, or to Pavia. His tenants helped him out; when he had things to do that meant he couldn't take Shiloh with him, he would either leave Shiloh with one of them, or one of them would come up to the house to stay with him. Shiloh helped around the house, slowly taking over the housekeeping, which Killian allowed because he seemed to need something to do. One of his older tenants asked him what he intended to do about Shiloh, and he told her he didn't know yet. She told him Shiloh was a good boy, but fragile, and that he needed someone strong to look after him. Killian had to agree with her assessment, and then she surprised him by suggesting that he should be said person. Killian still wasn't sure what to think about the idea.

Killian spent a lot of time talking to Natalya and Ignacio about his newly discovered sexuality—even discussed it with Georges and Kelia. Rimalian society was generally accepting of any kind of pairing that might come up, because oftentimes psionic bondlinks were at the root of them. Marriage in Rimalian society wasn't limited to one man and one woman. A woman was traditionally allowed up to four husbands, if she could provide for them and the other husbands agreed. Some marriages were complicated arrangements where a second husband wasn't the husband of the wife, but of the first husband. Almost every conceivable romantic arrangement was generally acceptable to Rimalian society, under the right circumstances. His friends did warn him that the humans weren't always so accepting or civilized. In many places, two men or two women couldn't openly show affection unless it was clear they were related. Some places were better than others, and if Killian truly was gay, or bisexual, he would need to bear that in mind when he was outside the Rimalian enclaves.

Celie arrived at the beginning of the third week, just after lunch. It was the end of the month, so Killian was in his study, going over accounts. Shiloh answered the knock on the door before fetching refreshments, followed by all three dogs. Killian wasn't surprised when Shiloh didn't speak to their guests. Since Kelia questioned him, Shiloh'd only spoken to Killian or Jaden, or when Araminta called. He didn't speak at all if anyone else was in the room or within earshot.

"Shiloh, stay, please," Killian called when Shiloh would have left them to their discussion. Killian walked out from behind his desk and held his hand out to Shiloh. When Shiloh took it, Killian led him over to the couch where Celie sat, encouraging him to sit with her. "I asked Celie here to help you. She's a *Tii-su.*"

Shiloh gave him a startled look before glancing at Celie. Killian went on, "I know some of why you are in so much pain, Shiloh, and it's tearing you apart. You never sleep a full night, you're losing weight, and you never talk, except to me, Jaden, and Araminta, and only when we ask a direct question. You're hurting more than I know how to help. A *Tii-su* is the only other thing I can think of to help you recover." He brushed his lips lightly over Shiloh's forehead, and then let go of him. "Her assistant and I are leaving. Celie is blind. At the very least, you'll need to talk to her to help her around."

Killian quietly escorted Celie's assistant, Penny, out of the study, after telling the two on the couch that he was taking Penny over to Lady Nedai's.

Driving down towards his tenants' homes, he stopped by one. He knocked on the door, and then stuck his head inside the door. "William?"

The friend he'd met the night he'd arrived at the Jonai estate had recently married one of his tenants, much to Killian's pleasure, and he had asked Killian to officiate. William and Carys were a good match. Several months after that horrible week, Carys had Hunted William, and William had been conveniently easy to catch, much to the entire area's amusement. Even Lady Jonai had teased him about making her work a little to catch him, but William hadn't wanted to play games. Because Carys' family hadn't really been prepared to take William in if she caught him, William had spent the first two weeks he was Carys' fiancé with Killian. Now married not quite a year, he was a blissfully happy young man.

William called back from up the stairs. A minute later, he came downstairs, drying his face. Now sixteen, William was filling out a little more, although Killian noticed William's face was unusually pale.

"Are you okay?" Killian asked, as he stepped into the house.

"Yeah I'm fi—" William blanched even more and raced for the kitchen, heaving into the trash can. Killian followed him and gently supported his friend with one arm while pulling his phone out. He called Carys and ordered her back to her house, telling her William needed her. She told him she'd be there in five minutes or less. He assured her that William wasn't hurt, and he would stay there until she arrived.

Penny had followed Killian into the house, and now she handed Killian a soft, wet towel. Carefully wiping his friend's face, Killian asked, "How long have you been sick?"

"Oh, about a week now," William said with a rueful grin, leaning against Killian weakly. Killian helped him over to the table and Penny dug around in the refrigerator, coming up with some lemon-lime flavored soda.

"Do you need a *Tii-su*? Why didn't I know about this? Carys hasn't said anything about you being sick." Killian was angry and worried, wondering why he hadn't been told. It was his responsibility to see to the health of those on the estate, and he couldn't do his job if they didn't talk to him.

William patted his hands, his touch-sense calm and happy. "Don't be mad. We've been gleefully keeping it to ourselves; we didn't want anyone to know yet."

The cheerful words and tone confused Killian even more, although Penny began to smile happily. William dropped the other shoe for him.

"We're pregnant."

Killian stared at him for a minute and then whooped aloud. Carys walked in about then. She grinned fondly at her husband, and went to him and laid her hands on his shoulders. "You told him?"

William shrugged, smirking. "He was upset. You didn't tell him I was sick."

Carys refused to take all the blame. "Hey, neither did you!"

"Oh, shut up, both of you," Killian groused, as he hugged first William, then Carys. "Congratulations, both of you, but why hide this?"

"We just wanted to enjoy it ourselves for a little while, before we set our families off," William answered.

Killian thought about it. "Oh Deity and stars, your mother is going to be useless for a week, Carys," he said with a laugh.

Carys laughed, agreeing. Her mother had gone wild planning the wedding, and William and Carys both hadn't cared, they'd just let their parents do what they wanted. Carys' mother, and William's father, had both lost their minds. Killian could just imagine what their reaction to their first grandchild would be.

"Please, can you wait to tell her until the end of next week? I need her to focus on the fields at least that long."

"Is William being sick why you called me?" Carys asked.

Killian nodded. William patted her hand where it rested on his shoulder. "It's just morning sickness, just at a new time, that's all. Go on back to work, although I would appreciate it if you could cook the hamburger for me tonight. The raw meat is what set me off."

Carys nodded. "I'll try, but ..."

"Oh yeah, if it sets me off, it might get you, too. I'll figure something out, love, go on back to work," William told her.

"Carys, make yourself a prenatal appointment in the morning, alright?" Killian told her, as she moved to leave. "And don't worry about the meat, I'll cook it for you." William and Carys both threw him a grateful look.

"We've got one for late next week. It is why I asked for the afternoon next Thursday."

"Oh, okay, then. See you later."

"Why'd you stop by and without your new shadow?" William asked.

"Lady Celie is here, and I'm taking Mistress Penny over to the Nedai. I wondered if you might go up to the house and hang out, in case Shiloh needs someone?" Killian asked. "Celie is there, but I don't know how things are going to go, and Celie asked me not to be there for their first talk."

William nodded. "Of course. I might bring him back down here afterwards though, okay?"

"Sure, I think it's good for him to see you two together. He needs to know there are good women out there," Killian agreed.

William grinned, then covered his mouth and lunged for the trash can again.

Killian looked at Penny. "Is this normal? I mean, he's not the one who's actually pregnant."

Smiling, Penny shrugged. "I'd say he's having sympathetic symptoms. Many men have a few, some never, and some seem to do the whole bit. Even human men have been known to have sympathetic pregnancies." She gave William a cheerfully wicked grin as she rinsed out the towel he'd used earlier. "I've even seen a couple of men go through labor pains with their wives."

William gave her a horrified look. "Oh, Deity, help me."

Killian couldn't help it, he laughed hysterically at the whole situation. William was usually so cheerful and relaxed. It was amusing to see him so rattled.

William punched his arm in disgust, although there was a small smile trying to break onto his face. It took a few minutes for Killian to get himself back together, but he felt better for the happy news and laughter.

•   •   •

Shiloh stared at the closed door of the study for a minute before turning back to Celie. She was tall, and what he figured would be called pleasantly plump. Her face was unlined, although he figured she had to be in her nineties—around early middle-age for most Rimalians—and she had clear, sparkling brown eyes. He swallowed nervously. "Hello."

"Hello, Shiloh." Her voice was soft and carried a faint accent he couldn't place, although he figured it didn't matter. He didn't know whether he should be angry with Killian or not. "You could be angry with him, but it wouldn't change the fact that he called me. In all honesty, there's so much pain and fear swirling off you, I'm surprised he didn't call sooner." She held out her hand. "Come Shiloh, share with me what hurts, and we'll see if we can make it better."

Shiloh stared at that beckoning hand, with its faint tracery of veins, and then slowly took it. Maybe Killian was right and he did need a *Tii-su's* care. The nightmares only got worse every night.

The first thing he felt was warmth. Not the warmth of Celie's hand in his, but the warmth of her mind. Then he heard her voice in his mind, asking him to show her everything that had led to his being in Killian's care. He did, even including his discussion with Kelia. The overwhelming sense of betrayal he felt that his parents had known about Anan's past and arranged to marry him to her anyway was what hurt him most, besides the fear the Council would require him to honor the agreement.

Why don't you want to honor it? Celie asked.

Anan doesn't really want me; I'm not even a person as far as she's concerned. I'm something for her convenience, and a means to gain money towards recovering her estate. And ...

And ...?

I don't think she's changed, Celie. I would never be safe or valued. If I had children with her, they would never be safe or valued. If she decided I was inconvenient, she'd put me aside. I think she wouldn't care if I told her no, either. She certainly didn't care that Killian told her no.

What of Killian?

What about him?

He's part of what's causing you so much pain, Shiloh. Celie's voice continued to be quiet, soft and accepting, making it easier to accept her intrusive questions.

Shiloh cringed. He didn't want to talk about that. He felt a brief burst of anger at Celie's amusement at his reticence; his feelings for Killian were special and not for dissection.

Ah, but the fact remains that you must, if not with me, with someone. Your new love for him is a large part of what's hurting you, which in turn hurts him.

Why would it hurt him? That was a ridiculous thought.

No, not ridiculous. Killian loves you as well; that is quite evident to me, although I don't think he realizes it yet. Not in those terms. You are a little more self-aware on some levels. It's not that he's an insensitive clod. He's just been so busy surviving that his emotional growth became a little delayed in some ways. We Tii-su were aware of it, but as long as it wasn't hurting him, we had no reason to disturb his peace of mind.

He just feels sorry for me, and hates Anan, Celie. That's all.

No, that's not all. You're right, to a point, and he's a wise one to know and admit it, he does feel sorry for you, and there is still some lingering hatred of Anan. From his point of view, her actions led to the destruction of his life, and he's not entirely wrong. It's unfair to place all the blame on her shoulders, however. Anan isn't responsible for Janet's actions, after all. But the fact remains, he cares for you, because you're you. Not just because you're someone he can save from Anan, or just because he thinks your parents did wrong by you.

Shiloh thought about that for a long while. *Let's say you're right, but there's a vast difference between loving someone and being in love with someone.*

And you've fallen in love with a man you don't think wants you.

Yes.

Let me give you another perspective, Shiloh. Perhaps you have fallen in love with a man who has no clue about any kind of love, other than for his siblings, a few friends, and his lands. Love he doesn't differentiate. To him it's all the same, except that he places more value on people than lands or things. Now you enter into the picture, and there's something new in his heart, but he doesn't know what it is or what to do with it. He knows it's possible for people to be in love, because he's been fortunate to have the example of Natalya and Ignacio, as well as William and Carys, but he doesn't really understand it.

Celie paused a moment to give him time to digest the information and then continued.

Add to all that, the fact that he has given you Sanctuary. He is bound to see to your needs, without taking advantage of you. You're under his protection, and there you must remain until Kelia deems otherwise. There is also the fact that technically, you are still engaged to Anan, and any kind of romantic relationship between you and anyone else would be inappropriate, unless and until that is ended.

I know.

And that's a big part of why it hurts, yes?

Yes. Why doesn't Killian at least say something, though?

Maybe he doesn't know what to say. He may feel there is no point in bringing up something which will only hurt you both right now. I will tell you in confidence, because it may help you, and will not harm him, that Natalya called me after Killian asked her for a guest room for me. She told me Killian is very innocent in many ways. That he has never been attracted to anyone before, at all. She's of the opinion that he just operated in a kind of asexuality until he met you. She doesn't know if he's gay, straight, bi, or only notices you out everyone on the planet.

How could that happen?

I would guess a large part of it began with Anan's assault on him. It's quite common for sexual assault victims to become uninterested in sex for a while. Some only a few months, others, years. It depends on circumstances in many cases. Rape may be about power, but it uses sex to get it, and that creates some serious hang-ups. That is part of why rape is so severely punished in our culture. The victim suffers for a lifetime from it. Natalya thinks that's how it began, and it became a natural state for him, because there was nothing to change it.

So it's like he's ten again and just now noticing boys?

Something like that.

What do I do?

First, you must heal yourself. Your sense of betrayal at your parents' hands is every bit as important as this, and you can't hide from one in favor of the other, Shiloh. All your hurts need to be addressed, and I think perhaps you need a little training among the Tii-su. I think your touch-sense has gotten stronger, probably because of age and stress. Sometimes our abilities get stronger as we get older. You've felt hunted and hounded for months now, and I think your abilities have grown stronger in an attempt to help you survive. I'll begin training you, and we'll go from there.

What will training do?

It will let you have better control over what you do and do not pick up, so you can maintain normal relationships without too much strain. Even as we've talked, I've picked up on so many background pieces of knowledge that you've picked up over the past few years, things you don't even know you know, but plague your mind, anyway. You need to be taught to shield yourself from that. Rimalians are very good about avoiding skins without comment, but humans aren't, and there are times when touch is unavoidable. Would it not be better to shield yourself if you wish?

Oh, I get it. Celie?

Hmm?

Am I judging too harshly? My parents, Anan, everyone?

You have every right to feel as you feel, Shiloh, no matter how others perceive the situation. There are those that wouldn't understand why you're upset, and others that would think you're not mad enough. It is possible you judge your parents a little harshly, but I think it is because you do not accept that your parents may have been fooled by Anan. Anan, I think, hasn't changed at all, and you do not judge her harshly enough. How we see things often changes with experience and information. Only time will answer that question truly for you. How you feel today, may be different tomorrow.

How long will I have nightmares about Anan killing Killian, or my dogs being butchered by my father, and everything else that has me screaming in my sleep?

I think that as you deal with your fears, the nightmares will fade. They're your subconscious trying to work out your issues, that's all. All those nasty little things that have preyed on the back of your mind are coming to the forefront. I can, however, set things up to give you a few nights' peace. Not a permanent cure, per se, but a few nights actual rest will do you good. Your mind is chasing itself in circles, viciously biting itself and then crying because it doesn't understand what it did to get hurt. I think we can short-circuit that pattern. Maybe your mind will ... uh ... reboot itself into a healthier pattern.

How many nights?

Oh, I think three. Then we'll wait a week and see what happens. Come on, we've been at this a while, and we're both tired. We've done enough for now.

How long are you here for?

A few weeks, I should think. Maybe longer. We'll just have to see. There's no timetable in healing this kind of pain, Shiloh. And even after I go home, you are welcome to call upon me anytime you feel the need. Now, let's go take care of young William, he's throwing up again.

William? He's sick?

Only sharing his wife's morning sickness, although I think we're not supposed to know. But he's thinking very loudly about it right now.

Shiloh blinked as he found himself aware of physical reality again. He jumped up at the sound of someone being sick outside the study, in the hall. It was a good thing the hall floor was tile …

7

LATER THAT DAY, after they were settled in for the night, Shiloh decided to talk to Killian about some of the nightmares that awakened him every night. Celie had promised him three nights without nightmares, and this seemed to be the best time to talk about them without repeating them when he tried to sleep. Killian was in the study, doing his paperwork, so he went and made their hot chocolate, bringing the mugs to the study.

Killian looked up from his desk and smiled when Shiloh set his mug down beside him. "You seem a little better," he said.

"I think I do feel a little better. Maybe because Celie promised me no nightmares tonight?" Shiloh mused as he sat on the couch.

"Maybe. There were a few nights where Georges did that for me. Something about giving my mind enough actual rest to look at things rationally," Killian said as he picked up his mug and stood, crossing the room to sit down beside Shiloh.

Shiloh chuckled a little. "Celie called it a reboot."

"As good a term as any. What's on your mind?"

Shiloh took the opening, telling Killian about the nightmares, and how he was feeling about his parents. The only thing he didn't bring up was how he was falling in love with Killian.

Killian listened quietly, giving in to the urge to hold Shiloh to his side. Holding Shiloh as he slept every night had become an exercise in torture, because his body always reacted to Shiloh's proximity. He taken to wearing his baggy jeans and longer shirts, leaving them untucked. He'd come to terms with his attraction to Shiloh, although he knew nothing could come of it, at least while he was providing Sanctuary. Earlier, William had taken Shiloh and Penny back to his house, so he could make his wife's dinner. Killian had used the chance to speak privately with Celie. She hadn't told him much—he hadn't expected her to—but she did tell him the two of them should use this time to get to know each other. She also told him to continue taking care of Shiloh as he had been, and that Shiloh and Killian both needed all the TLC they could get.

Once Shiloh had talked himself out, Killian stood. "Come on, let's go to the couch in the den, it's more comfortable." He took Shiloh by the hand and led him to the den, and grabbed the blanket he'd taken to leaving on the back of the couch for Shiloh. He sat down and gestured for Shiloh to get comfortable. Shiloh laid down, snuggling close, his head on Killian's leg as usual. Killian spread the blanket over him and settled back, getting comfortable. Killian stroked Shiloh's head, sometimes playing with his short braid. Shiloh's hair fell to his waist in thick waves when it was loose, Killian knew, but he left it in its braid. Killian always let Shiloh sleep as late as he could, since his sleep was often interrupted, and he knew Shiloh would be embarrassed if someone saw him with his hair loose. He smiled as Shiloh's hand snaked out and found Killian's own braid, and the end of it was dragged under the blanket where Shiloh could hold it to his face. It wasn't long before both men were sound asleep.

•　　　•　　　•

The day after Celie arrived, Kelia called Shiloh and Killian into the village to meet with her, Anan, and Shiloh's father, Ewan.

When they arrived, she told them she was turning the matter over to the Council for mediation, as well as giving them her recommended course of action. When Ewan questioned why, and pointed out he was denied his inheritance until his son married Anan, she informed him that stipulation was one of the reasons she was turning it over to the Council. She told them to go to Rimalia for the Council meeting and the business would be settled then. In the meantime, she forbade them from having any contact with each other. When Anan had smirked, Kelia glared and made sure she wasn't misunderstood. She didn't just mean that Anan and Ewan couldn't contact Shiloh; it also meant that Ewan and Anan couldn't contact each other. Killian had wondered why that had angered Anan so much; although he had the impression Kelia had been amused.

The following five weeks continued much the same. Shiloh still had days where he didn't talk much, but those quiet days now lacked the broken, hopeless quality that had so concerned everyone. He gradually began to show his natural, spritely personality. He continued to talk to Celie every day, and occasionally Celie brought Killian into those sessions. Shiloh spent more nights actually sleeping in his room and fewer retreating to the den.

His gradual return to good health showed in the dogs as well; they returned to their usual playful, high-spirited selves. The estate children often took off with the dogs, returning them at dinnertime after having run them ragged. All the children enjoyed the dogs so much Killian wondered why none of his tenants had any. He found out one day while talking to Mary, Carys' mother, that his own mother had not allowed the tenants to have pets, and they had continued to obey the stricture. Since many of his tenants were there with him and Mary, he told them all to spread it around the estate that if any of them wished to have a few pets, they were quite welcome to do so. He did, however, draw the line at any of them owning lions, tigers, or bears. With laughing calls of "Oh, my!", he left them to their work, pleased at how happy they were.

Shiloh was often seen in the fields, pestering everyone to teach him what they were doing. It meant there was a little less progress as a result, but Killian turned a blind eye to it, glad to see Shiloh wasn't so withdrawn all the time. Besides, willingness to learn should always be encouraged.

He and Shiloh spent nights quietly, sometimes just talking, other times playing with Jaden, or speaking with Araminta—who seemed relieved Shiloh seemed much better—and giving into their attraction a little and snuggling on the couch in the den after Jaden went to sleep. Although they never talked about it, they firmly kept their actions to just sitting closely, having separately come to the conclusion there was no point in discussing their attraction to each other until the Council had made its decision. Neither mentioned the number of cold showers they both took, either.

8

THEY ARRIVED AT RIMALIA two days before Council was to meet, partly to spend time with Araminta, and partly because Shiloh had never been and Killian thought it would nice to show him around a bit. Shiloh tried to be interested, but he was too worried about what the Council would decide to really be able to focus. Araminta was allowed to come stay with them at the Larrestes house while they were visiting, which offered a welcome distraction. They'd left the dogs with William, and Shiloh had asked Killian to take care of them if the Council made him go with Anan or back to his father's house, so they couldn't be held hostage against him. Killian had agreed, mostly to keep Shiloh from worrying. He didn't like it, but he understood the request.

The day after they arrived, they were informed by messenger that both Anan and Ewan had also arrived. That ratcheted Shiloh's stress level to the point Killian dragged him into the study and just held him in his lap until Shiloh fell apart again and let it all out. Celie came in and, getting his permission, she used her abilities to soothe Shiloh, quieting him a little. They didn't sleep much that night.

Shiloh's first sight of the Council building stunned him. It had to be the most massive structure he'd ever seen. If the architects had intended anyone who approached should feel like the most insignificant creature in the universe, they succeeded. The black basalt stone was smooth and well maintained. The huge edifice was unbroken at the ground level except for the entrances, which were just oversized doorways. It had few windows; Killian and Celie had told him the structure had been built with sieges in mind, to protect the island's more at-risk residents, children, and the elderly. Despite several human invasions over the millennia, it had never been breached.

Once inside, Shiloh followed Killian to the Council chamber, an arena type room, where the entire group met for their quarterly meetings. Moving to the small area reserved for petitioners, Killian ensured Shiloh and Celie were comfortable before going to take his place with the Council on the low dais. Araminta sat by his side; as the future *Artris*, she needed to be well-informed.

Shiloh found the Council fascinating. As he watched, he could see who got along well, who hated each other's guts, and who didn't really care either way. He also noticed that despite these differences, or maybe because of them, the *Artris* still managed to be civil towards each other, and they actually listened, for the most part. After the Council finished with all the other business, Kelia brought the matter of Shiloh Zahirris requesting Sanctuary of Killian Larrestes, from Anan Nyirej and Ewan Zahirris.

When asked why she'd not mediated the situation herself, Kelia briefly explained everything she'd learned, and many nodded, agreeing that it was complicated enough that perhaps more than the Magistrate's attention should be paid to it.

The Council proceeded to question Ewan, and then examined the will for themselves, with many expressing surprise that there was no provision in the will to keep Anan from selling Shiloh's birthright inheritance, a small estate in North Carolina.

Shiloh sat stunned. He had no idea he was to have inherited anything, let alone that it would have gone to Anan upon the marriage. At least now he understood how marrying him would get her a good bit of the money she needed to recover her own birthright estate.

One of the *Artris*, Lady Solentai, spoke up. "Lord Shiloh, were you aware of your inheritance?"

Shiloh shook his head as he stood to answer. "No, my Lady. Had I known, I would have immediately retreated to it, with none but the Council to gainsay me."

Kelia told the Council she believed Ewan and Anan had conspired to keep Shiloh ignorant of his resources in order to pressure him into the marriage. Over Anan's and Ewan's protests, Lady Kierstai advised them they should probably stay silent, as anything they said could lead to them being asked to Verify it, and the consequences of lying would be severe. Both quickly shut up, Ewan looking ill and Anan looking angry.

Shiloh looked at Celie for support; she patted him gently. Then Lady Kierstai asked why, other than her attempted rape conviction in the past, Anan was so unsuited to Shiloh. They were both unattached, young, and healthy. Kelia replied that as Shiloh was gay, marriage to a woman should not have ever been considered for him unless there was a strong need for a peace bond, which did not apply here. Lady Jarvai turned to Ewan.

"Did you know of your son's orientation?" she asked.

Ewan stood. "Yes, my Lady, we did."

"Did you, Anan?" Lady Jarvai stared intently at the woman, almost as if she was seeing right into her.

Anan stood as well. "Yes, I did, and I told him I didn't care, that he could have a male lover if he wanted," she answered insolently.

Shiloh stood again, angry.

Lady Solentai looked at him. "You have something to add, young Lord Zahirris?"

"What she said is true—as far as it goes. What she didn't tell you is that she said I could have any lover she took, and was bored with. She forbade me to find one I actually wanted," Shiloh replied as calmly and respectfully as he could manage. He was torn between wanting to run to Killian and hide in the bigger man's embrace, and wanting to take the Guards' swords and cut Anan's smug, menacing head off. Somehow, he found the strength to do neither, standing in place, outwardly calm.

"This does not seem to have been properly arranged on any level. Young Lord Zahirris, why do you fear for your good welfare in Anan's care?" Another *Artris* spoke this time. *Matthew, Lady Sorai,* Shiloh noted.

"I am a very strong touch-sensitive, my Lady. There have been a few times over the past few years where I have come in skin-to-skin contact with Anan, and the things I felt ... sensed ..." He looked at Kelia questioningly.

"Go ahead, tell them everything you told me when I questioned you," Kelia encouraged.

"She doesn't want me, my Ladies. I'm just a thing, a convenience for her plans to recover her birthright. I would catch flashes of hatred toward a young man that I later discovered was Regent *Artris* Larrestes. Anger that he had cost her so much. I didn't understand it at the time. She sees me as something she can use and abuse, and as long as we're married first, no one can tell her differently. I have no *Artris* to speak for me. The few females that remain in my Clan do not seem inclined to step up and do their duty, which appeared to feature strongly in her plans." It was a relief to finally have it all in the open. Even so, he almost took a step backwards when Anan stood again.

"He's just a hysterical male, easily swayed by others. He's been in Lady Larrestes' charge for weeks. The Regent could have convinced my fiancé of anything by now."

Celie stood now. "Do you mean to suggest, Anan Nyirej, that I would allow a patient in my care to be brainwashed?"

Anan froze.

"Your patient, Lady Celie?" Lady Kierstai asked, watching everyone carefully.

Celie looked toward Shiloh for a moment, asking permission to discuss their sessions with the Council.

He nodded. "Go ahead, Celie, I trust you."

"Shiloh became quite distraught over the betrayal of his parents, both in them knowing about Anan's past and not telling him, arranging the marriage anyway, and in Ewan's threatening to kill his dogs if he didn't go through with it. His depression became severe enough that Lady Larrestes called upon me to tend to him."

Noticing Celie seemed to be facing the wall just to the side of the Council, Shiloh gently turned her a little more towards them. No one said anything, although there were a few fond smiles.

"We've spoken every day since I arrived. His mind is his own, his beliefs his own, his feelings his own."

Gathering his courage, Shiloh dared speak up again. "Ask her if she's changed. Ask her what her intentions towards Lady Larrestes are. What her intentions are towards me. What her intentions for my estate are."

Lady Jarvai and several others, including Kelia spoke quietly for several minutes, then broke off into other groups, speaking some more. Eventually the entire group had discussed his request.

Lady Jarvai spoke again. "These are valid questions, Mistress Nyirej. We require answers to them. First, your intentions for the estate once it passes into your control?"

Anan began to look hunted. There were several full-blown *Tii-su* in the room, one of whom, Kelia, was a *Sennrojai* on the Council. On top of that, several other *Artris* were sufficiently sensitive to know when they were being lied to, even if they couldn't sniff out the truth directly.

Kelia caught the errant thought from Anan that she shouldn't have bothered chasing Shiloh; he'd proved too much trouble. Kelia couldn't help it. She smirked just a little and shared the tidbit with Celie, who psionically chuckled, commenting it was too late now.

Anan tried anyway. "I withdraw my claim to Shiloh as husband."

Anan's statement shocked Shiloh. Was she able to do that?

"If that was what you had wanted to do, you should have done so before it was brought before the Council," Milossa said sternly. "Indeed, the way this will is set up, Ewan would then have grounds to bring you before us for denying him his inheritance."

"Answer the original question, Anan Nyirej," Natalya ordered.

"I wish to sell it.

"Why?" Lady Solentai asked.

"Because I was forced to sell my birthright, in order to pay reparations," Anan answered angrily. She stood with her fists balled, as if she wanted to strike out.

"So you would deprive your fiancé, and your prospective children, of their rightful inheritance, instead?" Lady Torraï's eyes showed her disapproval clearly, over her face veil. In a moment of misplaced idle curiosity, Shiloh wondered why she wore it; the custom had never been common for females. Surely it wasn't because of her nearly space-black skin. Among Rimalians, such dark, Ancient-toned skin was a mark of rare beauty.

"I have the right to do as I wish with my property," Anan replied defiantly.

"True," Lady Jonai agreed. "But you must have more care with the inherited property of another, especially birthright properties that are not truly yours. If you and young Lord Zahirris married, his inherited birthright estate would become the birthright of your eldest daughter, or your only child. Tradition requires that these properties be preserved. "

"But it becomes mine when I marry Shiloh, and I can do as I wish with it," Anan replied, still standing with fists clenched, getting angrier.

"Let's move on to the next question," Milossa suggested. "What are your intentions toward young Lord Zahirris?" Milossa also watched the female closely. What were they looking for? Shiloh wondered.

"What do you mean? I am supposed to marry him, what else could be asked for?" Anan asked.

"Do you like him?" Natalya asked, with a quiet kind of cheerful malice.

"Why would that be necessary?"

"Do you want him?" This question came from Lady Ertrai, an older woman, who had seemed content to watch until now. "I mean sexually. Is he attractive enough to you that you would want to have a sexual relationship with him?"

Shiloh blushed deeply at the question, and squirmed in his seat. Celie patted him again as some of the Council members smiled benignly at him, apparently pleased with his embarrassed reaction.

Anan looked at her oddly. "He would be adequate to that purpose, I suppose."

Angry on Shiloh's behalf, Killian struggled not to say anything, but he didn't want to egg her on. If he was reading his fellow

Council members right, she was digging herself a nice hole all by herself. And they seemed pleased by Shiloh's modesty. Besides, her intentions towards him were next to be questioned and he would have a chance to speak then.

"Would you treat him with respect?" Lady Sorai asked.

"He's a male. Why would I waste respect on him?" Anan's tone was equally confused and angry. Obviously, men, in her worldview, just weren't worthy of respect.

Every male on the Council, and a majority of the females, all stood up angrily in protest. Saul, Lady Nerris, had his hand on his dagger. "It is a waste to respect a male?" he asked softly, threateningly.

Anan looked wildly around, aware she'd put her foot in it, but not really understanding why.

"SIT DOWN!" Milossa ordered. She stood and stared sternly around at the Council members until slowly, reluctantly in many cases, everyone sat down. The four men on the Council—Killian, Richard, Matthew, and Saul—were the last to sit, all still glaring at Anan.

Milossa gave everyone a few minutes to compose themselves before she spoke again. "Obviously, Mistress Nyirej, we need to speak with you about the lessons you missed as a child. I would have thought, however, after your punishment five years ago, you would have learned that men deserve respect and care from women."

"All that showed me was that you were willing to believe the lies of some hysterical little tease, who cried a little and you all felt sorry for him," Anan replied haughtily. "You left me with permanent scars over what some insignificant little male said one night because he didn't think I spent enough money on him, or whatever his problem was, and he cried rape. And you idiots believed him."

The room was silent for a minute while nearly everyone in the room stared at her in disbelief.

Kelia stood. "Lady Jarvai?"

"Yes, Lady K'Arith?" Milossa answered.

"*Tii-su* Georges is here on the island, and we can bring Marabel Solentai here if Mistress Nyirej would like to revisit that decision. I know she appealed once, before the flogging was administered, and then she later appealed the reparations. Both times, the decision was upheld. One person in the group who that listened to her appeal on the flogging informed her she should be glad it was such a light sentence. If she truly believes we were 'fooled' by a spiteful or hysterical male, both of them are right here, we can Verify it again."

"Lady Larrestes, are you willing to endure another Verification of the incident?" Milossa asked.

"I am," Killian said, without hesitation. He had nothing to lose by telling the truth again. And maybe this time, something would be done to protect other males from Anan.

"Anan Nyirej, are you willing to endure another Verification of the incident?" Milossa asked.

Anan stared at all of them. She was caught, and everyone knew it. The mind doesn't lie. Perception of memories may change, but the memories themselves do not. Snarling with hatred, she shook her head.

"You are before Council, you must speak," Milossa reminded her. "And be careful what you say, because it will be the last time that the incident of five years ago will be addressed in this fashion."

Anan remained silent a while longer, glaring at all of them. "It wasn't right; he didn't deserve seventy-five percent of my inheritance."

"I didn't deserve to be sexually assaulted, either," Killian answered coldly. "You had no right to touch me when I told you no. I had to drag my dagger across your face for you to even start to let me go. Some of the wounds you left on my body got infected. They scarred. You deserved your punishment, Anan Nyirej, and there were many times I wished you'd been put to death."

"I should have killed you when you tried to refuse me my rights as your fiancée," Anan spit out angrily.

"We would not be having this conversation if you had. The time when that was permissible is millennia past," Milossa commented. "You would not have been flogged. You would have been put to death for murder."

Shiloh watched all this, feeling like it wasn't even about him anymore. Anan's hatred of Killian was getting the best of her, and he could see many on the Council recognized that. Was his asking for Sanctuary being used to punish Anan further?

Celie quieted him. *She brought this on herself, by not being honest with you, and forcing you to feel the need to ask for Sanctuary. She could have just relinquished her claim to you, before the Council was involved. Ewan could have then petitioned the Council for help to gain his inheritance. Smart, careful women write their wills to avoid these problems, not cause them. The Council didn't seek this, but they are going to use it, since they would already be at home with their families, otherwise. Kelia is particularly cranky; because of this fiasco, she's been separated from Saul for entirely too long.*

"Young Lord Zahirris, how do you feel about marrying Mistress Nyirej? Can you now honor the arrangement of your mother's choosing?" Lady Ertrai asked kindly. She gave him what he figured was supposed to be a reassuring smile. "Have your doubts about your future with her been eased and laid aside?"

Shiloh swallowed hard to shift the lump in his throat. He stood again. "No, my Lady. I still see a woman who cares nothing for me or any children I might have had with her. I have no wish to marry her, or, indeed, any woman. My mother, father, and Anan all knew this. I feel that my mother betrayed her duty to see to my future in the best manner for me. My father betrayed his duty to ensure I was aware of my own inheritance." He spoke as calmly and strongly as he could manage, not wanting to have to repeat himself. For a moment, he wished he were curled on the couch with Killian, watching the weather, drinking hot chocolate, and petting his dogs. "My Ladies, if I cannot trust her with my dogs, how could I trust her with my children?"

Anan glared at him, her dislike of Killian spilling over onto him, but he didn't care. Killian had shown him more caring in the short time he'd known the man than he'd known in all of his life. The idea of being forced to be with Anan in any way was simply abhorrent. A realization popped full-grown into his mind: He would rather die than marry Anan. He sat down in shock, basically dropping into the seat. Several heads snapped around to look at him, and Celie put an arm around his shoulders. He stared at Killian; their gazes locked.

"You would truly rather die than marry Anan?" Lady Ertrai asked, making him realize that every person in the room with sufficient sensitivity had heard his thought, it had been so strong.

Killian's face blanched, fear crossing his face before he schooled it again. Araminta didn't bother hiding her response; she left her chair and ran to him, climbing into his lap. Shiloh closed his arms around her instinctively, appreciating the comfort offered.

Shiloh somehow managed to look away from Killian, to Lady Ertrai. "Yes, my Lady, if suicide is my only option, I will take it, and I will make sure that Anan does not get my estate. They deserve a Mistress that will do her best for them, and I deserve a spouse who values me as a person worthy of respect. I never expected her to love me, or be my soul mate or anything like that. But I will not be sold for a convenience."

"Even if the Council commands the marriage?" Lady Jonai asked quietly.

Shiloh looked at Lady Jonai. "Yes, my Lady, even if the Council commands the marriage. She only inherits if the marriage is consummated. I can prevent that."

Shiloh wasn't sure, but he thought he saw approval in the eyes of many *Artris*. Some just looked irritated. One of them spoke now. "Let's just vote on this and get it over with. They've both said their piece, and that girl is lying more to herself than to anyone else. The boy is obviously not a very biddable male. I don't know why she'd want him anyway."

Shiloh noted there were more than a few smothered smiles at the woman's comments. Maybe she was known for having more conservative opinions?

The Council fell into groups. Shiloh watched as Killian approached Milossa and spoke quietly with her for a moment. Celie, who indicated she needed to go back and listen, gently nudged Araminta from Shiloh's lap. Shiloh watched as groups fell apart and reformed with different members and how people moved around, talking to each other. This went on for two hours, much to Shiloh's amazement. Through the rest of the deliberations, Killian stayed in his seat, not participating, although Araminta floated from one group to the next, listening closely. Killian must have decided to abstain from the vote, and Milossa had obviously agreed that he should, since she allowed him to just sit, watching. Anan glared at everyone from her seat. Ewan sat, his head in his hands. Confusion, anger, and pain swirled off him so strongly, Shiloh could feel it. He wondered if he should care more about his father's distress, but he found he just couldn't right then.

Finally, the groups coalesced back into their original positions and sat down again. The stragglers who brought their findings to Milossa finally took their seats as well and Milossa sat quietly under everyone's watchful eyes.

"Shiloh Zahirris, the Council has come to a decision regarding your Sanctuary. The actions of others have placed you and this Council in an untenable position. Saving you from an unwanted, deceptively arranged marriage would punish your father further than he deserves, and not to do so would reward such arrangements more than Anan deserves. So the Council has decided upon a course of action that will address these issues, without the loss of anyone's life." Milossa spoke in a clear voice that Shiloh could not have ignored if he wanted to. "Shiloh Zahirris, you will marry Anan Nyirej."

Anan grinned widely as Shiloh's heart plummeted to his feet. Stunned, he stared at all of them. Did his needs, wants, opinions, fears, his life mean that little then?

"Don't get too happy yet, Anan Nyirej. You will divorce him one hour later. Neither of you will leave this room or be out of our sight during that time. The marriage will allow Ewan Zahirris to gain control of his inheritance. Ewan Zahirris, you owe reparations to your son, for the threat to his animals as blackmail, and for failing to tell him of his birthright. The amount will be ten percent of your inheritance. Following the divorce, Anan Nyirej, you may leave in peace, owing and owed nothing, gaining nothing, with the admonishment to be honest about yourself to any you may consider marrying in the future. Males are amazingly forgiving creatures, but not if they are mistreated or deceived. Shiloh, you will also be free to leave, owing none, owed only the reparations from your father."

Shiloh began to breathe again.

Milossa went on. "Shiloh, you will, however, be known to have been divorced by Anan, not the other way around, do you understand this?"

He knew she was asking if he understood he might have trouble in the future because some would not want to marry a man divorced by his wife. Many would question how he'd been such a failure, even though the story of tonight's happenings would soon be gossip fodder. Only contract marriages could be dissolved without fault.

"Yes, my Lady, I understand."

"You will be free to take charge of your birthright, but you will be known as a divorced male. Are there any objections to this?" Milossa asked.

"Why should I agree to this?" Anan demanded.

"Because you have no choice, unless you seek to defy the Council," Milossa replied calmly. "You will not profit from deception if we have anything to say about it. Perhaps the next time you seek to marry, you will be upfront about your mistakes."

Anan stared, and then finally dropped her gaze, anger coming off her in such waves Shiloh could feel it, even though she was on the other side of the room from him.

No one objected. Shiloh could deal with the bad reputation if he could avoid suicide. He might catch shit, but he wouldn't be touched by Anan, and he would be free to live his life as he wished, with whomever he wished. This nightmare was almost over. He looked at Killian and his heart broke all over again.

Killian's family estate was in Italy, and Shiloh would be returning to the States, to North Carolina. He was going to gain his freedom and his safety, and lose the man he'd fallen in love with. Looking into Killian's eyes, he knew that Killian knew it too.

9

THE NEXT TWO HOURS were somewhat anticlimactic. In short order, Shiloh and Anan were married. After an hour, long enough for the necessary people to honestly state the marriage had taken place and transfer control of Ewan's inheritance to him, Anan requested a divorce from the Council on the grounds of Shiloh's refusal to honor his vows and consummate the marriage.

Shiloh thought about speaking up, and then decided not to. It was petty revenge on her part, but at the same time, it was truth. Shiloh would've committed suicide before allowing that woman to touch him. The Council granted the divorce on those grounds, and Shiloh was free. By tradition, he was disgraced, but he was free in practical terms.

It was late before he, Killian, and Araminta arrived back at the Larrestes house on the Island. It would be three days before a *Sennrojai* would be able to send him back to the estate in North Carolina. Unless he could think of something, that was all the time he would have with Killian.

Killian smiled when Araminta dragged Jaden upstairs with their dinner, which Jaden had put together, a stew that would keep in the crockpot. The household caretakers had also politely retired to their own rooms. Killian and Shiloh were left alone in the kitchen. Shiloh suspected a friendly conspiracy.

The two were quiet as they ate their stew, needing a little quiet just to process the day's events.

Eventually, Killian spoke. "Better, now?"

Shiloh nodded. "Mostly. There's just one problem now."

Killian tensed. "What would that be?" he asked hopefully.

"I've fallen in love with you, Killian. And I don't know what to do now ..." Shiloh said softly, watching Killian's reaction closely.

Killian closed his eyes, as if he was in pain. Killian stood up and held his hand out to Shiloh. Shiloh stared at it for a minute, then took it slowly, standing slowly, not resisting as Killian drew him closer. Looking up at the man he'd come to love, Shiloh stepped into his arms. The embrace did not feel comforting this time. As Shiloh no longer needed Sanctuary, neither of them had to ignore the attraction and need that had developed between them. Killian tipped Shiloh's head just a little, and kissed him, very, very softly.

Shiloh moaned as Killian gave him the sweetest, softest, most erotic kiss he could imagine. It was light years beyond what Shiloh had imagined for his first kiss. He'd thought he would feel awkward, scared, or just plain stupid, but he felt none of these. He felt cherished, loved, and desirable. Shiloh put all his love for Killian into the kiss, wanting him to feel the same thing from him.

Only when they needed to breathe did they end their first kiss. Killian stared in wonder at Shiloh. "Come to my bed?" he asked in a tentative whisper. "Please?"

Shiloh nodded, too overwhelmed to speak, his touch-sense flaring brightly with Killian's emotions and intent. It wasn't really late enough to go to bed, but neither cared. Each knew the other intended to make good use of the time they had. Shiloh happily followed Killian upstairs to the *Artris'* suite.

The *Artris'* suite had a massive four-poster bed in it. When Killian looked at it, he laughed softly.

"What's so funny?" Shiloh asked as he held Killian's hand, rubbing his thumb over the back of it.

Killian pointed to the sheets. "They were cotton this morning. Someone put silk sheets on there for us."

Shiloh blushed and squeaked. "Really?"

Killian nodded, and drew him close again. "You don't have to stay in here with me if you don't want to."

Shiloh smiled. "I know. I want to. This feels right. You feel right, Killian."

He reached up as Killian faced him, and touched Killian's face. Killian closed his eyes at the touch, stunned. If anyone had demanded that he describe the emotions he felt as Shiloh caressed his face, he would have failed miserably. They were too overwhelming, too strong to separate. For the first time in his life, he wanted to be touched in a sensual, sexual manner. It was exhilarating. It was terrifying.

Shiloh shivered as Killian's hands slid along his face, cupping his head. "Can I loosen your hair?"

Shiloh nodded, afraid to speak for fear of ruining the moment. He could sense the love and lust Killian had for him, and it took his breath away. Killian took his time unraveling the braids in Shiloh's hair, fingering the tangles loose. Shiloh then returned the favor, gently massaging Killian's scalp, getting a few soft moans in return. They twisted their hands in each other's hair, the soft, wavy masses clinging to their hands and faces.

Shiloh tipped his face up to Killian, silently asking for another kiss. Killian obligingly dipped his head, very lightly licking the seam of Shiloh's mouth, wanting a small taste. He moaned as Shiloh opened his mouth to him, and shyly licked back. Killian opened up to Shiloh, swallowing the gasp of pleasure Shiloh gave him.

For long minutes they kissed, and nuzzled. Killian gradually moved them both to the bed, and they toppled onto it together, staying wrapped around each other. They touched gently, sensually, but somehow; they didn't ignite like Shiloh thought they would. He found himself lying on his side, tucked into Killian's side, both of them shirtless, content somehow to just cuddle. The exhaustion and sleepy contentment that emanated from Killian explained much of the reason. Killian's arm held him snug against Killian's body, and Shiloh reveled in the fact they fit perfectly together. Shiloh nuzzled at Killian's hair where it lay over his chest, inhaling the clean scent of it.

Killian tangled his fingers in Shiloh's hair, loving the soft silky thickness of it sliding over his fingers. Their petting became more and more languid as exhaustion from the emotional upheavals of the preceding weeks caught up with them. They slept peacefully, never leaving each other's arms.

.   .   .

It was dark when Shiloh woke up. A quick glance at the clock told him it wasn't even two in the morning, and a soft, faint snore told him Killian was sleeping soundly. Shiloh didn't try to move though, not yet. On one hand, he needed to use the bathroom, but on the other, it was so perfect lying there, snuggled so tight to Killian, that he just didn't ever want to move again. Finally, his bladder threatened him with an embarrassing occurrence if he didn't get up, so he did, as quietly and carefully as he could, not wanting to wake Killian. Coming back, he found Killian sitting up, yawning, apparently waiting his turn. So much for not waking him up, Shiloh thought. When Killian went to the bathroom, Shiloh slid into the bed, wriggling under the covers until he lay in the warm spot left by the other man.

Killian came back to see the nervous look on Shiloh's face, and knew it probably matched his. He lay next to Shiloh, taking his hand, and bringing it to his lips, pressing a soft kiss into Shiloh's skin. Shiloh was so beautiful, Killian thought as he put his arm around the smaller man.

Shiloh leaned his head into the crook of Killian's neck, letting himself sink into the intimacy of the moment. After all of those nights on the couch, it felt like the most natural thing in the world to let Killian shelter him, and Shiloh wondered if Killian felt the same way. "What time is it?" he whispered softly, afraid a normal tone would dispel the intimacy between them.

Killian answered in a whisper, too. "It's only one thirty in the morning. We've a long time before we need to be up."

"Killian?"

"Yes, Shiloh?"

"Do you want ...?" Shiloh blushed, not even able to complete the question.

Killian snorted softly, squeezing Shiloh closer. "Yeah, I want, but I want it right, too. Does that make sense?"

Shiloh nodded. "What's right to you?"

"I don't want to be rushed. I don't want you to feel rushed into it," Killian answered softly. "Come on, Sprite, let's lay down and get comfortable."

"Sprite?" Shiloh questioned a little incredulously.

Killian grinned as he pulled Shiloh close to him. "You are so sweet and happy so much of the time, you seem like one of the sprites the humans speak of, come to play among the Rimalians."

Shiloh blushed again, pleased at that description. "You make me feel safe. Safer than I've ever felt." He settled in, laying his hand on Killian's chest, right over his heart. "I'm afraid to lose that security, but in less than three days we're going to be on opposite sides of the world."

"We don't have to stay there, Sprite," Killian answered gently. "I want you in ways I didn't even know were possible until I met you. But I also don't want this to be a fling. I've never wanted anyone, until I met you."

"I want you, too, Killian. What do you suggest?"

"We can visit each other. If you like, I can come visit you in a few weeks. Then we can figure it out from there."

"Really, you would come visit me?" Shiloh asked, surprised. Why would he do that?

Killian seemed to read his mind. "Because I want to see you. I want to see what we could have together." Killian held Shiloh tighter. "I don't want to never see or hold you again. I can't bear the thought."

Shiloh kissed the shoulder under his cheek, feeling Killian's breath hitch. "I don't want that, either. I was so scared this was all I'd have of you ..."

"And now that you know I want more than these few days with you?" Killian asked softly, his voice hopeful. Shiloh could sense Killian was afraid Shiloh wouldn't want more.

Shiloh shifted up so he was braced on an elbow, looking down at Killian's face. "I want more than a quick fling, Killian. I want to know where this goes for us." He leaned down and laid his lips against Killian's, moaning when the kiss deepened. This time he licked at Killian's mouth hungrily. Killian opened to Shiloh, moaning as Shiloh's tongue swept in, tasting eagerly. Shiloh's body tightened. Their bodies hard and leaking, they moved instinctively. Combined with the deep kisses, it only took a few minutes of rubbing against each other for both of them to come, swallowing each other's cries.

Panting, Shiloh collapsed on top of Killian, shocked at how quickly that had happened, and how good it felt. Suddenly Killian laughed, and Shiloh found himself grinning foolishly. He looked at Killian. "Good?"

"More than good, my little Sprite." He kissed Shiloh again. "More than good."

They cleaned themselves up, then returned to the bed, spooning together. They both knew they had more to work out, more to talk about, but they didn't want to lose the afterglow of such a surprisingly sensual lovemaking, preferring instead, to sleep.

The last thing Shiloh felt and heard was Killian's lips on the back of his neck, kissing and whispering, "Good night, Shiloh, my beautiful little Sprite."

10

S HILOH'S NEW ESTATE MANAGER, Sherry Ertrai, greeted him upon his arrival at the airport. He let her drive while he sorted recent events out in his mind.

Only that morning, Lucretia had taken them back to Killian's estate. Then Killian had taken Shiloh to the airport in Italy, so as to not attract any attention from human authorities about how Shiloh had gotten back into the country. Rimalians preferred to avoid questions like that; it just made things easier in the long term.

His estate, a plantation in a rural area outside a small city in North Carolina, was a working farm, with its income coming from cotton and the supply of organic produce to local shops. The house itself had been built in the 1680s, one of the oldest surviving structures in the States. The Morgaine House had been built by a Jarvai family group and, later, sold to the Zahirris. A huge, grand old place, it could proudly boast to never having been worked by slaves.

The Zahirris were a very small clan now—Shiloh was one of the few left, and fewer of them female. Shiloh did have a female cousin, the daughter of an uncle, but as her mother's heir, she could not become the Zahirris heir, despite being the only one in the bunch Shiloh would want to see as *Artris*. Perhaps that was why his mother had been so determined to see him married to a female; she'd wanted a granddaughter she could make heir.

During the drive, Sherry told him of recent events on the estate, including a birth for which he was invited to the christening later in the week. She also covered the histories of the various tenants. Sherry's family had worked the estate for over two hundred years, and the population currently included families from the Jarvai, M'Ilvith, Solentai, and Torrai Clans. Not all were Rimalian; some were descended from indentured human servants who had married and stayed.

As they drove down the estate drive, he noticed a few tenant houses being torn down.

"I'm sorry, Sherry, I must have missed something. Did you tell me why these houses are being torn down?" he asked, flushing at his inattention. Most of his mind was in Italy, wondering what Killian was doing.

She smiled politely. "They were too storm damaged to salvage. I decided to house the families in the Morgaine House until we could build something, or perhaps buy some mobile homes for them. The houses weren't safe, and Lord Ewan wouldn't give me any direction. From what Lady Jarvai told me, it wasn't until a few days ago that you knew the estate was yours." She sighed, and then pulled the car over and parked. "My Lord, I'll be honest, you'll have your hands full. We all knew that the estate went to you, but since you never visited, never showed any interest, we assumed you didn't give a sh— dang."

"So I'm going to catch a certain amount of shit, aren't I?" Shiloh mused.

"Yes, sir, you will. I've explained to everyone what really happened, but not everyone will believe it. Especially since your ex-wife was here many times, particularly in the last six months, making it very clear we were all about to lose our homes and livelihoods. I even called your father, but he said she could do as she wished as the property would soon be hers."

"Anan did what?" Shiloh asked, stunned.

"She's had four different appraisers out here. She stayed for a week or so every time, and always left the entire estate in disarray. I've managed as best I can, but when your father said to obey … well, let's just say that there's been a certain amount of willful obedience, even on my part." She blushed a little.

"How bad is it, Sherry?"

"We're barely going to get by, this year and next. We knew she wanted to sell the place for the money, and we decided we weren't going to lose our homes without a fight. We've tried to stay solvent, yet, at the same time not worth selling. Been two years that way. We lost a few customers, but most knew what was going on, and we worked out certain arrangements, off the book deals, with the difference going into discreet investment funds. With a little help, the legalities have been dealt with, the taxes paid and such. It's all legally accounted for, it's just not registered as being part of the estate. Before Lady Jarvai called me, I was trying to decide whether or not to cash it in to rebuild the storm-damaged houses. Thankfully, Lady Jarvai's call a few days ago meant I could postpone the decision for you to make."

"So, basically, you've been embezzling from the estate, to keep the estate and run it?"

Shamefaced, Sherry nodded. "Yes, my Lord. I'll understand if you find it necessary to replace me, but I have both sets of books ready for you to look over."

"One thing at a time, Sherry. Let's get to the house. I'm sure you've had a long day, and you did all the driving." A sudden thought caused Shiloh to freeze. "When was the last time Anan was here?"

"Three weeks ago. She wasn't happy, I can tell you." Sherry didn't seem to know whether to be proud, embarrassed, or both. After his experiences over the last few months, Shiloh could understand the feeling.

"So you've been making all the decisions without support since *Senki*'s death?" he asked.

"Yes, sir. When I asked Lord Ewan about it, he said there wasn't any point in him doing anything, since the estate would be changing hands again soon enough. I even asked when you would be coming to inspect your new property, and he told me you had better things to do than worry about something you weren't keeping long." Sherry sighed. "I heard that same thing for nearly three years."

As they drove up to the huge house he hadn't seen in almost five years, Shiloh ran his fingers through his hair. It was all such a mess! "I've been trying to avoid getting married that long. For a while I was able to claim a mourning period for *Senki*, but after that ..." Shiloh shuddered.

"But now you come to us under the disgrace of divorce?" Sherry asked delicately, blushing again.

He shrugged. "It got *Senka* his inheritance and me my freedom from that psychotic bitch, Anan. I know that there will be some that treat me disrespectfully, but as long as it isn't any of my tenants, I'll deal with it." He looked around as he got out of the car. A crowd stood on the front lawn. "There aren't many young people among them," he noted, more to himself than Sherry.

There was definitely a dearth of young adults in the crowd of tenants. "Some have moved away entirely, some are in college, and others have taken jobs elsewhere to bring money back to their families," Sherry told him.

Shiloh nodded to show he'd heard, and then stepped toward the crowd. "Hello, all."

People who'd once greeted him with happy smiles now just gave him a grim look. Most did bob their heads in greeting. He sighed. Yeah, he was going to need help. He didn't know the first thing about running an estate, because he'd never been taught. But Killian had told him about some of what he had dealt with, so he knew whom to call. At least he would have one friendly voice, other than his estate manager.

"I understand Mistress Sherry has informed you all I was unaware of my inheritance until a few days ago. I also understand that my ex-wife has caused a certain amount of trouble for you, which you have fought back against in your own way. I'm not going to stand here and tell you what you should or shouldn't have done. You were here and I wasn't, so all I will say is that she is no longer your worry. If she sets foot on this property, I give you leave to remove her from it, forcefully if necessary."

"You would ban your wife from the estate?" one of the older women, one he didn't recognize, asked incredulously. She must have been new.

"Ex-wife, and yes I do. She had no rights to do as she did."

"So it's true, our new lord is disgraced," the same woman said, her disgust clear in her voice.

"I don't see it as a disgrace, and I won't listen to that crap from my tenants. My 'disgrace' as you put it, has not only bought my freedom, but just might save your home," Shiloh retorted. "I have no intention of selling the estate. Anan was going to, and with no care for what might be done with it."

The people in the crowd exchanged uneasy glances and then began to melt away, back to their homes, some of them walking into the House.

Dispirited, Shiloh sighed. What a wonderful beginning to his new life.

·   ·   ·

An hour later, Shiloh was in the *Artris'* suite, which included his bedroom, a guest bedroom, a sitting room, a closet so large it could have been a bedroom itself, and a full bath. The bathroom had been remodeled to have a huge garden tub and shower big enough for two. Wondering vaguely who had done the remodel, he took out his cell phone and called Killian. With a six-hour time difference, it would be about three in the morning in Italy. Killian would be sleeping, but Shiloh was under orders to call when he went to bed.

"Hello, Shiloh." Killian's sleepy voice made Shiloh shiver. For three nights they had slept comfortably together in Killian's bed—not out on the couch, so propriety could be observed—making out a lot, exploring each other a little, but stopping far short of where they wanted to. They had agreed to go slow, regardless of what their hormones wanted. It had been wonderful torture and Shiloh wanted nothing more than to be right back in Killian's bed. The huge four-poster he was sitting on felt cold. What Killian would look like in it, hair loose, and naked ...?

"Hi, Killian. I miss you," he said quietly.

"I guess it didn't go well." There was a rustling sound, like Killian was sitting up.

"Let's see ... Anan has been causing trouble on the estate for at least a year, the manager began embezzling from the estate to make it harder for Anan to sell it and, of course, I'm a disgraced male and I'm in charge and I'm clueless." Shiloh sighed. "*Senka* did nothing for or with the estate since *Senki* died, so now I get to play catch-up on the last three years." Tears stung his eyes. Shiloh shook his head; he didn't have the luxury of crying anymore, there was too much to do. "Killian, I don't have a clue where to start, and I'm not sure how much help I can count on from the tenants. I don't know what's been said in the past few years, but people who were always happy to see me in the past could barely even look at me today."

"First thing is, don't make any decisions in a panic. That was the first thing JoAnne and Natalya taught me. You need to sleep tonight and then call me in the morning, okay? I'll try to help you sort things out," Killian told him, his low, friendly tone calming Shiloh immensely. "Now what's this about Anan?"

"She's brought in at least four appraisers over the last year or so, Sherry said, and apparently the last time she was here was about three weeks ago," Shiloh told him. "Why would she visit if her rights to the estate were unresolved?"

"You need to call Lady Jarvai and tell her about this, and Ewan's mismanagement," Killian told him. "You also need to decide whether to call the Magistrate about your manager."

"That one I knew. Sherry told me she'd understand if I chose to replace her. She apparently kept official records, designed to make the estate look bad, and then the real books, including accountings of the embezzled money. We're going to sit down and go over both sets of books," Shiloh said.

"What the hell?"

"I told you, she was trying to make it hard for Anan to sell the place. Ewan told her to do as Anan said because the place was going to be hers as soon as we married. Anan apparently came in acting like she already owned the place ... These people used to be pretty content and happy, and now ..." Shiloh fell silent. He didn't know if he was defending Sherry's actions or just repeating the information.

"You're tired, love, I can hear it. The time difference is getting you, I think," Killian said softly. "You should sleep for now, Sprite, and call me when you're in your study tomorrow." His voice was warm and soothing in Shiloh's ear.

At the reminder of the time, Shiloh yawned, and then nodded, even though Killian couldn't see him.

"Yup, you're yawning in my ear. Call Milossa and tell her you've discovered Anan has been interfering on the estate, even while you were under Sanctuary. She needs to know."

"Okay. I love you, Killian."

"I love you too, Sprite. Call me when you get up." After the reminder, Killian hung up.

Shiloh sighed, and did as Killian told him, calling Milossa, who was quite cross at being woken up, and even more annoyed when she learned why. Shiloh told her everything he'd learned so far, and that he'd phoned Killian for help. She reassured him that had been a wise decision. After he yawned in her ear the fourth time, she chuckled and told him to sleep.

Giving her a sleepy "Yes, ma'am," Shiloh hung up on her; asleep before he even fell over on the bed.

•　　•　　•

It was ten o'clock the next morning before he woke up, and much to his surprise, Killian was sitting on the bed next to him with his girls. He rubbed his eyes, thinking it must be a dream, but no, both Killian and the dogs were still there when he opened them again. He reached out to Killian, expecting him to vanish.

"Killian?" he asked as he touched Killian's smooth jaw.

"Hey, sleepy Sprite." Killian kissed Shiloh's questing fingers. "It's about time you got up. We've been here for two hours."

"How?" Shiloh sat up, grimacing as he realized he was still wearing his shoes. Eeww. He didn't want to think about the condition of his socks after wearing them for nearly twenty-four hours straight.

"Lucretia brought myself, the girls, Natalya, Milossa, Kelia, and a few others to investigate the issues with the estate, and Anan, themselves." Killian gently cupped Shiloh's chin. "I don't suppose I could talk you into a kiss?"

"If you don't mind my mouth tastes like fuzzy things with eyes are growing in it ..." Shiloh told him, smiling softly.

Killian grinned back and leaned forward. Their mouths met gently, and they sighed. Tongues tangled, then they drew back reluctantly. Killian rubbed their noses together. "Nah, there might be fuzzy things in there, but they don't have eyes yet."

Shiloh laughed a little and crawled into Killian's lap, needing the comfort. "I'm so glad you're here."

"It's not to stay, love, but I'm glad, too." Killian wrapped his arms tightly around Shiloh and Shiloh relaxed for the first time since he woke up the day before. He'd hated leaving Killian. They cuddled for a few minutes, getting ready for the day.

"Let's take what we can get." Shiloh stood up and stretched, knowing Killian watched him hungrily. "If we need to get to work, you've got to not look at me like that."

Killian grinned. "I can't help it. But you are right. You know where your study is?" Shiloh nodded. "We'll meet you in there when you've showered and everything." He kissed Shiloh again and left the suite.

11

T HE COUNCIL MEMBERS spent most of the day investigating the situation with Shiloh, Anan, and the estate. Sherry agreed to a Verification of her actions, and those present, including Shiloh, were assured that all of the money squirreled away had indeed been properly accounted for and used only to benefit the estate. Sherry's actions were excused as an extreme effort to preserve the estate she was charged with managing. Shiloh informed the Council members present that he had banned Anan from his estate, and they agreed it was warranted, telling him they would inform her themselves when they went to question her about her actions. She had committed a grievous breach by continuing to try to prepare the estate to be sold when Shiloh, and by extension his property, had been protected by Sanctuary.

The tenants watched warily but seemed willing to wait and see what happened. They were markedly cold towards Shiloh, though, and it hurt him more than he wanted to admit. Shiloh listened as the Council group spoke with everybody, studying how they handled the tenants. He was a fast learner, and he wanted to do right by the estate. It was his home now.

Killian stayed close by, although not too obviously. Shiloh didn't argue about it either. This was Bible Belt area, and he had no idea how accepting his tenants would be. Some Rimalian enclaves were influenced more by local human beliefs than others. The tenants seemed to be having trouble with his being divorced, so he didn't need them having kittens because he was gay, too. Right now, he needed them to work to bring the estate back to its proper state. There would be time enough to fight about his sexuality once the estate was back on its feet.

Shiloh invited the Council members to stay at the estate, and they accepted. He and the housekeeper—who turned out to be the woman who had made the 'disgrace' comment—made up rooms for everyone, including the guest room in his suite for Killian. Hopefully Killian wouldn't sleep in it.

The housekeeper's attitude was sullen and just shy of disrespectful towards him, as had been the attitudes of most of the tenants. Lucretia winked at him before she retired for the night, making him blush. She didn't say anything against his obvious plans though, just patted him and told him not to worry; he was an adult and no longer bound by certain restrictions, since he was technically a divorced male. Although Killian was also an adult, because he had never been married, he had to be more careful. For now, though, his tenants would probably assume Killian's unmarried status was why he was sharing Shiloh's suite. Lucretia advised him to let them assume the arrangement was to protect propriety, for now.

When Shiloh finally went to bed, he was just as exhausted as he'd been the night before. Killian met him in his bedroom and pushed him towards the bathroom. "Come on, Sprite, into the tub with you."

Shiloh managed to get undressed while Killian ran a hot bath for him. "I don't know why I'm so tired. I slept for what, nearly twelve hours?"

"It couldn't possibly be because of all the animosity thrown your way today, could it?" Killian asked sarcastically. "I know you're new to this, but you need to put your tenants in their place, sooner than later, love."

"But I need them to run the farm. The estate won't survive if the farm is untended," Shiloh protested. He couldn't afford fights he would lose.

"On one hand, you're right." Killian kissed the back of Shiloh's neck, and then helped Shiloh into the tub. Killian picked up a washcloth and got it soapy. Sitting on the step set into the tub, Killian began to wash Shiloh's back. "But here's the flip side. The estate doesn't survive if you don't take charge of it, either. You've got the purse strings and now you're here, regardless of what others have done in the past. You spent more than a month on my estate, bouncing around, sticking your nose into everything. Put what you learned to good use, love."

"That part's easy, but most of these people have known me since I was in diapers."

"When was the last time you were here?"

"Almost five years ago."

"Would you have let them treat you like this then?"

Shiloh blinked. Killian was right. He would have taken strips out of them if they'd treated him so disrespectfully the last time he was there. "You're right. I wouldn't have let them get away with this 'so sorry' snide insult bullshit." He sighed as he thought about the difference between now and then. "I didn't realize how much of that 'I'm just a worthless male' attitude I'd internalized the past few years." Surrounded by Anan's psionic miasma as she'd pursued him, somehow part of him had begun to believe her views of his value, and they came to the fore when he got depressed. Maybe he should call Celie and ask her to come?

Killian turned him and kissed him gently. "You've never been worthless, Shiloh."

"Thank you, love," Shiloh said, kissing Killian back, basking in the touch-sense of his lover. Celie had taught him how to shield himself better, but it still wasn't automatic. After the psionic battering of today, it was wonderful to be able to relax that side of himself.

Once Shiloh was clean, Killian helped him out of the tub and dried him thoroughly. Shiloh let him; it was nice to be pampered.

"Come on, let's get you to bed. I already rolled around in the guest bed like I slept in it. I'm hoping, though, I don't have to." Killian leered comically.

Shiloh grinned, and put his arms around Killian's neck. "Take me to bed. Although, I don't think I'll be awake long."

"That's okay, Sprite. It'll be good just to hold you." Killian helped Shiloh into the bed, and set the alarm for early the next morning. Then he slid in under the covers with Shiloh, spooning himself around him. "We're going to go question Ewan tomorrow, and then Anan, then Lucretia is taking all of us home."

Shiloh sighed. A night alone with Killian and he was too exhausted to do anything with it. The snuggling was good, though, he thought as he pressed himself back into the curve of Killian's body, so comforting after today. He let Killian's love soak into his skin, and tried to return it in a way that allowed Killian's touch-sense to pick up how much Shiloh loved him, as well. They had agreed not to hide their feelings from each other anymore. "When will you be able to visit?"

"In a few weeks, for about a week, maybe ten days." Killian nuzzled the back of Shiloh's neck. "Will those tenants still be living in the house?"

"I don't know, Kil. They don't have the homes that're supposed to be provided for them, so ... And I don't really want mobile homes on the plantation. I know they're just as good as stick built these days, but I want to keep buildings on the estate as close to original as possible, for the most part. I want to rebuild their houses when I can."

"Well, we'll just play it by ear then." Killian kissed the back of his neck. "Sleep, love, we've had a long day." He closed his own eyes, as something in his chest settled. This was where he belonged, with Shiloh. He didn't know yet how they were going to make it work, but he was determined to try. Shiloh's soft snores were the last thing he heard.

•   •   •

The next morning, after the Council members had left, Shiloh sat at his desk looking over the notes he'd taken the night before. He and Killian had woken up early enough to have a good snuggle before they had to be seen out and about.

Shiloh's face heated as he thought about the way Killian had touched him, after blushing furiously as Killian admitted to watching some things on the Internet. Things he wanted to try. Try he did, and Shiloh shivered with remembered pleasure as he grinned. He really loved Killian's learning curve.

The housekeeper, the older woman who'd made the comments about his divorce, walked in without bothering to knock. Shiloh frowned as he looked up from the papers. Lorretta hadn't been housekeeper the last time he'd been there; in fact, she hadn't even been on the estate. It was time to deal with her attitude. He watched as she desultorily began to dust.

"Excuse you, Mistress Lorretta," he said coldly.

She glared at him. "What?" As an afterthought, the woman added, "Sir?"

"Sir?" He raised an eyebrow. "Is that the proper address for me?"

She stared at him haughtily for a moment. "You may own the estate, but you are still a disgraced male. Your wife divorced you because you refused to honor your vows, little male. You do not deserve the title of 'Lord.'"

Shiloh nodded as if he might agree. "My disgrace doesn't matter. That you would listen to gossip and not ask me for the facts tells me that I shouldn't trust you."

"I honor my agreements, unlike some here," she retorted.

"But you have not kept the agreement that you treat the owner with proper respect, Lorretta."

She finally began to look worried. "I treat you with more respect than you deserve. Sir."

"In your opinion, not mine. You are relieved of your duties, Mistress Lorretta. I will arrange a severance and, in case the work you did previously was better than the half-hearted effort I've seen, ask Mistress Sherry to write a reference for you. But I want you gone from the estate within the hour. You may leave." Shiloh turned his chair until his back was to her. Pulling out his cell phone, he called Sherry and ordered her to his study. The study door slammed shut.

A few minutes later, he heard an angry voice, then a calmer one in the hall outside his study. Sounded like Lorretta expected Sherry to gainsay him. She could try, and he could dismiss her, too. No way in hell was he going accept being treated like this.

A moment later, there was a knock. He waited a minute, then called out, "Come."

Sherry walked in, looking perplexed.

"Thank you for coming promptly, Mistress Sherry. We need a new housekeeper, and I was curious to see if you had any recommendations. Otherwise, I will advertise elsewhere."

"Excuse me, Shiloh, but—"

Shiloh cut her off mid-sentence. "I think that a return to formality is in order, Mistress Sherry. I had hoped that if I was just my usual self that I would get at least common courtesy in return, but since that isn't the case ... I told you I wouldn't tolerate disrespect from my tenants. I guess they didn't listen when you warned them," he said calmly. He waved her to a seat to indicate that he wasn't angry with her personally.

"I see, my Lord." She studied him for a minute. "And Lorretta's dismissal?"

"Is an example. If she can't even be bothered with such a base courtesy as knocking before entering someone's office when they're working, what other courtesies will she ignore?" He sighed. What would be the best way to walk the line between putting them in their places and keeping their cooperation? "There is too much to do for this estate to tolerate petty bullshit, Sherry. I'll bet the list I compiled yesterday isn't even close to everything that's been neglected, whatever the reason it happened. I need to be able to trust you all as much as you need to trust me."

"I grant that you have a point, but it isn't that easy for them," Sherry said carefully.

"Can you explain to me why?" he asked. "The comment Lorretta made about me not honoring my vows gives me a clue, but is that the whole of it, or is there more?"

She sat thoughtfully for a while, but Shiloh didn't push. He could afford to give her time to figure out how to answer politely. "My Lord, do you have any idea at all of what's been said about you the past week?"

"Only Lorretta's comment a few minutes ago. I figure Anan is running around telling anybody and everybody I refused to honor my vows, which is sort of true, and sort of isn't."

"How do you mean, my Lord? You did marry her, correct?"

"Yes, but only to satisfy the Council's command and *Senki's* will. I never wanted to marry Anan in the first place. I was forced to the altar and ran from it. I requested Sanctuary from Lady Larrestes almost eight weeks ago. The Magistrate turned the matter over to the Council."

"Why didn't Lady Larrestes adjudicate the matter, my Lord?" Sherry looked confused. He could understand that, since anyone who had authority enough to provide Sanctuary normally also had the authority to adjudicate the matter. Shiloh quickly detailed events for her.

"You were only married for an hour?" she repeated incredulously, chuckling. "And the lack of consummation was why Anan didn't get the estate?"

"Exactly." He shook his head sadly. "*Senka* owes me reparations for failing to tell me of my inheritance, and for blackmailing me. Anan got to marry me, but was also forced to divorce me. I got my freedom and kept my virtue and property, if not my reputation. I will get the estate back on its feet, but how I do that depends entirely on y'all. I don't want to tell everyone to leave; almost all of you were born here and this is your home. But it's my home now too, and I won't tolerate being treated as a pariah in my own home."

She nodded agreeably. "You should know it's being put about that you and Lady Larrestes are lovers, that you disgraced yourself before your marriage. Word has it that Anan divorced you partly because you were no longer virgin."

"I don't care," Shiloh said with as nonchalant a shrug as he could manage. "He might, though, and I hear he's pretty good with a blade. Anyone who wants to repeat that rumor may wish to have a care, since he'll be back in a few weeks."

"May I ask why?"

"Sure. We've become very good friends. He's not even a year older than I, only a few months really, but we kind of bonded because of Anan." He grinned suddenly. "Wow. I finally realized something Anan was good for: I have a new friend because of her. Anyway, he'll be here for a week or so."

"I'll spread the warning. Will he be sharing your suite again?"

"That would be best, wouldn't it, since he's a never-married male?" Shiloh shrugged.

"It would take care of the who's visiting his bedroom thing," Sherry agreed. "It's just …"

"There will be some who will believe the moon is green cheese despite clear evidence to the contrary," Shiloh said derisively, understanding what she was getting at.

Sherry fell into that thoughtful silence again. He had learned several things about Sherry in the last two days: she was well-liked and trusted by his tenants, and she tried to gather as much information as possible before making a decision. "My Lord, this may be delicate ground, but you said Lady Larrestes was also Anan's victim?"

Shiloh sighed. "Do you know how he became Regent?"

"We heard that his mother killed his father in front of his younger siblings, and the Council ruled it murder and executed her. Lady Nedai spoke for the Larrestes for a time, and he was approved Regent some time ago, until his sister is considered old enough and ready to be *Artris*." Again, Shiloh explained what happened.

Sherry sat, stunned. "Did Lady Elizabeth know?"

Shiloh gave her a grim, sober look. "They both did, according to Lady K'Arith. She told *Senki* herself," he answered quietly. "And none of them told me."

She got up and went to the sideboard, where a decanter of brandy sat, with glasses. He said nothing as she poured a drink and swallowed it down. Belatedly, she looked at him for permission, and he waved the silent question away. She raised a glass, asking if he wanted one and he shook his head. She poured herself another and brought it with her back to her seat. He wondered if she felt odd sitting on that side of the desk when, for a few years now, she'd sat on this side of it.

"So that was what the Council meant by Anan not profiting from deception," Sherry said as she settled into her chair.

"Yeah. The Council questioned her about her intentions, not only towards me, but my birthright and Lady Larrestes. They weren't happy with any of her answers."

They were both silent for a time.

"So do you have any recommendations for a housekeeper?" Shiloh asked. "I don't care about gender, just ability."

"Actually, I know a young man who's in college right now, his first year, but he's not happy there. He went because there just wasn't anything for him to do here that he's happy with. I also suspect that he won't have any issue with your divorce."

"What's his name?"

"Keith Torrai. He scandalized his parents by not moving with them when they left, and he gets some shit because he's unmarried but doesn't work to protect his reputation like some around here think he should," Sherry answered. "No one can ever point out an instance where he's actually behaved badly, though; he even lives in a male dorm."

"So he's skirting that line but no one really thinks he's crossed it," Shiloh said with a smile. "What's his number?"

She gave him the number and he wrote it down. A male strong enough to buck convention like that without losing his reputation should be able to handle the politics of being a housekeeper just fine. Then Shiloh handed Sherry his to-do list and suggested she take it and add to it anything he missed, as well as her suggestions about how the jobs should be completed, if she had any.

Shiloh picked up the phone to the sound of Sherry softly closing the door behind her.

12

T WO DAYS LATER, Shiloh and Keith headed into the city
together.

When Shiloh received a cashier's check for three hundred thousand, he had gulped in shock. He hadn't known his father's inheritance was worth three million. According to the United States, Shiloh wasn't old enough to set up a bank account on his own, and too many people had access to the estate account for him to feel comfortable depositing the money there. Granted, neither the United States nor any other government on Earth was aware of the alien culture that lived amongst them, so Shiloh supposed they could be excused for treating him as a child. After all, humans matured more slowly than Rimalians. Therefore, since Keith was of age as far as Uncle Sam was concerned, he would help Shiloh set up a bank account.

Shiloh had been delighted to find he and Keith got along great, and they had plans to get the house into shape. Keith certainly hadn't been offended, as Lorretta had been, by Shiloh's wish to maintain his own rooms.

Thanks to Keith, after two hours of paperwork and red tape, Shiloh possessed a bank account he could access at need, a temporary debit card, and as a few thousand in his pocket in cash. The first place they headed for was the hardware store. Shiloh admitted it might be a little paranoid, but he would feel better if the locks on the house were changed, including adding a locking doorknob to his suite. Until he felt more comfortable with the situation on the estate, he would just lock his suite and his study when they were vacant. They bought new doorknobs for every entrance to the House, as well as for the *Artris'* suite, Shiloh's study, and Sherry's. Only the three of them, Sherry, Shiloh, and Keith would have keys for every door, with the exception of Shiloh's suite. Only Keith would have a spare key to the *Artris'* suite.

He had already discussed with Sherry having a security firm look the house over and make a few recommendations for improving its security. Since this was an extremely low crime area and incidents on the estate were rare, she'd been surprised, but said she'd call around and ask for quotes. She said it might mean allowing humans to come in and look the place over. He said it was fine as long as she escorted them.

After the visit to the hardware shop, they stopped to have lunch, and talked, getting to know each other better and discussing what else was required for the House. Then they went shopping, since Shiloh needed some more clothes. All he had was what Killian had bought him, and he needed some he wouldn't care about ruining. To help him manage the Estate, he also bought himself a good laptop and a Wi-Fi device. He couldn't keep borrowing Sherry's. Although he enjoyed being out and about, Shiloh was happy to get home.

They spent hours changing doorknobs, not finishing till late, but Shiloh wanted it done before they went to bed. Finally, Shiloh was able to go to bed feeling safer. The fear that Anan might have keys to the house had led to some bad nightmares. Sherry denied Anan possessed keys to the house until Shiloh pointed out Ewan had owned a set and it was highly likely he'd given them to her. Sherry conceded the point, and helped install the new locks in her personal time after she'd finished for the day.

Shiloh pulled out his phone and called Killian. They woke each other up every night; when Killian started his day in a few hours, he'd call back, waking Shiloh.

Killian's sleepy voice answered, making him smile. "Hello, Sprite."

"Hi, love, how was your day?"

"Long. Oh, before I forget, you should expect a call from the Council in the next day or so."

Shiloh knew better than to ask why, since Killian probably couldn't tell him. "Okay, thanks. We replaced a gazillion doorknobs today, with only a minimum of cussing," he told Killian.

Killian chuckled. "Are you sure you did it right, then?" Shiloh heard faint rustling. He pictured Killian sitting up in his bed and settling back against the pillows.

"Yeah, I'm sure they don't wiggle and the keys work, so ..." Shiloh smiled, although Killian couldn't see it. "What are you wearing?"

"What?"

"I've decided to instigate a bit of phone sex, and from what I understand, it begins with 'What are you wearing?'" Shiloh grinned as he heard Killian choke. He loved surprising the man. "Breathe, baby."

"Deity help me. Where'd that idea come from?" Killian asked, laughing.

"From being seriously horny and hearing your voice," Shiloh answered with a giggle. "Well?" he asked as he heard more rustling. What was his love doing now?

"Well, what?" Killian teased.

"What are you wearing?" Shiloh repeated, as expected.

"Nothing, now," Killian told him.

Shiloh gulped as he pictured Killian's tall, muscular frame, nude.

"Shiloh ..." Killian's soft, seductive voice broke into Shiloh's trance.

"Huh?" he asked, his mind still a little stuck on Killian getting naked to have phone sex with him.

"You're wearing too many clothes. Take them off." Killian's voice held a hint of command that had Shiloh obeying without a thought.

Putting the phone down, Shiloh scrambled out of his clothes, glad he'd already locked the door. He picked the phone back up. "Now I'm naked, too," he said cheerfully.

Killian groaned. "Good. I want you to lay down with me."

"I wish I could," Shiloh said as he lay down, stretching out on the slightly rough bedding. That was something he should have done in town, gotten himself some nice sheets for himself. Then again, for this bed, he'd probably have to look online. He had a sudden, very brief fantasy of Killian in this bed with him, on soft silk sheets. Oh yeah, now he definitely had to buy some. It would be worth it, though.

"I wish you could, too, Sprite. I haven't been sleeping well with you gone." Killian's admission gave Shiloh a ridiculous case of the warm fuzzies.

"Me either, although I hope that at least tonight I won't have nightmares about Anan being able to get into the house." Shiloh shuddered at the thought. "I'm laying down, was there something you wanted me to do?" he asked, preferring to get back to something a lot more fun—playing with Killian.

"I want you to touch yourself," Killian ordered, his voice falling back into the seductive caress Shiloh loved. That tone being breathed against his bare skin felt incredible, and Shiloh let himself imagine Killian was there, doing exactly that.

"Where?"

"Your nipples. I love how the lightest touch has them hard under my fingers."

"Only when you touch them, Kil." Shiloh's breath came faster as he rubbed his nipples, enjoying the little zings of pleasure they sent shooting through his body. Killian had actually made him come just by playing with his nipples. His body tightened as he remembered that night.

"Pinch them, Sprite. I want to hear your pleasure when you play with those tasty little nips." Moaning, Shiloh obeyed, loving that prim, proper Killian enjoyed talking dirty. It had kinda surprised them both how much of a turn-on it was.

"I want your mouth, Kil, please."

"I'm going to suck those pretty nips until they're aching, Sprite. Then I'm going to lick them until you are writhing under me, begging."

"Please, please ..." Shiloh begged, easily falling into the fantasy. Oh, that felt so good. He managed to tuck the phone so he could hear and touch his aching cock at the same time.

It was as if Killian could read his mind. "Oh no, I didn't say you could touch your cock, Sprite." Killian's voice still held that sex-on-a-stick tone, but he was breathing harder. Shiloh imagined Killian touching himself, stroking himself. "Keep playing with your nipples, love, I want you to come without even touching your dick, just like the other night."

"Oh, God," Shiloh breathed as his body tightened further.

"You feel so good under my hands, taste so good I want to eat you," Killian murmured to him. Shiloh pinched and twisted his nipples more, and imagined Killian's tongue licking them, teasing. "Can I, Shiloh? Can I bite those hard, pert little nips?"

"Yes, please, bite me; suck me, anything you want!" Shiloh answered desperately, pinching them again as he remembered feeling the heat of Killian's mouth on them. He cried Killian's name as he came, cum landing hotly on his stomach and even his neck. He dimly heard Killian cry out his name as he came, too, and Shiloh focused a little more on the phone, loving the sounds of Killian's pleasure. "Oh, Deity, Kil."

Killian's voice was hoarse as he chuckled. "I agree, Sprite." He chuckled again as Shiloh giggled happily. "I think I love phone sex with you."

"I know I do." Shiloh sank into the bedding, feeling boneless. The spunk drying on his skin started to feel sticky but he didn't care. He felt all tingly, and Killian's still heavy breath was in his ear. "So much better than 'How was your day, dear?'"

Killian laughed. "Oh yes, although, you already told me how your day was, dear."

"So did you, dear," Shiloh teased back. "I can't wait until you get here, Killian."

"Who knew three weeks could seem that long?" Killian asked plaintively.

"And the week you'll be here will go by too quickly," Shiloh added with a sigh.

"Ten days. We'll work our asses off all day—and play all night," Killian corrected.

"Ten days?" Shiloh repeated. "Good. I want all the time I can get with you." He sighed again. "Any ideas on how we're going to do this?"

"Not yet, but something will come along. I won't be Regent *Artris* forever, after all. Araminta will take over in a few years, and I'll have fewer responsibilities."

"I don't know, I think you'd go nuts not handling things. You're good at it." Shiloh yawned as Killian did. He giggled again, feeling bubbly. "Our brains are complaining about lack of oxygen."

"And lack of sleep. Go on to sleep, Sprite. I'll talk to you in a few hours." He yawned again.

"I love you, Killian." Shiloh turned onto his side, pulling the sheets over himself. His eyes drifted closed as Killian told him he loved him, too. He barely remembered to close the phone to end the call.

•   •   •

Sitting in his study, Shiloh thought about his phone call with Killian the night before. He had just come to a decision about something when his cell phone rang. Seeing that it was Milossa, he answered promptly.

"Hello, my Lady. How are you today?"

"I am well. And you?"

"I'm working on it," he said with a small laugh. "Things have much improved since I replaced the housekeeper, at least in the house."

"We heard about that. Lorretta actually complained to the Council about your dismissal of her," Milossa told him.

He blinked in surprise. "Why? Did I forget something I was supposed to do? I gave her a severance, and Sherry wrote a far better reference for her than I would have done. We arranged her travel to another estate willing to take her on."

"No, you were quite generous given her behavior towards you. She was reminded that it is one thing to think your boss is a disgraceful waste, but smart people do not tell them so, and in their own homes, at that." She made an odd sound, which sounded kind of amused and kind of rude. "You had every right to dismiss her. For that matter, you have every right to dismiss every tenant on the estate if you must."

"Yes, but given what Anan's done to my reputation, on top of being divorced, I'd have a hard time replacing them." He sighed. "They're being more respectful, which I can deal with. I'm hoping that if I give them some time, they'll see the bullshit was never true, that I'm still the same person they were happy to see years ago."

"Perhaps not quite the same, but yes, I see your point. That is a very wise decision."

Shiloh found himself flushing at the praise.

"There's a purpose for calling you this morning, Shiloh. You are ordered to come to Rimalia in three days. You will bring your estate manager, Sherry, your housekeeper, and five witnesses from your estate. I suggest you draw them by lots; that should squelch any claims of coercion or whatever. Lucretia has volunteered her services, but it is traditional to have a gift for the *Sennrojai* who provides travel for you and your party regardless of how well you know them. The gift is not necessary for emergencies, of course, just so that you know for the future."

Shiloh was too shocked by the order to be able to focus on it right away. He considered Lucretia instead. "It will be nice to see her again but, my Lady, what would I get her?"

Milossa made a sad sound. "I happen to know that she recently lost her pet, her only companion, a dog. Perhaps the breeder from whom you got your pups might have another litter ready for adoption? I noticed that she was quite charmed by your girls, as I understand you call them."

"Yes, my Lady. I'm afraid I treat them kind of like my children. How long is recently, though?"

"A few months. Don't worry, I wouldn't have made the suggestion if I didn't think she was ready for a new dog," Milossa assured him.

"More like two dogs, my Lady. Some breeds don't like being alone, more so than others, and Boxers need playmates. They're very high energy dogs, so if that would frustrate Lucretia …?" Shiloh asked delicately.

"On the contrary, a few wild pups to chase after would do her some good, I think," Milossa said with a laugh. "And their playfulness will help her smile again."

"My Lady?" Shiloh asked cautiously, afraid to ask a question he wasn't sure he wanted the answer to.

"Yes, Shiloh?"

"Why am I being summoned to Rimalia? Did I do something wrong? Am I not doing something I'm supposed to?" he asked in a nervous rush.

"The Council will inform you of why when we meet in three days. However, I will tell you you're not in trouble. As for the other, it's entirely possible that you're not doing something you should, or doing it wrong. But I don't know, I'm not there. I'll give you a bit of advice, Shiloh. Do the best you can and make no apology. Your best sometimes isn't enough, and that is true of everyone, not just you or me. But as long as it is your best, you have nothing to be ashamed of," Milossa told him, the warmth in her tone reassuring Shiloh greatly.

"Thank you, my Lady. What time should we be ready?"

"At ten in the morning."

"We'll be ready."

After the necessary courtesies, he hung up. When he began to shake, he picked his phone up again and called Killian.

As soon as Killian answered, he spoke. "I've been ordered to Rimalia in three days."

"I know, love," Killian replied, sighing. "I'm sorry but I can't tell you why."

"I know. I'm sorry I'm freaking out," Shiloh apologized as he tried to calm down.

"Just breathe, love," Killian soothed. He hummed a little, knowing it helped Shiloh when he was out of sorts.

"I'm alright," he said eventually. "I think."

"Yeah, well, getting called to Rimalia to face the Council out of the blue can be pretty startling. Are you going to stay with me?" The suggestiveness in Killian's tone made Shiloh smile.

"Is that an invitation?"

"Of course. I understand if you would rather go to the Zahirris house ..."

"No, I don't think so. My father is there currently, I believe, and I just don't want to deal with him. The estate is in bad shape because of all his—Senki's—and Anan's combined bullshit. I'm not sure I could trust myself to be civil. Not to mention Senka has made it perfectly clear how little he cares for me." Saddened, Shiloh sighed. "I'd rather spend time with you guys. Are you bringing Jaden?"

"I hadn't planned on it, but I can. I'm sure he'll be happy to see you, too." Shiloh could hear the smile in Killian's voice.

His heart finally calmed from its racing, and he was able to take deeper breaths.

"Are you bringing the girls?"

"I don't know. Is it acceptable to ask Lucretia when she's already got to bring so many others? I didn't even know that it's custom to give gifts to *Sennrojai* when they provide transport."

"You can ask, the worst she'll do is tell you no. But unless there's someone there the dogs will obey, it's not an unreasonable request," Killian replied.

"They listen to Keith, and some to Sherry, but otherwise ... No, not really, and those two are coming with me. I don't suppose you can tell me why about that either?'"

"Council business, love. I'm sorry."

"Don't apologize for something that doesn't need it, Killian. I know there's a lot you can't talk about unless they're on the Council," Shiloh assured him. "Are you busy right now? I didn't mean to interrupt ..."

"It's okay. I was just taking a break. I'm recovering from Hypercane Mary." Killian laughed.

"William and Carys finally told them?" Shiloh grinned.

"Not intentionally. They went over to Mary's for dinner and both were hit with morning sickness. Mary was both dancing around because she's going to be a grandmother and cussing them out for not telling her sooner." Killian laughed hysterically as he described the whole scene. By the time he was finished, Shiloh was chortling hysterically, as well. Having met Mary, a human married to a Rimalian, he could well imagine the pint-sized woman's antics.

There was a knock at the door, and, even though he was still laughing, he managed to call out, "Come."

The door opened quietly and Keith entered, shutting the door behind him before giving Shiloh a quizzical look.

He waved Keith to a seat. "Keith just came in."

"All right then, I'll let you get back to it then. I know you can't say it back right now, but I love you, Sprite," Killian said softly. They had decided to wait a little time before revealing to others that they were seeing each other.

"Yeah, you're right, I do. I'll talk to you later and see you in a few days." Shiloh hung up.

Keith jumped right in. "What's so funny?"

Shiloh grinned and explained about Hypercane Mary, Keith's laughter joining his. "So you're going to see Lady Larrestes in a few days? I thought he wasn't going to be here for another couple weeks?"

"In three days, you, Sherry, five witnesses, and I are expected on Rimalia," Shiloh replied. "I have no idea why. It could have to do with Anan's crap, but wouldn't they have told me if that was the case?"

"Well, does Sherry know yet?"

"Nope, I was only just informed myself." Shiloh picked up the phone on his desk and asked Sherry to join them. A few minutes later, during which Keith got them all some tea, Sherry joined them. Shiloh quickly related the details of the call with Milossa.

"It could have nothing to do with Anan and everything to do with you, Shiloh," Sherry said. In private, they were informal, although when out and about she addressed him more formally.

"But Milossa said I wasn't in any kind of trouble," Shiloh protested.

"Sherry smiled. "Trouble isn't the only reason people are asked before Council. You are one of the few Zahirris left. It could be that they wish to speak to you about keeping your line alive. Since Elizabeth died, the Zahirris haven't had an *Artris*; your cousin can't do it, she's already heir for her mother. The other females are obviously too spineless and careless for at least one of them to step up and take the job on. The Zahirris can function without an *Artris*, for a time, since it's a very small clan, but it's the duty of the Council to keep lines alive."

"But what's that got to do with me?" Shiloh asked.

"Well, it's not out of possibility they will ask you to endeavor to have a few daughters, since you are the son of the last *Artris*," she answered.

Shiloh stared at her with such shock that Keith got up and poured him a brandy, holding the glass to his lips. He swallowed the liquid down, coughing as the liquor burned his throat. He waved away a second glass. The Council knew he was gay, and with his shredded reputation, just how the hell was he supposed to have children?

"There's no point in worrying about it right now. We'll find out in three days," she said, getting up again. "The rest of the security bids on the house should be arrive by tomorrow morning."

"Okay, thank you. Find me when you've got them."

"Will do."

13

F OR THE SECOND TIME in as many weeks, Shiloh found himself in front of the Council. He was nervous but tried to reassure himself with the fact that none of the Council members appeared angry. Lucretia, and her new puppies, sat beside his group.

He hadn't been able to find any Boxer pups available locally, not even at the Boxer rescue, although he did find himself making a financial donation. The rescue supplied him with the number of a woman who was looking for good homes for her litter of pit bulls. When he and Keith visited, they found the dogs well-cared for, well-behaved, and obviously well-adjusted, all signs they were born to a good home. He chose two females from the litter, and to Shiloh's delight, Keith took one of the males and suggested there were others on the estate who might be interested in the remaining four pups.

They promptly took them to the same vet the estate used for the farm animals, the Prewitt Veterinary Practice. Dr. Liam Prewitt assured Shiloh the pups were in perfect health, and gave them all their shots. Lucretia had been very pleased to be given the pups, actually hugging Shiloh for such a thoughtful gift.

They waited patiently as each of the Council members confirmed there weren't any matters more pressing than the issue concerning Shiloh. There were not.

"Lord Shiloh Zahirris, come forward, please," Milossa called.

Shiloh made his way forward warily, facing the Council's low dais.

"Recently, you brought to our attention certain inequities in your father's management of your birthright. You also brought to our attention Mistress Anan Nyirej's attempts to take over an estate that did not yet belong to her, at a time when you—and by extension, your property—were under Sanctuary." Milossa glanced around the chamber briefly. "Anan Nyirej has ignored the Council's command to be here, and we will deal with that momentarily. Lord Ewan Zahirris is in no fit state to be here. Lady K'Arith placed him under the care of the Tii-su earlier this week."

At Shiloh's startled and worried look, Milossa reassured him. "He will be well physically, but he is in need of care. Your concern does you credit, given his treatment of you."

"My Lady, what's wrong with my *Senka*?" Shiloh asked.

Kelia answered quietly. "He is broken mentally, Lord Shiloh, severely enough to require intervention. This decision was made when we went to question him about his mismanagement of your birthright. The Council also decided not to inform you until we reached a decision about the entire matter."

"I see." He didn't really, but he'd be polite. From a few smiles he caught, they didn't believe him but weren't going to say anything.

"Lady Lucretia, if you would be so kind as to grab Mistress Anan?" Milossa asked with a smirk.

Lucretia nodded and two minutes later, Anan stood before them, naked and wet. She had apparently been showering.

"How dare you!" she screamed.

"You were warned, Mistress Anan. You were told this would be the result if you chose not to attend on your own," Milossa reminded her.

Shiloh was shocked at the sight of Anan's body. Her torso was covered by the scars of her flogging. Strangely, he also felt like there weren't enough of them. He looked away, not wanting to embarrass her further. A Council Attendant stepped into the private chamber of the *Artris*, and came back with a plain, beige robe. Anan pulled it on hastily.

"Mistress Anan Nyirej, it is the Council's decision that you pay reparations to Shiloh Zahirris and the tenants of his estate for your unwarranted takeover attempt," Milossa told her.

"I told you, Lord Ewan said I could do as I wished," Anan reminded them mulishly.

"But you also knew he didn't have the right to give you that permission," Lady Nyirej reminded her in turn. "Your actions show that the two of you conspired to deprive Lord Shiloh of his birthright. Although this matter had been thought settled, the fact that we now know you took another appraiser and at least one buyer to the estate while Lord Shiloh, and by extension his property, were under Sanctuary means we had to reconsider the case. You knowingly broke Sanctuary, Anan, and you will suffer the consequences."

Anan spluttered indignantly.

"Quite true," Milossa agreed. "If you had not broken Sanctuary, we would not have grounds to reconsider the decisions previously made. So your punishment is two-fold. You will pay reparations to the tenants for the extremes you pushed them to in order to protect their homes from your actions. You will also pay reparations to the estate and Lord Shiloh Zahirris directly for the amount of work Lord Zahirris will have to undertake to repair the damage to his property. The second part of your punishment is that you will be publicly flogged for breaking Sanctuary. Sanctuary is one of our most sacred traditions and you completely disregarded it. This cannot be allowed to go unpunished. The flogging will take place tomorrow morning at eleven in the town square. There will be no appeal."

"How much are you going to let Zahirris soak me for this time?" she asked snidely. Anan's openly disparaging question caused several Council members to glare at the woman.

Milossa and the rest of the Council looked at each other, seeming to confer silently.

"Well now," Lady Matthew Sorai commented as he sat

back in his chair. "We had decided on only half of your current worth, distributed evenly, but perhaps your attitude needs a little adjusting."

"The Council will deliberate for five minutes," Milossa stated. They stood and fell into small groups that slowly interchanged. Shiloh walked over to Lucretia, who was stuck keeping a watchful eye on Anan.

"Why didn't she keep her mouth shut?" Shiloh whispered, not wanting to interrupt the Council's deliberations.

"Because some people are too stupid to live," Lucretia answered as she leaned down to rub the ears of one of her new pups.

Keith shook his head, amazed at the woman's apparent lack of common sense. "Wow, she keeps this up, and they'll bankrupt her." The others in the group nodded.

"The Council is tired of having to correct her behavior," Lucretia said softly. "If this doesn't teach her to behave reasonably within society, they will take far more extreme measures."

Five minutes later, the Council members retook their seats.

"The suggestion is that since Mistress Nyirej seems displeased with losing only half of her financial worth, she shall be fined two-thirds instead. Is this acceptable to the entire Council?" Milossa asked, looking at her fellow Council members for confirmation. Every single one agreed, their gazes on Anan, as if daring her to say anything. "Very well. The total reparations will now be in the amount of two thirds of your worth, Anan. You will be escorted to the bank where you will have a cashier's check made out for the appropriate amount. The check will then be delivered to my office this afternoon by you and your escort. Any attempt to avoid full, honest payment will mean you lose the lot. Is this understood?"

"It is." Rage flowed off Anan to such a degree that Shiloh had to repress a shiver.

"You may sit until we are done with our business. Then Lady Lucretia and Lady Ertrai will accompany you to your bank."

Milossa turned back to Shiloh, clearly dismissing the woman and anything to do with her. "Lord Shiloh Zahirris, the Council has deliberated on certain needs of your Clan since you were last before us. We have come to a decision.

"Your Clan requires an *Artris*. The few remaining eligible females finally asked the Council to choose a new *Artris*, the best thing, I suppose, since it appears that none of them believe your Clan is worth risking life or limb to care for it." Milossa shot a glance toward a group of three females that sat with the rest of his tiny Clan. They gave angry, arrogant looks back. But Shiloh agreed with Milossa. If any of them had been willing to accept the risk of being *Artris*, and not just sought the privilege of it, they would have stepped up by now. "It has been decided that you are best suited to that position." Milossa's calm statement was met with nods from the Council.

Disbelieving, Shiloh stared at her for a moment, swaying on his feet. He locked his knees to keep from falling on his ass in front of everyone. "Why me?"

His question was echoed by outraged exclamations by his kinswomen.

"Because you are willing to learn, and willing to work, both of which will be needed. You arc willing to make difficult decisions for the sake of others, even when those decisions are not in your best interest. This has been demonstrated already by your short tenure at your estate. None of your cousins have all of these qualities. You do. As of this day, you are Lady Zahirris, *Artris* of your Clan, with all privileges, rights, and responsibilities. While the Council is aware you have a male gender preference, it does not preclude you from attempting to have children. As long as your heir is genetically yours, it doesn't matter how you manage it." She grinned with wicked glee. "At least your options these days are less distasteful than they used to be. All of your children, and grandchildren, will retain the Zahirris name after marriage, regardless of gender."

"You were asked to choose between us!" one woman protested, standing up. Her name was Gaili, if Shiloh recalled correctly.

"Each of you have had ample time to claim your Clan's Matriarchy, Mistress Gaili," Milossa answered sharply.

"In fact," Kelia added, "when I came to you, Ruth, and then Orlie, to seek someone to speak on Lord Shiloh's behalf, as any female in his Clan could have, each of you stated it was not your problem to deal with. You chose asking the Council to decide for your Clan, not out of concern for the well-being of family members who might be distressed by infighting, but because none of you were willing to work for it, or fight for it."

"In more plain terms, you didn't choose this course out of civility and to help preserve the few remaining members of your Clan, but out of sheer laziness," Richard, Lady Jonai concluded with disgust.

"But you forgot that when the Council is asked to decide succession, the Council is obliged to look at the remaining members of the ruling bloodline of a clan first, even if all that remains is male. Lord Ewan cannot be considered due to his ill-health. That leaves Lord Shiloh," Milossa said.

Shiloh blinked, too stunned to think for a moment. "What of my *Senka*?"

"You will need to take charge of your father's inheritance and see to his needs. The properties will remain in his name. He is not to be deprived of his inheritance. However, we are agreed he doesn't have the wherewithal to manage it. This task will be yours. We recognize you are untrained for this task, so you will be given all appropriate help," Milossa told him. "Lucretia has volunteered her services to enable you to visit each property easily and quickly. Regent Lady Larrestes and Lady Dana Xeltrai have offered their assistance in teaching you to manage your new responsibilities. Fortunately none of the other Zahirris clan properties have suffered as your birthright has, so you should have little trouble with them. Whatever their failings as kinswomen, they are not poor managers of your Clan's properties, and we do recommend that you retain them in their current positions."

"We will discuss your father's condition privately, Lady Zahirris," Kelia told him. "I will visit Ewan with you today so that you can be assured of his well-being and the necessity of this step."

"Tomorrow, there will be a feast in your honor to celebrate your becoming *Artris*." And with that, Milossa called the meeting to an end.

Shiloh was stunned by everything, and Killian had to help support him as several of his new fellows surrounded him.

14

T HE FOLLOWING NIGHT, Shiloh found himself in the midst
of an island party he wasn't of a mood to enjoy. The *Tii-su* felt
Ewan had suffered a breakdown and, when added to his lifelong
depression, this meant he simply could not manage things for
himself. Along with the fact that he blamed his son for pretty
much everything that had gone wrong in his life, his bitterness
and dislike had crystallized into an intense hatred of his son. The
Tii-su were unsure if they would be able to help him out of that.
Apparently, he'd fixated on his hatred of his son to the point that
he had begun to allow the clan properties to suffer, which was
why Shiloh had been given the handling of Ewan's estate.

The confrontation with Ewan directly after the Council
meeting had been angry and painful. Milossa, Kelia, and Killian
had accompanied him, for which he was grateful. Ewan's
accusations about Shiloh's taking everything away from him,
including his home, were painful but helped prove to Shiloh the
necessity of both his guardianship and his father's treatment.
The irrational male refused to leave the Zahirris Clan House, but
Shiloh was willing to tacitly cede it to him, much to Milossa's

approval. At Kelia's suggestion, Ewan was confined to the clan residence on Rimalia. If he wished to leave Zahirris House, he could not just go to another clan property and take up residence without Shiloh's permission. Shiloh didn't want his father sneaking away elsewhere and wreaking havoc. Plus, it would ensure the man received the treatment he needed.

Milossa had turned over the reparations check, which ended up being for a little over two million dollars, later that same afternoon. The sizable amount meant each of them—including Lorretta, since she, too, had been affected by Anan—would receive roughly twelve grand in US dollars.

Last night, when everyone else in the Larrestes House had gone to bed—including those who had come with Shiloh—Killian had quietly led Shiloh to his bedroom and held him close while they talked. Then, and only then, Shiloh had his own mental breakdown, crying over all of it: his father's rejection and hatred; having to work so hard to pretend everything was okay when he felt isolated in the first place; and the knowledge that as *Artris*, that isolation would get worse.

Killian's heart ached, knowing his bubbly Sprite was slowly being destroyed by his circumstances. The carefree, happy person who'd worked so hard to come back out after Anan's and Ewan's behavior, was slowly disappearing again.

Killian asked Shiloh to call upon Celie again, and Shiloh promised he would, not wanting to fall into the depression that had so consumed him the first few weeks he'd known Killian. Then Killian had tucked him under the covers, and held him close, calming him, kissing him every time Shiloh awoke from nightmares.

Pretty much everyone on the island had watched Anan's punishment that morning. She had been given one hundred lashes, delivered—as was custom—by a woman drawn by lot from the crowd. Then the *Tii-su* came and took her away for treatment of her wounds. Shiloh had found it difficult to watch, but he did it. What stunned him more than the violence of her punishment was the level of animosity the crowd held for her. Sanctuary was sacrosanct; if one was stupid enough to break it, one paid a very high price indeed, since it existed to protect all in need of it, no matter rank or position.

Now there was a big party going on, and all he wanted to do was go home with Killian and for them to lock themselves in Killian's bedroom, never to come out. He didn't want the party and he didn't want to be *Artris*. Shiloh understood that becoming *Artris* was an honor; he was honored so many of the Council thought so highly of him. On the other hand, he didn't want the responsibility. He just wanted to make a home for himself on his own little estate and live his life out in peace, hopefully with Killian.

Jaden unsteadily walked up to Shiloh where he sat on the outskirts of the party, looking shell-shocked. Shiloh shook off his self-pity and grabbed the boy, drawing him into his lap, and hugging him.

"What's the matter, Jaden?" he asked softly, as he grabbed a young male who paused by them, looking shocked by the emotions Jaden broadcast, and ordered him to get Killian and Araminta. The young male nodded and hurried off. Shiloh was horrified by the level of pain and despair he felt coming off Jaden. What could possibly have happened?

The people around them began to quiet as they became aware of Jaden's anguish, offering silent support while Shiloh projected calming, loving thoughts.

Jaden buried his head in Shiloh's neck, crying, and he cuddled Jaden close, rubbing his back and making soothing noises. "Shh, little one, it'll be okay ..."

Jaden just shook his head and cried harder.

Killian finally made his way through the crowd, followed closely by Araminta, who already had tears running down her face in reaction to Jaden's distress. She joined her brother in Shiloh's lap, wrapping herself around the still sobbing boy.

Killian knelt in front of them all, caging the children, since Shiloh's lap wasn't really big enough for both. "What's the matter, Jaden?" Killian asked softly.

"He found his *Miisen* tonight, and he rejected Jaden," Araminta answered fearfully.

"Oh, Deity," both men breathed, staring at each other. Shiloh winced as he heard Killian call for Kelia, psionically screaming for the woman. The crowd, which had drawn close, moved back, instinctively making space just before Kelia, Lucretia, and a few other *Sennrojai* and *Tii-su* appeared in their midst. With Killian's nod of permission, Kelia touched Jaden gently, seeing everything that happened.

Shiloh studied the crowd watching them; it wasn't prurient interest, it was genuine concern, but still, perhaps it was best to go somewhere private. Lucretia seemed to agree with his thought and the next thing he knew, he was sitting on the couch in Killian's den.

Finally Jaden spoke, his voice listless. "He said we weren't lifemates, that I was sick and twisted to say something like that. He said he didn't ever want to see me again, to stay away from him."

"Who was it, love?" Killian asked gently. He still held all three of them. Lucretia and Kelia sat nearby broadcasting a sense of support and acceptance. Rejecting a *Miisen* bond like that could have serious consequences, including driving both mates insane. Jaden hadn't fought it, but his mate was apparently trying to.

"Jimmy Masrei, from Shiloh's estate," Jaden said, hiccupping softly.

"Deity help that boy." Shiloh knew the male; his parents were tenants. Jimmy was a good, decent young man, at fifteen, but he'd been raised to hate a great many things normally accepted by Rimalians. He did not have his majority, however, because of serious developmental issues that amounted to mild retardation. His parents were the worst kind of evangelicals, though, the fanatical kind that gave the good, decent ones a bad name. There had actually been requests from several tenants to kick the elder Masrei off the estate, but Shiloh hadn't had time to figure out how to do that and also help Jimmy who, being unmarried and not considered an adult, would have to go with them if they left.

Kelia looked at Lucretia, who nodded; Shiloh assumed they'd spoken psionically.

Suddenly, Jimmy appeared in the room. Kelia caught him when he would have bolted, holding him gently but firmly. "Oh no, boy, we need to sort this out."

"He isn't my *Miisen*, no way, no how," Jimmy said, tears streaking his face. He flinched as Jaden cried out in pain at those words.

Jaden's agony at the rejection knifed through Shiloh, so strong they all flinched. The emotion even overwhelmed Shiloh's painstakingly maintained shields. He felt someone else shield him, for which he was grateful. This could turn into a disaster.

"Jimmy, why do you say that?" Kelia asked carefully. He struggled in her hold, but she restrained him easily.

"H-he's a m-male, my Lady," he answered softly, stuttering in his distress. Jimmy's gaze seemed drawn to Jaden, who hid in the sheltering arms of his siblings and Shiloh, his whole body shaking. "Ma says she's found a good woman for me to marry."

Surprised, Shiloh raised an eyebrow; this was the first he'd heard of a betrothal. As the owner of the estate, Shiloh should have been informed of any coming marriage, since he would either have to provide the new couple with lodgings or find a new tenant to replace Jimmy.

Lucretia stepped over to Jimmy and tipped his chin up, so he had to look in her eyes. "Gender has nothing to do with lifemates, James. Nor does having a *Miisen* prevent you from marrying another. Have you not been taught this?"

"Ma said that the girl she's marrying me to is my *Miisen*. That she'll make sure I stay on the right path, since I'm too stupid ..." Jimmy wasn't struggling in Kelia's hold anymore; he just stood there, a defeated slant to his shoulders.

Shiloh sighed. This was why he hadn't evicted Cheryl and Arnold Masrei yet. He'd hoped to alter the boy's low opinion of himself with the help of several others on the estate. The Masrei were tenants Anan had brought onto the estate four months before Shiloh asked for Sanctuary, and because Ewan had said she could do what she wanted, Shiloh and the others were kind of stuck with them. It wasn't that they were bad workers, because they weren't, but they preached near constantly about how pretty much everything, up to and maybe including breathing, was a mortal sin. Being told they were going to burn in Hell because they didn't fear God's wrath enough was galling for people who believed in a loving, compassionate Deity.

The adults looked at each other. How the hell were they going to solve this?

Jimmy flinched again as Jaden still sobbed hysterically. Shiloh and Killian weren't really that sensitive unless they touched someone, but some things were too powerful not to be aware of. They, along with the two *Sennrojai*, could feel Jimmy's struggle between everything he'd been taught and the fact he could feel Jaden's pain, and newborn self-hatred at knowing he was the cause of it.

Jimmy broke free and reached for Jaden. The others moved enough to let him, but Jaden recoiled this time, trying to hide behind Shiloh, Killian, and Araminta.

Jimmy fell to his knees, hanging his head. "Please, Jaden?" he begged softly.

"No, you'll hurt me ..." Jaden drew himself up into a ball. They could feel him psionically retreat within himself as well, trying to make himself numb to protect himself against such unbearable pain.

Kelia psionically "grabbed" Jaden, not allowing him to withdraw too far into his own mind. *Oh, no, Jaden. You can't break the bond unless you're willing to kill the both of you. I know you hurt so much you want nothing more than to die, but do you want James' death?*

Jaden wailed and screamed both vocally and psionically, as Jimmy screamed with him. Kelia and Lucretia held onto both of them as more *Tii-su* entered. They too, joined in, preventing Jaden's incoherent wish to die from coming to pass. The two lifemates were slowly moved to the center of the group, with Shiloh, Killian, and Araminta holding them, the *Tii-su* surrounding the small family. Killian and Shiloh refused to let go of either Jaden or Jimmy, both talking to them, repeating over and over that this could be worked out, that they didn't have to face this alone.

Gradually the psionic storm quieted, Jaden no longer seeking death to alleviate the pain of Jimmy's rejection, along with Jimmy's guilt, fear, and confusion calming enough for his own death wish to fade. Jaden still wouldn't allow Jimmy to touch him, though, and Jimmy didn't try very hard, clearly feeling he deserved to be rejected, in turn. And Jimmy had withdrawn within himself, although not as far as Jaden had tried to go.

David Correai walked in, joining the group surrounding the two traumatized males, his mind a calm comfort in the flood of psionic pain.

Killian and Shiloh had no idea how he got there and they didn't care. If anyone could save these two boys, it was David. "He specializes in helping bondmates of any kind to repair their bondlinks." Araminta had once told them during their phone chats early in her training.

David touched both young males tenderly. *Ssshhh, little ones. You've done yourselves serious hurt here, haven't you?* he projected soothingly. They both crawled into his arms, somehow managing not to touch each other. No one tried to force the issue; they all just continued to lavish the two with love, acceptance, and support.

It's okay, I know how much you hurt, but if you want it to stop, you have to heal each other, not just yourselves.

He'll hurt me, Jaden whimpered, pressing himself further into David's side.

I don't want to hurt you! Jimmy cried, doing the same. David's gift had them both instinctively reaching out to him for help, without even realizing they were doing it.

David cradled them both close, but he didn't force them to touch each other either. *It's okay, little ones, it's okay, we'll work through this. You both have good reason to be afraid, but I'll help you. Will you trust me?*

Both looked at him for a long time, and then they slowly nodded.

He nodded gravely back. *Then take each other's hand.*

Fear showed on Jimmy's face, but he tentatively held out his hand to Jaden, although it shook badly. Jaden stared at Jimmy's hand like it was some sort of contact poison, but then he, too, slowly reached out to touch Jimmy. As they finally grasped each other's hand firmly, Shiloh found himself sharing a sigh of relief with Killian.

For another three hours, everyone stayed right where they were on the floor, offering up support as David helped the two young males begin to repair the damage they had done to each other. Finally, Jaden allowed Jimmy to draw him close and they sought comfort in each other's arms. The boys were trembling, exhausted, and still in an incredible amount of pain, but they were alive, and now they were finally fighting to survive together. They lacked the joy that should have been present for newly discovered *Miisen*, but Shiloh finally knew they'd live. They weren't going to have an easy time of it, but they'd get through.

Killian, Shiloh, take them to bed with you, Araminta, too. Do so every night for the next few days at least, maybe even a few weeks. They will need a massive amount of support from all of you. And they shouldn't be left alone either. They need to stay together and you need to stay with them. Under no circumstances are either of them to be left alone with Jimmy's parents.

Of course, David, Shiloh and Killian replied in concert.

I want you all to stay here on the island for a couple of days before you go back to Morgaine house. Go to bed for now, we all need to sleep. I'll be back in a few hours to work with them again, David told them. "Go on then," he prompted gently, vocally, when they were slow to move.

Thankfully, Jaden allowed Jimmy to carry him, tucking his head under Jimmy's chin. Shiloh picked up Araminta, and Killian supported him as they followed with the younger males. Killian didn't normally lock his bedroom door, but at Shiloh's urging, he did this time. Hopefully the boys would feel more secure with the world locked away from them.

After settling the injured pair in the middle of Killian's bed, the rest of the family crawled in with them. They tucked the children between them, touching them tenderly.

Caressing each other's faces, Shiloh and Killian silently communicated their love for one another. They stayed awake until the other three were asleep, then let themselves follow, hands clasped over their family.

•   •   •

The next five days were exhausting. Normally a very happy, calm, and accepting child, Jaden became fearful and distrustful, even lashing out at Araminta and Killian. Terrified of what would happen when his parents found out about Jaden, Jimmy became prone to crying jags. David and the other *Tii-su* were in constant attendance, often giving Shiloh, Killian, and Araminta a chance to get away and regroup for a few minutes.

Sherry, Keith, and the others were sent back to the estate with instructions to say nothing to Cheryl and Arnold Masrei about what was going on with their son. Well aware of the beliefs of her cousin, Lady Masrei seconded the order, calling Cheryl herself to tell her Jimmy had been ordered to stay in Rimalia by the Head of the Council, at the request of the *Tii-su*. Since Milossa had indeed made that request, no one was lying. Cheryl and Arnold were also assured Jimmy was properly chaperoned; considering there was always at least one male adult with them, this was the truth too.

Shiloh and Killian frequently reached out for the reassurance of each other's touch, even though circumstances didn't allow them much time to just hold each other. David finally granted permission for the small family to return to Shiloh's estate the next day. Natalya and Ignacio had joined them frequently, providing support not just for Jaden and Jimmy, but for Killian, Araminta, and Shiloh, as well.

Satima Rosetai, another *Sennrojai*, arrived to work a little of her own magic on the injured lifemates. She ordered everyone else out of the House, telling them to take a break, not just from the situation but each other as well. The group scattered. Taking advantage of the order, Killian asked Shiloh to walk with him to a small meadow not far from his house.

Shiloh happily agreed, grateful to get just a little alone time with Killian. His girls followed along, running about, barking, and joyfully exploring, as Killian snagged Shiloh's hand and led the way. They found a nice tree to sit beside at the edge of the meadow, Shiloh snuggling under Killian's arm as they lavished attention on the dogs, since they'd been somewhat neglected over the past few days. They both laughed as the pups raced around the clearing before coming to get petted, and doing it over again.

"Are you okay, love?" Shiloh asked Killian as they watched the dogs run wild.

"I'm not sure. I've never heard of such a thing. I mean, your parents don't choose your *Miisen* for you. I've heard of people having issues because of the gender of their *Miisen*—but never rejection of a *Miisen* based on it ..." Killian sighed. "I know Jimmy has developmental issues, and that Cheryl has taught him to believe certain things, but it's really hard for me not to be angry at him for hurting my little brother so badly. Then it's hard not to be mad at Jaden for hurting Jimmy back so badly ..."

"I know what you mean. Jimmy is the only reason I haven't evicted Cheryl and Arnold by now, given the complaints I've gotten. And since you know how things have been on the estate for me with my tenants, you know they've been seriously disruptive. Yet at the same time, every single tenant who has asked for their eviction has also asked me to find a way to help Jimmy ..." Shiloh sat up as an idea hit him. "Wait a minute! Lady Masrei is still on the island, right?"

Killian nodded. "Yes, she's been trying to help. Why?"

"As *Artris*, can she take custody of Jimmy? Remove him from his mother's care?"

Killian's eyes widened in surprise. "Yes, she can, if she feels it's in his best interest. It's rarely done, but ... And David, Kelia, the others, they all agree it's best that Jimmy remain at your estate for the time being, since he feels at home and safe there," Killian told him. "We can go talk to her right now."

"No, first things first." Shiloh shifted, straddling Killian's lap and winding his arms around Killian's neck. "You've been right here and I haven't been able to kiss you in days."

Killian found himself smiling as he looked into those green eyes he so loved to watch. "That's terrible, Sprite. Have I been neglecting you?"

"No more than I've been neglecting you, love," Shiloh answered, loving the way Killian's hands slipped under his shirt to rub the bare skin of his back. He wiggled his hips a little, feeling his body and Killian's respond to their closeness and movement. He leaned forward just a little and Killian's mouth met his in the hungriest kiss they'd ever shared. They kissed for long minutes, pressing themselves close. The hunger slowly gentled into something more tender, healing. For nearly an hour, they kissed and nuzzled languidly, letting their love for each other heal all sorts of hurts from the past few days they hadn't even realized they had.

With a certain amount of regret, they eventually left the meadow, followed by contented, tired pups, to go talk to Lady Masrei.

15

WHILE ON RIMALIA, Shiloh met with Lady Masrei. Killian also arranged for Natalya to look after his estate in his absence, since Jaden and Jimmy both were going to need him continually for the next few weeks. Killian wasn't too worried about his tenants; the estate was well run and in good shape, everything flowing smoothly. If there were any issues, Natalya would deal with them and keep Killian informed. Lucretia and Satima had both volunteered their services if necessary to take him back and forth if something major happened. The other Larrestes estates already had managers, or were run by their owners, all of whom were informed that if they needed their Regent, he could be found at Morgaine House for the time being.

The decision had also been made to tell Jimmy's parents that Jaden and Jimmy were *Miisen*. Nobody doubted that Arnold truly cared for Jimmy, but he was a very traditional male and wouldn't ever go against his wife's decisions. Considering her devout evangelical beliefs, they weren't too sure just how Cheryl would react to her son having a male *Miisen*. Shiloh had received many reports of Cheryl behaving quite affectionately towards him, yet she'd also been overheard saying incredibly cruel things to him. Even when she praised the boy, she tore him down.

The ingrained need to please, his thirst for Cheryl's approval, and his parents' evangelical teachings had clashed with Jimmy's instinctive need to accept his *Miisen*, and it had all boiled over into the trained response. Lucretia had reported that when she had grabbed Jimmy, it had been off one of the few sea cliffs on the island, which had not been anywhere near where Jaden left him. The young man had gotten pretty far in a short time. They had all shared a stunned silence when they realized just how close these two young males had come to dying that night, because the confusion, guilt, fear and pain had driven Jimmy to commit suicide without any conscious thought on his part. If Lucretia hadn't grabbed him when she did, he might have succeeded, killing them both.

Upon their arrival back at Morgaine House in the US, Sherry came out to greet them all—along with Cheryl, Arnold, and quite a few of the other tenants who were still living in the main house. With so many tenants hanging around, not much work was getting done, but Shiloh let it go. They were all concerned for Jimmy, and sometimes that was just more important than work that would still be there in an hour or two. Keith informed him he had rooms prepared for everyone, since Lady Masrei had accepted Shiloh's invitation to stay for a few days, and David and Tristan Rustei were staying to help with Jaden and Jimmy. Jenaia Jonai, one of Tristan and David's other two lifemates, and also a *Tii-su*, would arrive the next day.

Cheryl glared at Jimmy, who flinched, then at Shiloh. "What the hell has been going on?"

Shiloh decided to start as he had to go on. "Is that proper address for an *Artris*, Mistress Masrei?" he asked coldly. He knew that while he, Killian, and the *Tii-su* had been dealing with the crisis, the rest of the Council had been informing every Zahirris property of the changes in Shiloh's status.

Cheryl blinked and, not having expected that, backpedaled a little. "No, sir ..."

"Sir?" Shiloh asked, pushing.

Cheryl glared at him but knew better than to deny him the proper address a third time. "My Lady," she said snidely.

"Hmmm." Shiloh watched her, considering. He waited until she shifted slightly under his stare before he continued. "To answer your question, Cheryl, young Jimmy has found his *Miisen*."

Cheryl's eyes widened, she looked over at Araminta and Lady Masrei, the only females in the group. "Which of you two claims to be my son's *Miisen*?"

Jaden stepped forward and gently took Jimmy's hand. "Neither of them do. I am his *Miisen*," Jaden spoke softly but firmly. The two had made strides in their acceptance of each other, but the initial rejection and resulting pain and confusion still was an issue. However, Jaden would reach out to touch Jimmy now, and Jimmy didn't shy from it, and Jaden allowed Jimmy to touch him as well, so there was progress.

"That's impossible. My son would never have a male *Miisen*; he's not one of those perverted, damned creatures that flaunt God's will," Cheryl said.

Irritated, Lady Masrei spoke up. "Cheryl, *Miisen* are Deity's will—we have no control over who our lifemates are, if we are lucky enough to have one." She glared at her cousin. "You should be thanking Deity that Lucretia saved Jimmy before he succeeded in committing suicide. Your teachings have so warped and scarred the boy that he rejected his *Miisen*, sending both him and Jaden into a suicidal tailspin."

"There is nothing wrong with my teachings to my son. I've made sure he's a proper, God-fearing young male who would never disgrace himself, or me, by committing such a dreadful, hideous mortal sin." She glared at Jimmy. "James, come here. You," she pointed at Jaden, "whoever you are, stay away from my son, I won't have you trying to pervert him into damnation."

"No." Jimmy and Jaden both answered, softly but firmly. Jimmy looked terrified at defying his mother, but Jaden stood beside him, and Lady Masrei, Killian, Araminta, David, Tristan, and Shiloh stood with them, subtly offering support.

Cheryl's jaw dropped and Arnold looked stunned. Jimmy had never defied either of them. "I am your mother and you will, by God, do as I say. Get away from him. I've made the final arrangements for your marriage to your true *Miisen*, a good woman who will keep you on the righteous path. Come, James, you know you're too stupid to go believing everything strangers tell you."

"I've heard enough," Lady Masrei said. "Cheryl, I am removing James from your custody."

"On what grounds?" Cheryl demanded angrily.

"Emotional abuse. You have shown no concern that your son nearly committed suicide, and your calling him stupid and perverted only cements my decision. No, Cheryl, for his own health, I'm removing him from your custody. Your raising of him nearly led to the deaths of both your son and Jaden Larrestes." Lady Masrei glared at Cheryl. "I want the contact information for the woman you think you're marrying James to; I will decide for myself whether it is a suitable match. Has James even met this female?"

"Of course not. Why would he? He's a male, and a stupid one at that. I would be remiss in letting him make such a decision," Cheryl answered, surprise briefly replacing the indignant look on her face.

"Why have you not informed me of this impending arrangement, Mistress Cheryl?" Shiloh asked calmly.

"Why would I tell you? You're merely a male. It's not your place to be involved. We won't even begin to get into your lack of honor," Cheryl answered, completely unconcerned.

Angered by the continued lack of respect, Shiloh stepped forward, hand on his dagger. "You will apologize for that insult, or you will bleed."

Cheryl blinked again, taken aback. "You're a male; you can't challenge me. And there's no honorable woman that would defend you, you are disgraced."

"I am *Artris* Zahirris. I have the right to Challenge regardless of my gender. I don't need a female to defend me." Shiloh's hand remained on the hilt of his dagger.

"Not to mention," Lady Masrei added, "I know quite a few women, myself included, who would be pleased to defend Lady Zahirris' honor, were it necessary." She smirked at the stunned look on Cheryl's face. There were a few titters throughout the crowd. They were enjoying seeing Cheryl get her comeuppance.

Cheryl swallowed as she realized that if she didn't apologize in an acceptable manner, she would have to fight to defend the insult she'd given. She might be bigger than Shiloh, but the entire estate knew that he tried to find time to practice his training every day. She might have been taught when she was younger, but she certainly didn't practice. Cheryl stared at him and didn't like what she saw. He was willing to bleed to defend his own honor, but she wasn't willing to bleed to insult it, and everybody there knew it.

She got down on her knees and bowed her head, baring the back of her neck to Shiloh in the traditional manner. "I apologize, my Lady."

Shiloh didn't move his hand from his dagger. "And your claim that I have no honor?"

Clearly reluctant, she hesitated. "I was wrong, Lady Zahirris. Your honor is unstained."

Shiloh waited for a minute, then nodded. "I accept your apology. I won't a second time." It was a formal way of stating that you got away with it this time, but next time, you wouldn't be able to get out of the fight.

"Yes, my Lady." Cheryl stood up and Shiloh slowly removed his hand from his dagger.

Shiloh looked at Jimmy, who had watched the whole thing with a stunned look while Lady Masrei stood behind him and Jaden, a hand on each of their shoulders. Jaden still held his hand.

Lady Masrei shook her head. Shiloh glanced at Killian who shook his head as well. Shiloh sighed; they were right, Cheryl wasn't going to accept the pairing and if she didn't, Arnold wouldn't.

"Cheryl and Arnold Masrei, you are relieved of your duties to this estate and to me as owner of this estate. I ban both of you from returning without prior permission from me," Shiloh announced. "Sherry, Keith, please use as many assistants as you need to both assist them with gathering up their rightful belongings and then escort them off the estate."

"But I apologized!" Cheryl objected.

Arnold fell to his knees in shock, staring in disbelief at Shiloh.

"And I accepted your apology, Mistress Cheryl. However, your behavior during your tenure here has been such that, in the short time since I took possession of this estate, I've had numerous, repeated complaints. You have every right to believe as you wish. However, you do not have the right to browbeat people with your beliefs of their damnation simply because they don't believe as you do. The only reason I didn't evict you immediately was my concern for James, who has slowly begun to thrive here despite your treatment of him. Since Lady Masrei has taken him into her custody, I need not fear for James' good health and can now take the appropriate steps to return peacefulness back to this estate."

Her shoulders slumped, Cheryl turned Lady Masrei. "My Lady?"

The *Artris* shook her head. "It's his estate. He can evict anyone he wishes. If you like, I have a property that could use good help, as long as you don't behave disruptively. Gather your belongings and I will assist you to get there."

Shiloh turned to Lady Masrei. "None have, nor do I, complain of their work ethic. All I have spoken to have claimed them good, productive, honest workers. I have even been told they are willing to help their fellows, an always-welcome trait. However, their religious ... uh ... evangelizing is not welcome here, and they have not listened to any exhortation to stop. I have feared that the matter would become bloody next."

She nodded. "I understand. This is not the first time." She turned back to Cheryl. "I wish you would understand the difference between welcomed opinion and browbeating."

"What of my son?" Arnold spoke for the first time, looking pleadingly at Lady Masrei.

"James will be staying here. The *Tii-su* believe he and Jaden both will recover best in the care of Ladies Zahirris and Larrestes, as well as in the influence of the good people of this estate. I have seen nothing to doubt the *Tii-su* judgment." Lady Masrei was gentle as she spoke to Arnold, but there was no doubt she believed what she said. "Arnold, I have no objection to supervised visitation with your son, for both you and Cheryl, but it will not be for some time. James is grievously injured, and I believe that injury is directly the result of his upbringing. You and Cheryl failed to teach him the truth about lifemates, which led to great injury done both to Jaden and James. They need time to heal."

Cheryl was too stunned to protest. Sherry indicated that several of the other tenants come along to escort them, as per Shiloh's orders.

"Lady Zahirris, I give you the fostering and guardianship of James Masrei, my cousin. Do you accept?" Lady Masrei asked formally.

Shiloh gave her a slight bow as tradition demanded. "I accept, Lady Masrei. I will care for him to the utmost of my ability."

She nodded. "Then, if you don't mind, I'm going to go assist with Cheryl and Arnold." Shiloh nodded back, and she leaned down to give Jimmy a gentle kiss on the top of his head and then gave Jaden one as well. "Don't worry, Jimmy, you're in good hands. Go now, you and your lifemate could use a nap."

David spoke. "I noticed Cheryl and Arnold went to the House. Is there somewhere else the boys can rest?"

One of the tenants stepped forward. "This way, milords. I have a guest room the younglings may use."

Tristan nudged Araminta to follow her brother, his *Miisen*, and *Tii-su* David. Then he turned to Shiloh. "Well then, my Lady, could I con you into the nickel tour of the estate?"

Shiloh managed to chuckle. Although a blatant tactic to keep Shiloh from coming into contact with Cheryl and Arnold before they left, he agreed. There had been enough drama, no need to encourage more.

16

THE FOLLOWING THREE WEEKS were tiring, but not as much as the first week with Jaden and Jimmy. Although the two boys and Araminta continued to sleep between Shiloh and Killian every night, they slowly began to spend time on their own as the weeks progressed.

Jenaia, Tristan, David, and occasionally their fourth mate—whom Shiloh was surprised to discover was Matthew, Lady Sorai, an extremely rare occurrence—spent a great deal of time with them. It soon became obvious they were going to have issues being apart. The three *Tii-su* believed that Jimmy's initial rejection of Jaden, and then Jaden's rejection of Jimmy, had caused both to develop a fear that bordered on a psychotic phobia of being separated from each other. For now, it wasn't an issue, but it could become so later on in their lives if they didn't learn to function alone. Jenaia surmised it would be years before they would feel secure enough in each other to even try. Her recommendation to both Killian and Shiloh was to have Kelia examine them in a few years, and if she felt they were ready, for her and her *Miisen* Saul, Lady Nerris, to work with them. Kelia and Saul had separation issues of their own, and they were the only ones Jenaia knew of that might be able to help Jaden and Jimmy effectively.

When Lady Masrei visited next, they discussed the best way to proceed. It was decided the two would be kept together and split their time between Shiloh's estate and Killian's, perhaps even visiting Lady Masrei on occasion. The two would continue to work around the estate doing chores well within their capabilities—Jaden, because of his age, Jimmy because of his developmental issues. Although they worked well together, they were still supervised closely due to bouts of suicidal thoughts; there were just too many ways to get hurt on a working farm. Even when they were allowed to be alone, the *Tii-su* kept close psionic track of them, on a few occasions shutting both down into a forced sleep before they could injure themselves or each other, physically or emotionally.

Shiloh and Killian often found themselves working together in Shiloh's study. Since Killian had already volunteered to help Shiloh learn the ropes as *Artris*, he took the opportunity to do just that. He taught Shiloh how to manage several estates remotely, what questions to ask, and how to find out who best to talk to on each one. While he told Shiloh there were many things he wouldn't get unless he was onsite, Killian also assured him that teams of *Artris* had already inspected each Zahirris estate and found every one of them but Shiloh's birthright functioning as it should, and Shiloh's estate was slowly getting itself back in order.

"So you have some time before you need to go to each one yourself. And Dana and I will go with you for your yearly inspections, and you will come with us for ours."

By the fifth week, Jaden and Jimmy had improved considerably. The acceptance and support from everyone had a tremendous healing effect on both younglings. As they healed, Shiloh and Killian were able to steal more than a few minutes alone time, and Araminta returned to Rimalia to resume her training.

By the sixth week, *Tii-su* David decided the boys could sleep alone, although they remained in Shiloh's suite in case they needed Shiloh and Killian. Shiloh and Killian didn't engage in any making out or heavy petting, because they never knew when the boys would come crawling into bed with them, but they appreciated being able to sleep next to each other again. The three *Tii-su* gently teased the two about being 'so close and so far', but they both felt oddly okay about it; they were learning more about each other in this extremity than they would have in months or years of a more normal courtship.

By the end of the eighth week, Jaden and Jimmy had managed to sleep a few nights without crawling in with Shiloh and Killian, and it had been several weeks since they'd fallen into such a negative loop that they tried to hurt themselves.

At twelve weeks, Jaden and Jimmy were returning to their usual selves more and more, although neither was as easily entertained as they had been. Before he returned to his own estate, David did place a few inhibitions in their minds, which would force the boys to seek help rather than harm themselves; this normally wasn't done with *Miisen*, but the circumstances were unusual. With that precaution, David felt they had recovered enough to be left to heal themselves and each other without so much interference from the others in their lives, although David did "order" Killian to stay another two weeks in the US, before he returned to his own estate. Considering the sheer amount of damage they had done to themselves, the boys were recovering very quickly.

Lady Masrei had been concerned about the age difference: that Jimmy was physically fully adult—including having the normal sexual responses—while Jaden was only barely entering Rimalian adolescence. She wasn't worried Jimmy would find Jaden's childish body attractive, but since the two couldn't be separated ... Jaden might be exposed to sexuality in a far more graphic fashion than books and learning films from school. Normally, even with as interlocked as lifemates' minds were, an adult Rimalian who had a child *Miisen* could keep the child out of the more sensual areas of the adult's mind and experiences. James just did not have that ability, as his own mind was still quite child-like. David had chuckled quietly, explaining he'd already headed that problem off at the pass. He had placed a light inhibition against masturbation in Jimmy, and placed a light hypnotic suggestion in Jaden's mind to simply "not see" any erection Jimmy might have. It would further delay Jimmy's sexual and mental maturity, but better that than Jaden be exposed prematurely, especially considering that although Jimmy might physically be ready for sex, because of his slower mental development, it wasn't even in the back of his mind yet. David told them that by the time Jaden reached adulthood at fourteen, Jimmy's mind would have caught up a little more completely with his body.

As part of their treatment of the two, the *Tii-su* had worked extensively with Jimmy to undo his mother's teaching that homosexuality, and that sex not intended for procreation, were sins. The *Tii-su* also carefully mentioned to both males that there was nothing wrong if they found themselves attracted to each other later on, that it was normal and healthy, when they were both old enough. In the meantime, the light psionic inhibitions would help preserve both their innocence, until they were both old enough to decide for themselves. David wouldn't even have to go undo it; the blocks were constructed to gradually fade as the two got older, allowing them to progress naturally.

Because Jimmy needed more stability than Jaden, an informal custody arrangement was developed. The two would split their time, year by year, until Jaden was fourteen. Then Jaden would most likely decide where they lived. At ten years old, Jaden was still a child, albeit a very mature one, and entering adolescence for a Rimalian. As such, along with being the son of the last Larrestes *Artris*, he was accustomed to a certain amount of responsibility, and it wasn't long before he asked Shiloh what his responsibilities would be while he was on the estate.

All in all, the *Tii-su* were certain the boys would be fine, leaving everyone sighing in relief. However, the incident had sent shockwaves throughout Rimalian Society. With the fact Rimalians were beginning to integrate more with human society due to a higher density of population, the *Tii-su* and *Sennrojai* decided to quietly teach all the children and young adults how important it was to accept your *Miisen* and protect that bond, no matter the gender of one's *Miisen*. No one wanted a repeat of the near tragedy.

One of the odd benefits of the situation with Jaden and Jimmy was that Shiloh's relationship with his tenants greatly improved. The other was that his tenants picked up on the relationship between Killian and Shiloh and seemed to approve, even conspiring to give the two a few minutes alone time fairly regularly. It took a while for Killian and Shiloh to catch on, but when they had, they'd laughed their asses off.

17

A WEEK INTO Killian's "vacation," one of the children came running into the house screaming for help, that several women were trying to kidnap Jimmy. Shiloh, Killian, Sherry, and Keith had been in Shiloh's study, going over the estate accounts, using it as a teaching opportunity for Shiloh. The four of them scrambled out of the house, bringing their daggers out.

The scene they found stunned them. Several women surrounded Jimmy and Jaden, and were themselves surrounded by the tenants. *Great,* Shiloh thought. *A hostage situation.* Jimmy and Jaden clung to each other, even as two of the three women tried to separate them.

Shiloh strode forward followed by the others, the crowd letting them in and closing behind them. "What goes on here?"

"I am Amalie Nyirej, James' fiancée, Lady Zahirris. Today is our wedding day and I'm here to collect. These are my attendants." She indicated the two women with her.

"Lady Masrei denied the arrangement, Mistress Nyirej. At the present time, James isn't capable of entering such an agreement," Shiloh said as calmly as he could. He didn't really care if the women got hurt but he didn't want anything to happen to the boys.

"Lady Masrei isn't his mother, and Cheryl assures me that James is capable enough of entering into marriage. James comes with me, to marry, then we will return to take our place among your tenants," Amalie replied. She said it like she thought Shiloh would agree to that, like it had already been agreed upon. Did she really think Shiloh was that stupid?

"You need my permission to become one of my tenants, Amalie," Shiloh answered coldly. "Release them now, then seek out the Magistrate to register a complaint about Cheryl's bad faith arrangement."

"There's no bad faith. She's told me of your trying to pervert a decent young male. She also said that it was unlikely that you would allow him to leave as he wishes. Therefore, we are taking him. He belongs to me, now. You have no say in it, Lady Zahirris," Amalie replied haughtily.

"NO!"

The denial was psionically and vocally screamed by both Jaden and Jimmy. Before anyone else could move, Jaden had taken his dagger and stabbed Amalie in the back, dropping her like a rock. Jimmy, following his *Miisen*'s lead, drew his blade and stabbed the woman who kept trying to pull him away from Jaden as Jaden stabbed the third woman in the stomach. The tenants all moved to grab the injured women, pulling them away, as Shiloh, Killian, Keith, and Sherry made for the boys. Shiloh found himself thanking Deity the two had been allowed their daggers back.

As Sherry and Keith grabbed Jaden's and Jimmy's wrists, gently forcing them to drop the knives, Shiloh and Killian held the boys between them, in an attempt to soothe and calm them.

"Call the *Tii-su*," Shiloh ordered. "Assist the women, and someone call the Magistrate." He hugged the two shaking, terrified males tightly, listening to Killian murmur softly to them.

Within minutes, the women were being given first aid and several of the tenants had joined Shiloh and Killian in hugging and calming Jaden and Jimmy. Then the *Tii-su* and their assistants arrived, obviously with a *Sennrojai*'s help. The *Sennrojai* said they would wait for the call from the *Tii-su* and whisk them and their patients to the Hospital on Rimalia. No one wanted to answer questions in a human hospital if it could be helped. Many Rimalians feared *Sennrojai* and their psionic abilities, but Shiloh thanked Deity for them.

The Magistrate, who turned out to be Lady Ertrai, arrived courtesy of a different *Sennrojai*, a huge man Shiloh had never seen before.

The man concentrated on the group of *Tii-su* and the injured women, who suddenly disappeared. Then he turned his attention to the small group surrounding Jaden and Jimmy. Both of the males were still crying and shaking, but they were a little calmer than they had been. He focused on the boys; they slowly calmed as he approached.

He held his arms out. "Come here, boys." The man's voice was deep and rumbly, and the boys slowly moved toward him, letting him enfold them in his embrace. He looked at Shiloh. "Lady Zahirris, I am Catan Jinn. Hello again, Lady Larrestes." He and Killian exchanged nods. "I will attend these two, including Verifying why they stabbed those women, while you speak with Lady Ertrai."

Shiloh and Killian nodded, touching the boys gently before turning to Lady Ertrai.

She gave Shiloh a small smile. "Well, Lady Zahirris, you're certainly providing a lot of work for all of us recently."

"I suppose I could say it's not my fault, but I won't bother," Shiloh replied.

"Tell me what happened."

It took time, but eventually the whole story was shared. Lady Ertrai was very psi-sensitive and didn't need a *Tii-su* to tell her whether or not she was getting the truth; she could pick up on the lies herself.

Then Catan came over, still with his arms around the boys, and confirmed that Jaden had felt his *Miisen* under threat and had acted accordingly, and Jimmy had acted to protect Jaden from retaliation. Lady Ertrai received a call, then reported the *Tii-su* had gotten the viewpoints of the women as well. All three women were currently in surgery, and would be a long time in recovery, but it was believed they would live. Jaden and Jimmy both relaxed, as did Shiloh and Killian; Killian didn't know how his sensitive little brother would handle killing someone. He didn't think Jimmy would have coped well, either.

Shiloh thanked his tenants for coming to their assistance and told them to take the rest of the day off, other than looking after the animals. They all made a point to touch both Jimmy and Jaden gently before they wandered away.

•   •   •

Later on, Lady Ertrai and Catan joined Shiloh, Killian, Sherry, and Keith in Shiloh's study. The Lady Ertrai proceeded to tell them about the convoluted thread they had discovered.

Amalie was Anan's cousin, and Cheryl and Anan were friends. When Cheryl and Arnold had been evicted from their last home because of their pretentious preaching, Anan invited them to come to Morgaine House. After the Council had made their ruling, Anan had been pissed and had asked Cheryl to keep her informed of goings-on with the estate because she wanted to use the information to get revenge.

Anan and Cheryl had already decided to marry Jimmy off to Amalie so that Amalie could move onto the estate as Jimmy's wife and be available to cause trouble, when Cheryl and Arnold had been evicted. Amalie agreed because she liked the look of Jimmy; with his being borderline retarded, she believed he would be easily controlled and not cause her any trouble, just look pretty and do what he was told. Cheryl would simply tell Jimmy to beg Shiloh to let Amalie live on the estate with him and work there, since it was quite obvious to Cheryl that Shiloh had a soft spot for Jimmy.

At first, they had tried to solve the issue of Lady Masrei taking custody of Jimmy by contractual means, telling Lady Masrei that Amalie and Cheryl had already agreed upon the marriage and it was a binding contract. Lady Masrei pointed out she had a higher duty to protect Jimmy's good health than to allow an arranged marriage take place. Lady Masrei also told Cheryl and Amalie that they were welcome to bring the issue before the Council if they were unhappy with her decision. They apparently decided to just brazen it out instead. If it was a *fait accompli,* then Shiloh wouldn't throw Jimmy off the property and Amalie would be in the perfect position to help Anan get revenge.

Because Jimmy had always been such a biddable child, Amalie didn't expect resistance from him when she ordered him to come with her. Jaden's presence was seen as just a mere nuisance; as just another male, he wasn't a threat. They didn't believe Jaden was really Jimmy's *Miisen*; rather it was some sort of perverted excuse to take Jimmy out of Cheryl's custody.

Shiloh and Killian sat stunned.

Suddenly Keith burst out laughing. "Really?" He looked at all of them. "They really believe that flimsy crap?"

Killian began to chuckle. "I think that perhaps the Nyirej have been inbreeding just a bit much ..."

"Add to that, they all seem willing to believe the rest of us are out to get them," Catan added. "Well, not all of them. It's strange, one branch—fortunately the ruling branch—are quite sensible, and then the rest are just ... bizarrely odd. I wonder if it has anything to do with so many of those branches being psi-blind?"

"It's kind of hard to be a psychotic lunatic when you can feel the pain you cause," Killian mused.

They all shook their heads at the nonsense some people would believe.

"So what happens now?" Shiloh asked Lady Ertrai.

"I'm satisfied Jaden and Jimmy were acting in self-defense. Given the attitude they could sense from Amalie and her friends, and their own recent ordeal, neither one would really be able to recognize that you and Killian, as well as the tenants themselves, might have been able to handle it without bloodshed. Jaden saw a threat to his mate and he acted. The same with Jimmy. I should think being taken down by ten- and fifteen-year-old males should be punishment enough for those three. The story is already being passed around the Clans—quite deliberately. Lady Masrei has disowned Cheryl. And Anan ... I have recommended she be banished. Be thinking of who you'll give your Proxy to for that vote," she told them.

Killian and Shiloh both nodded. As her former victims, it would look better for them if they gave their vote on the matter to someone else. They spent a few hours talking quietly. Catan had made sure Jaden and Jimmy would sleep peacefully through the night, and he would stay for a few days to make sure they were coping well. Catan was quite pleased at their progress in some ways, though. They had acted instinctively in each other's defense, and that was as it should be between lifemates. He also felt the two were becoming a little more secure in each other. All in all, they were doing well.

18

KILLIAN SMILED as he followed Shiloh into his suite. They'd checked on the boys, finding them sound asleep, with Jimmy curled around Jaden protectively. Jaden had Jimmy's arms pressed to him, making Killian smile. Shiloh did the same thing with him. All three of Shiloh's dogs were curled up with the boys, although their stubby tails wagged happily when they saw Shiloh and Killian. Shiloh yawned and Killian took his hand and drew his love to their bedroom.

"Come on, Sprite, let's go to bed."

"Okay, love," Shiloh said as he yawned again.

Killian frowned slightly. His poor Sprite was so tired.

"Killian?"

"Hmm?"

"Why do you still call me Sprite?" Shiloh looked at the floor as he sat on their bed. "I'm not giggly or even all that happy on so many levels anymore ..." He trailed off as Killian knelt in front of him.

"You will always be my Sprite." Killian moved between Shiloh's legs. He wrapped his arms around Shiloh's waist and held him as Shiloh leaned over to kiss Killian's head and draped his arms around those broad shoulders. Killian pressed a gentle kiss to Shiloh's chest, right over his heart. Then he looked into Shiloh's eyes. "It doesn't matter what's going on, love, I know there's still that bubbly little Sprite in there, awaiting his chance to get loose and play with this poor befuddled Rimalian." They shared a soft gentle kiss. "Did you ever call Celie?"

Shiloh shook his head. "No, with everything with the boys ... I never got around to it."

"First thing in the morning, love, please? I don't ever want to see you like you were during those few weeks, ever again, okay? It scared the hell out of me." Killian traced his hand over Shiloh's face.

Shiloh nodded. "I will. Can I talk you into a hot soak with me?"

Killian's breath hitched and he shuddered. "Oh yeah, that sounds good." He loved to see Shiloh naked and wet. He reached over and grabbed a couple of heavy elastics off the nightstand, handing one to Shiloh. They both wadded their braids into messy buns, bound them with the elastics, and headed for the bathroom. They'd both washed their hair that morning and neither wanted their hair wet again. It took too long to dry.

Killian laughed as he watched Shiloh yawn again as he bent and started the water in the tub. "Are you sure you want to soak instead of go to sleep?"

Shiloh nodded as he yawned again. "I've wanted nothing more since those idiots tried to take the boys than to sit in a hot bath with you holding me. I don't want a long soak but ... I want it."

Killian nodded and undressed, watching as Shiloh undressed as well. He helped Shiloh step into the tub, and then he climbed in as well, settling Shiloh between his legs, holding him against his chest. He chuckled as Shiloh clasped his arms to him.

"Things are getting better, love," he said, nuzzling Shiloh.

Shiloh nodded. "I know. I just didn't want to be *Artris*."

"I can understand that. The Council kind of did the same thing to me that we did to you. At least, I know that in five or six more years I can get out of it, but you, love, unless you have a daughter that meets Council standards when she's of age, you could be *Artris* for life," Killian mused.

Shiloh sighed. "You're not helping cheer me up, love."

"I'm sorry, Sprite. It gets easier once you've got a handle on things, really, it does. And you've me and Dana to mentor you, and Evelyn Masrei, Natalya, Richard, and Matthew. Plenty of people to ask advice of. It will get easier in time, Shiloh, I promise." Killian kissed Shiloh's hair.

Shiloh turned his head, seeking Killian's lips. Killian leaned down that little bit needed and kissed Shiloh softly, passionately.

"Thank you, Kil. That does help." They kissed for several more minutes then returned to just cuddling in the hot water. Shiloh's head lolled to the side as he began to fall asleep.

Killian gently shook him. "Okay, Sprite, time to get out." Shiloh nodded and sat up, waiting for Killian to get out, and watching him get dried off with a sleepy kind of lust in his eyes. Then Killian helped him out and dried him off, chuckling as Shiloh moaned with pleasure, picked him up, and took him to bed.

· · ·

Hours later, Killian woke up to the most incredible sensation on his cock: hot, wet and *oh my stars that has to be a tongue* ... He opened his eyes and looked. Sure enough, Shiloh lay between his legs, licking his cock with a huge grin on his face. Noticing Killian had joined the party, he smiled even wider. Killian's heart turned over in his chest as Shiloh gave him another lick.

"You taste good, Kil."

Killian laughed, he couldn't help it. The Sprite was loose. "Hello, Sprite. What are you doing?"

Shiloh shrugged and gave the hard dick in front of him another lick. "Nothing important, just gonna get myself a snack. You go on back to sleep and ignore me." Then he swallowed the head of Killian's cock.

Killian's hips bucked, the pleasure indescribable. Shiloh placed his hands on Killian's hips to keep him from thrusting too hard.

"Sorry," Killian gasped.

Shiloh let go and grinned. "It's okay, love. You want me to stop?"

Killian shook his head, a little frantically. "Oh no, please don't stop."

Shiloh gave him the wickedest grin Killian had ever seen in his life and then sucked his cock right back into his mouth. Then Shiloh began to hum. Killian felt his eyes cross as his head dropped back onto the pillow he shared with Shiloh. He moaned and gasped.

Shiloh chuckled as he sucked on Killian's long, thick cock. From the things he'd found online and read, he knew he would be considered seriously lucky to have Killian's nine inches to play with. This was fun, and he'd never imagined Killian would taste this good. Killian's hips moved more and more as Killian gasped and mewled, his head thrashing. Shiloh used one hand to wrap around the thick shaft and his free hand to run his fingers over Killian's balls, noticing they climbed even higher under his touch.

"Shiloh!" was all the warning Shiloh got before Killian exploded. Shiloh swallowed as best he could, getting most of it, finding he liked the tangy, almost sweet taste. As Killian's body melted under him, he tongued that slowly softening shaft clean, licking his lips.

Killian lifted his head to watch, groaning softly. "Come here, Sprite." He reached for Shiloh who went gladly into his arms, sliding up Killian's body as Killian pulled him into a kiss. Killian took his mouth thoroughly, moaning as he tasted himself on Shiloh's tongue.

"My God, Sprite, where did you ...?"

Shiloh laughed as he lay on Killian's chest. "I looked up blow jobs on the Internet when I knew I was going to get to see you on Rimalia. I just never got to do anything with it till now. Instructional videos are useful." He was feeling pretty proud of himself, even though he was still harder than a rock. He jerked his hips, seeking relief. He laughed again as he found himself on his back, Killian braced over him, Killian's hand wrapped itself around his cock. Shiloh gasped as Killian squeezed and stroked him.

Killian smiled as he watched Shiloh. "You like that, Sprite? Like it when I stroke this thick cock for you?" Shiloh was almost as long as he was and just as thick.

Shiloh nodded frantically as he thrust into Killian's hand, loving the feel of Killian's callused palm on his sensitive skin.

Killian kissed him hungrily. "Mine, Shiloh," he said as he squeezed just a little harder, Shiloh's dick leaking even more, slicking things up, letting Killian's hand slide easily over him.

"Yours," Shiloh agreed on a gasp as his body tightened and he came, Killian's mouth swallowing his cry. Before Shiloh could catch his breath, Killian licked Shiloh's cum off his hand, then moaned and slid down so he could lick Shiloh clean.

"Deity, you taste good, Sprite," he muttered as he licked Shiloh, bathing his stomach and cock, even his balls. Killian was hard again after watching Shiloh come and tasting his cum, a strange combination of salt, bitter and sweet.

"Make love to me, Killian," Shiloh said softly, watching him.

Killian stared up at him, then moved back up his body to kiss him. He searched Shiloh's eyes and nodded slowly, kissing his beautiful Sprite. "Do we have lube?"

Shiloh nodded, flushing. "I um, I got that too, when ..."

Killian grinned. "You planned to seduce me while we were on the island?"

Shiloh blushed harder. "I love you and I want you, Killian."

"I love you too, Shiloh." Killian thrust against Shiloh. "And I think you can tell I want you, too." He felt Shiloh's erection against his, and he grinned. Thank Deity for still being in early adulthood—they recovered fast. He had a feeling they'd recover fast even after they had been together for eighty years, though. "I don't mean just for now, Sprite," he said softly as he braced himself so he didn't crush Shiloh under him. Carefully he rubbed Shiloh's cheek with a thumb.

Shiloh looked startled as he caught Killian's meaning. "You mean you want me forever?" He reached up to touch Killian's face tentatively.

Killian nodded. "I've wanted that for a while now, but I wasn't sure how you'd feel ..."

Shiloh breathed out, tears gathering in his eyes. He held Killian close. "Then maybe we shouldn't ..."

Killian drew back, puzzled. "Why not?"

Shiloh thumbed his lips, with a gentle, rueful smile. "Because I know you always wanted a traditional wedding, on the Island with Milossa officiating. You can't have that if ..."

Killian knew what he was talking about. The traditional wedding, on Council grounds and the Promenade and all, was reserved for virgin grooms, unless it was an approved exception, such as a *Miisen* being involved. All bets were off when it came to lifemates, which was one reason no one was batting an eyelash about Jaden and Jimmy sharing a bed now. It wasn't that he couldn't get married on the island if he wasn't a virgin, but he wouldn't be able to ask for it to be on the Council grounds or for the Head of the Council to officiate, since she wasn't related to him. His friends and relations might still take him for a Promenade, but any gifts would be bought by them, rather than gifted to him and his spouse by the shopkeepers.

He sat up, bringing Shiloh with him. "Is it important to you?" he asked.

Shiloh frowned. "I know how important that dream is for you." He looked down. "I put that dream aside a long time ago, and now, as a divorced male, I wouldn't get it anyway."

Killian tipped Shiloh's chin up to look into the clear green eyes he loved. They were stormy, clouded, not with pleasure, but with pain. "Why did you put it aside?" Killian had an idea why, but he suspected it needed to be said, and talked about.

"Anan. She didn't want the hassle." Shiloh shuddered. "I guess the real reason was, she didn't want to face Milossa."

"She probably knew Milossa would ask you if you knew Anan's past, if you knew what you were getting into," Killian said softly as he leaned forward and kissed Shiloh's nose.

"You're probably right. But she still refused to allow it." Shiloh moved so he knelt, straddling Killian's hips, taking Killian's face in his hands lovingly. Killian settled his hands on Shiloh's waist as they kissed and nuzzled for a few minutes. "I don't want to take that away from you. I don't know what I was thinking, planning to seduce you ..."

"Nothing I wasn't thinking, too, love," Killian answered with a chuckle. He touched Shiloh's face, holding it as Shiloh held his. "You're more important to me than what kind of wedding we might have, Shiloh. I don't need a Promenade or Milossa officiating. I just want you."

Feeling the truth of that, Shiloh closed his eyes and sighed. "I want you to have them though, Killian."

He tried to hide it, but Killian caught his feelings of shame and guilt. "Why do you feel guilty, love?" Killian asked, concerned.

"Because of me, there are a lot of people who assume you're not a virgin anymore, because of Anan's lies and because we don't even pretend to sleep in separate rooms—"

Killian cut him off with a soft kiss. "Listen to me, love. Due to Anan spreading lies, I've gotten shit about not being a virgin since I was thirteen. Once I became Regent, all those little niceties—like making sure I was properly chaperoned around strange women—went right out the door in favor of training me properly. I admit some of my new peers believed the stories at first, and treated me less than civilly. Most of them were decent enough to apologize for the slurs when they realized it was all lies, but it kind of inured me to that kind of shit. Besides, the last thing I wanted at the time was anything even resembling sex, and later I guess it just became a habit. JoAnne, Natalya, Georges, they all helped me believe that others' opinion of my chastity isn't important, except maybe the person I'm in love with.

"Then here you came into my life and turned everything upside down, and I couldn't even really kiss you because you were under my protection. I spent a lot of time talking to Natalya about you, you know." Killian gave Shiloh another soft kiss.

"You did?" Shiloh was surprised.

"She's my friend and mentor, and she's been all the mother Araminta and Jaden have had for the past almost five years. Who else could I talk to when I had no idea what was happening to me?" Killian smirked. "You were doing things to my body and dreams I didn't understand. She and Ignacio both helped me a lot, teaching me—and Jaden and Araminta—what they taught their own children: that sex wasn't evil or bad, or just an unpleasant necessity. They taught us it needed to be treated with respect, and that we needed to decide for ourselves when it was right for us. Yesterday, tonight, tomorrow, three years from now, or thirty, you're right for me, Shiloh. That's all that really matters."

Shiloh leaned his forehead against Killian's as he thought about that. Then he tried to figure out how to explain his feeling about it. "Maybe it's petty of me, but you deserve the wedding you've wanted for so long, and making sure you get it would kinda shove it down their throats." Shiloh made a frustrated noise. "But that's not it exactly, either. I know what it feels like not be able to have something you've dreamed of for a long time, what it feels like to be forced into giving it up." He sighed as he looked into Killian's eyes. "It's all mixed up together: knowing what you've wanted so long and wanting you to have what you want, knowing what it's like to be forced from it, and wanting to shove it down their throats that what they've been saying about you is all lies ..."

Killian's own throat was tight as he looked at his lover. Deity, he loved this man. He smiled tenderly, startling Shiloh, then he kissed his Sprite, trying to put all the love he felt for him into it. Everything Shiloh had just told him made him feel more and more loved, that Shiloh wanted to defend him so much. When they were finally forced to come up for air, Killian asked, "What do you want?"

"You happy, Killian," Shiloh told him. "I want to marry you, too. I was just afraid you wouldn't consider it since ..."

"Since I would catch shit for even thinking of marrying you. It's one thing to make a divorced male my companion, but to marry him? In my position? Is that what you're getting at?" Shiloh nodded. Then another thought struck Killian. "So you thought this would just be an affair, or at best a formal companionship?"

"I don't know. I just fell in love with you and was willing to take whatever you would give me." Shiloh looked down, then up into Killian's eyes. "It's not that I don't know you love me." He touched Killian's lips softly. "I can't help but know how much you love me, and I know you know how much I love you, but I didn't think you would want me forever." He looked down again as he dropped his hands.

Killian tipped Shiloh's face back up and kissed him gently. "I want you forever, Shiloh Zahirris. No one else, just you. If someone doesn't like it, then fuck 'em. They aren't marrying you, I am." He paused. "Unless you don't want to?"

Shiloh kissed him. "I always wanted that, Killian Larrestes."

"Good, it's settled. Now, about the blue balls we're both about to have?" Killian asked, teasing.

Shiloh laughed, well aware of the oddity of the Rimalian definition of "virgin." "Well, we already know how to have fun without intercourse." He turned serious again. "I want you to have the dream wedding you deserve, Killian."

"You deserve the same, Shiloh." Killian replied with a kiss.

"That's as may be, but my divorce precludes that. But it doesn't for you. Please, can we just let that be enough?"

Killian studied him for a few minutes, then nodded.

Shiloh breathed out a sigh of relief. "Thank you, love."

"I just want you happy, Sprite." Killian grasped both their erections, beginning a firm, fast stroke, smiling as Shiloh moaned for him. He could feel Shiloh's pleasure and relief and love.

Shiloh kissed him hungrily, hips thrusting in Killian's hold again. He began to play with Killian's nipples, grinning as he moaned at the touch. Then he leaned down a little and bit Killian's shoulder as they thrust against each other.

Killian swore, moving faster. "Come on, Sprite, come for me, now."

That was it; Shiloh came hard, crying out Killian's name, feeling the hot liquid splash of first his own cum then Killian's as he followed Shiloh over that edge, gasping Shiloh's name. Killian collapsed back on the bed, bringing Shiloh down with him. Shiloh nestled in, loving the buzz he got, not only from his own orgasm, but also the feeling of Killian's and knowing Killian was sharing his pleasure, too. It flowed back and forth, leaving them wired and looped at the same time. Killian knew he should get them cleaned up but he didn't want to move. This was perfect, right here. They needed to talk more but it could wait. He had only two goals this second: telling Shiloh he loved him one more time, and sleep.

I love you. They both said it as they fell asleep, not noticing they had communicated psionically instead of vocally. They just smiled and dropped off, content and loved, wrapped in each other's arms.

19

WHEN KILLIAN WOKE UP the next morning, it was to an empty bed with a note from Shiloh, telling him that he, Keith, and the boys had gone to town for a little shopping. It was signed, "Love, Sprite." He smiled as he crawled out of bed and headed for a shower, thinking about the reappearance of his Sprite early that morning. He'd been happy to see Shiloh's playfulness again.

It was almost nine thirty in the morning, a little later than he normally got up, but he didn't really care. Shiloh was going to marry him; that was the important thing.

Showered and having found a snack in the kitchen, and having romped with the pups for a few minutes, he went to Shiloh's study and sat down, pulling his cell phone out to call in to his estates. For a couple hours, he worked, checking and making arrangements as needed. Then he went outside to take a break while his managers and Mary at home faxed him copies of the estate books so he could check and balance them.

Killian was sitting on one of the benches outside when the shopping expedition returned. Many of the tenants had joined him, since it was lunchtime, and they were chatting amiably. Shiloh got out of the car and came over to him and, much to his surprise, knelt in front of him.

Shiloh blushed as he pulled a jeweler's box out of his pocket and handed it to Killian. "Killian, will you marry me?"

Killian stared at him, then smiled as Shiloh's blush deepened, even as he felt his own cheeks heat up. He nodded as he smiled more widely, feeling happy. "Of course I will, Shiloh."

Shiloh's answering grin was ecstatic and he nudged Killian's knee "Open it already."

Killian laughed, along with several others, and then opened the ring box. Inside were two matched rings, men's wedding bands. They were Black Hills Gold, the tri-color gold and leaf pattern beautiful. "They're gorgeous, Shiloh."

Shiloh plucked the rings out of the box, looked at them, then put one back and reached for Killian's hand. He showed Killian the inscription. *Always your Sprite.* Shiloh placed the ring on Killian's finger. Then Killian took the other one out and placed it on Shiloh's hand.

Everyone around them began to laugh and clap, with calls of "It's about time," ringing out.

Shiloh and Killian both blushed a little as they were congratulated. Jaden and Jimmy both hugged them, with the first truly happy smiles Killian had seen on their faces in months. Slowly everyone drifted off, and the boys wandered over to their favorite place to sit—a gazebo sitting in the small garden off to one side of the House—and Shiloh and Killian were left alone. They took each other's hands and cut through the House to the back garden, which was larger and had a several gazebos scattered through it. The one that had become their favorite sat along the far edge and was the largest—it not only contained a few benches to sit on, but it sheltered a tiny little pool surrounded by ferns. Indeed, the whole structure was scattered with ferns. It was beautiful and, Shiloh had discovered, expensive to maintain, but there wasn't anyone on the estate that wanted to lose it, including him. Some of the most peaceful moments of his life had been experienced in this gazebo during the last three months while holding hands with Killian.

They made their way to it, grinning when the gardeners congratulated them. Sitting down on their bench, Killian wrapped his arm around Shiloh's shoulders, and Shiloh leaned into him, sighing quietly as he settled. Killian kissed Shiloh's forehead—a sense of contentment emanated from Shiloh—and smiled. He hoped Shiloh got the same off him.

"Um, Killian?"

"Hmm?"

"I, uh, called Natalya this morning, after I talked to Celie." Shiloh sat up straight and looked Killian in the eyes. "I asked her if she would act as your mother ..."

Mothers usually gave their sons away and made the arrangements for the weddings, such as securing venues and catering if needed, whatever their sons wanted. Everyone went all-out for a wedding, and it wasn't unheard of for a Clan's *Artris* to lend a hand for arrangements if needed. Even peace arrangements were treated as a joyous, wanted marriage in the hopes that a happy beginning would become a happy life together. Technically, Araminta should be the one going to the Council asking the use of the grounds and requesting the Council's blessing for Killian, as well as making sure everyone who was invited got there. Getting everyone from both Shiloh's estate and Killian's would require the help of several *Sennrojai* at least, Killian thought vaguely as he considered what Shiloh had said.

"So why haven't I heard from her?" he asked with a smile.

Shiloh grinned. "Because I asked her to wait for you to call her and tell her we're getting married. And she said she'd be honored if that was what you wanted."

Killian immediately pulled out his phone and called Natalya. When she answered, he laughed. "So I hear you've already talked to my fiancé this morning."

She chuckled. "Yes, I have, and did he tell you what he asked me?"

Killian nodded, even though she couldn't see. "Yes he did, and I would be honored if you did act as *Senki* for me."

"Thank you, Killian. That means a great deal to me. Ignacio and I have come to love you three like our own ..."

Killian swallowed hard. "We love you, too, Natalya."

She gave an oddly shaky laugh. "This gives me an excuse to make off with Araminta again, too. Someone needs to teach her how to do it for when she has her own sons, after all. Now, I assume we're doing the whole traditional bit on the Island?"

"That's what Shiloh wants for me," he said with a smile for Shiloh.

She sounded a little puzzled. "Isn't that what you still want, Kil?"

"I just want him any way I can get him. He knows how much I wanted the whole traditional shebang and I'm not going to argue with him. It's not like it's too much of a hardship for me—" He waited a beat. "— other than blue balls."

There was a shocked silence on the other end, even as Shiloh burst out laughing, falling off the bench as he cackled hysterically. "I can't believe you said that to her!"

"Killian Larrestes! I do not believe you just said that!" Natalya burst out. "Great stars, I should never have introduced you to Internet porn. This is my fault."

"But it's been so helpful, Nat," Killian teased, watching as Shiloh turned bright red but kept laughing. "We've learned all kinds of things ..."

"I don't even want to know," Natalya said hurriedly with a small giggle.

Killian watched, amused as the two gardeners working today stuck their heads in to look at Shiloh, who was still on the ground, on his back, laughing uproariously. Killian grinned at them as he shook his head, indicating that they should leave it be. They grinned back and wandered off.

"Are you sure you don't want to know? Because—"

"No, don't tell me, boy, please." Natalya laughed at him. "I do take it from that rather bald statement you and Shiloh haven't explored each other too much?"

Killian found himself blushing. "Uh, no. I mean we're sleeping together but ..."

"Well, most of that has been with the boys, so no one will question that, but what about lately?" Natalya asked bluntly.

"Let's just say we had a long talk about it last night, when I told him I wanted him forever." Killian smiled at Shiloh as he quieted and tried to get up by himself. He had issues, though, because he'd start to giggle, which would make him clutch at his stomach, which was apparently hurting from laughing so hard. Killian got off the bench and sat on the ground, helping Shiloh to lay his head on his leg. "That led to the discussion about what kind of wedding ..."

"And that led to his insistence you get what you wanted for a wedding, which means no intercourse?" Natalya finished.

"Exactly." He poked Shiloh gently. "Good thing he's so sweet and cute or I wouldn't let him push me around so much."

Shiloh poked back. "You love me."

"Yes, I do. Natalya, Shiloh bought me a ring," Killian told her. "Matching rings, actually, and they're gorgeous."

Natalya laughed. "He told me. You know, Killian, your claim of virginity and its privileges is almost certainly going to be challenged, are you both prepared for that?"

"Yeah, I know. I've never done anything to be ashamed of and neither has Shiloh. As far as I'm concerned, he deserves the whole special rigmarole as much as I do—he's just as much a virgin as I am," Killian said, with an edge in his voice. Everyone on the Council knew Shiloh's marriage to Anan hadn't been consummated; it had been the whole point of keeping them in full view of the Council and the Assembly. But there were those who wouldn't pay attention to that fact.

"Alright, Killian, we'll deal with it as it happens, and I agree with you about Shiloh. We'll have to see what can be done. You two figure out exactly what you want and call me later, alright?"

They hung up. Killian looked down at Shiloh, who was now playing with Killian's braid. He smiled as he caught the glint of gold on his ring finger.

"What do you want for our wedding?" he asked Shiloh as he stroked his face.

"Me?" Shiloh looked confused.

"Yes, you. It's your day, too, love. Your real wedding day, regardless of anything else. What do you want?" Killian rolled his neck. He'd been sitting still too long that morning.

"I don't suppose we could get away with a long honeymoon?" Shiloh asked hopefully.

"We're *Artris*, love, we don't get such a luxury. We could combine things, though, touring about our estates and take a few days in each place just to play—see the sights and all." Killian smiled. "Although, we would have the first three days all to ourselves, with nobody bothering us."

"On the Island? Or could we go somewhere else?"

"Where do you want to go?"

"I actually want to just wander, where no one knows us or cares. Could we do that? For just a week or so?" Shiloh asked, sitting up and looking at Killian hopefully.

Leaning forward, Killian was met by Shiloh's kiss, and he sank his fingers into Shiloh's silky black hair.

Killian pulled Shiloh into his lap. He understood exactly where that request was coming from. For nearly six months, Shiloh had been living under close scrutiny, on top of the unrelenting pressure from Ewan and Anan before that. He could certainly see why Shiloh would not only want a break, but need one as well. "We can do that. We'll arrange things so we can just disappear for a few days." Killian was surprised at the level of relief he felt coming off of Shiloh at Killian's agreement. He promised himself he would find ways to whisk Shiloh away on a regular basis.

"Thank you," Shiloh breathed. He kissed Killian, and then tucked his head under Killian's chin, nestling close. "Killian, do you want children?"

"Yes."

"I always have, too, although I admit that the Council's orders kind of make me want to get sterilized ... but ..." Shiloh shrugged awkwardly.

Killian chuckled. "Well, I can understand the whole knee-jerk thing, but please don't, I would love to have a little you running around."

"But what about a little you?" Shiloh asked.

"My love, both of us individually have wealth enough to raise as many children as we want. I don't think there's any reason we can't secure the services of more than one surrogate. Additionally, there's no reason we can't adopt. We'll sort it out, love. We both want children, so we can leave the 'how and how many' for later, okay?" He kissed Shiloh again, then nuzzled him.

Both their phones rang, informing them that Anan was being brought before the Council—again—the next day. They were told to be ready at seven in the morning their time, as Catan would bring them to Rimalia, since he was still in the area. Shiloh was also told that Cheryl was on the Island.

When they both got off the phone, they looked at each other and sighed.

"Time to get back at it, okay?" Killian said. "Practice time. I want you to inspect the estate from top to bottom. Then we'll go over what you find."

"Only if you give me another kiss," Shiloh said, pretending to pout.

"Gladly."

20

THE NEXT DAY, they—including Jaden and Jimmy—all met in the Council Chambers about the attempted kidnapping. While they would need weeks to recover, Amalie and her friends were wheeled in on their gurneys. Anan, Cheryl, and Arnold were also in attendance.

Milossa Jarvai, as Head of the Council, began the proceedings. "Again, we are here because of the actions of Mistress Anan Nyirej, although admittedly she merely instigated recent events this time, as opposed to actually participating. However, it is patently clear that these events would never have happened if not for her encouragement." Milossa sighed. "In my years as *Artris*, I have met very, very few who are as unrepentant and recalcitrant as you, Mistress Anan. The last one, we hanged, as you might remember.

"You have been punished for your transgressions, and been given numerous chances to show that you have learned your lesson, but every time we turn around, we find that you are causing trouble yet again, bringing great harm to your victims. This time it is two young males who have already been greatly harmed by your friend, Cheryl. The Council meets to consider the

Magistrate's recommendation that Anan Nyirej be banished for the rest of her life."

Anan gasped. Banishment didn't just mean she would be shunned by Rimalians. She would also forfeit her remaining property and wealth and no longer be her mother's heir. She would lose everything that gave her rank and status. Since she didn't work, she would be penniless. She would receive no assistance from any Rimalian, although conceivably a *Tii-su* might act to save her life if need be, but that was a matter of their own conscience. She would no longer have the right to food, shelter, clothing, and medical care, as all Rimalian citizens did. She would be forced to support herself completely, if she could, rather than have the normal communal support they all depended on.

"Lady Larrestes, Lady Zahirris, first, I and the rest of the Council would like to extend our congratulations on your recent engagement. We all hope you have a long and happy life together. Second, I must ask who will bear your Proxy for this vote?" Milossa asked, ignoring Anan's angry stare.

Killian and Shiloh stood up. Killian indicated for Shiloh to go first. "Lady Xeltrai has agreed to be my Proxy, Lady Jarvai," Shiloh replied.

"Lady Nedai has agreed to be my Proxy, Lady Jarvai," Killian added.

"I accept your choices, my Ladies," Milossa said, indicating they should sit down. Now that they didn't have a vote in the matter, they were able to just sit and listen.

Lady Ertrai stood and reported everything, including reminding the Council of previous attempts to bring Anan's behavior back into socially acceptable boundaries. As none of their punishments seemed to have had the desired effect, she therefore saw only two options: banishment or slavery. She recommended banishment because slavery in Rimalian society was intended to rehabilitate a repeat offender in a carefully controlled and supportive fashion, and she did not believe Anan could be rehabilitated.

Lady Nyirej, whom Shiloh had discovered was a decent sort of woman, if very conservative, stood up. "Have the *Tii-su* made that call?"

Lady Ertrai faced her, shaking her head. "No, my Lady, Mistress Anan has refused to be examined. I have based my recommendations on her past behavior and her recent efforts and attitude, although, if the Council votes unanimously to force an examination, I will certainly not protest."

"I see. Thank you." Lady Nyirej sat back down.

Anan turned to Lady Nyirej. "My Lady, I am of your clan. You cannot allow them to banish me. I will have nothing."

"I have told you repeatedly I will not rescue you from foolish actions. I told you so when you begged to be spared the flogging you deserved, and the reparations you owed Regent *Artris* Larrestes, I told you again when you tried to claim a male who so obviously didn't want you. In that case, I even told you of a male that did seem interested in you—"

"But my Lady, he had no wealth, no property or standing—" Anan protested.

"If those are all you value, you deserve to lose everything, Anan," Lady Nyirej snapped, clearly beyond pissed. "Given your behavior, and the fact you obviously never learned to have at least a little respect for males, I'm glad for his sake he is too poor for you; it leaves him free to find a wife who will value him for his own sake, as a wife should. Sit down and shut up."

"Does anyone here speak on Anan's behalf?" Milossa asked quietly. No one moved and the silence was deafening. "Anan, you may speak for yourself. Can you give us one reason we should allow you to stay amongst our society? Can you reasonably justify your actions?"

"I have the right to avenge myself against those who have harmed me," Anan said angrily.

"Quite true, if you have done no harm to them first, Anan. I can think of no instance brought to the Council where you have been harmed first," Milossa responded.

"It started with that—that creature," Anan objected, pointing at Killian. "Sitting there among you, as if he had the right! Him and his false accusations!"

Killian stood, his hands moving to the buttons on the dress tunic he wore. "Shall I strip and show the scars I bear from your attempt to rape me?" he asked quietly. "Your actions led to my mother's. My siblings and I hold you partially responsible for the death of our father. Shall I call upon *Tii-su* Georges to verify the damage done to my siblings? Yet we never asked the Council to execute you for your part in our father's murder. *Senki* could have behaved properly, just as you could have. Yet we know, if not for you, our father would be alive. I wouldn't be standing here, as Regent, and it would probably be I who bears the stigma of a divorced male. Because I assure you, Mistress Anan, I would have sought a divorce the first time you hit me. And I have no doubt that would have happened. Shall we break down in minute detail, for all to hear, how your actions have led us all to this?

"Time and again you've been offered punishment and help. Correction for your behavior, and offers from the *Tii-su* to help you change your ways, so you can live among us without causing harm. Time and again, you refuse to accept that you need to change, and accept responsibility for your own actions, instead insisting the blame lies with me, or Janet, Lady Zahirris, or Lord Ewan. For years, I and my siblings have suffered nightmares because of you. I will bear scars the rest of my life that remind me every day of what you did to me. Lady Zahirris still has nightmares because of you. My brother and his *Miisen*, who were just beginning to cope with their new lives, have suffered a severe setback because you instigated the situation wherein James was nearly kidnapped.

"If the vote is to banish you, Anan, you have no one to blame but yourself. All you had to do was remember that your actions affect others and to have a little care in your actions. Since all you care about is yourself, I say all that will care for you is yourself." Killian's voice had remained quiet, calm the entire time, but as he sat and Shiloh took his hand discreetly, he knew Shiloh could feel the trembling Killian hid from the others.

Shiloh squeezed gently, trying to reassure. He got a small, gentle squeeze back.

Milossa waited for a few minutes, but even Anan was silent. Then she called for a vote. It was very clear the vote was unanimously in favor of banishing Anan. Then Milossa asked what time period Anan should be banished for. This involved far more discussion, and finally they arrived at a consensus.

Milossa turned to Anan. "Anan Nyirej, you are banished for one hundred years, during which you are not welcome among us, you have no status or rank among us, and any family holdings for which you may have any claim whatsoever are returned to the care and holding of your clan, to be distributed as your *Artris* sees fit. You are banned from contact with any of Rimalia, and we are banned from any contact with you. If at any time you disregard this ban, you may be put to death. If ever there is a change to this decision, you will contacted by my office, and my office only. It has also been agreed that, in fifty years, you may contact myself, or my successor, and request the ban be lifted. I will tell you now, if you have not tried to lead a decent, law-abiding life among the humans, such a request will not be considered. However, if you have learned to lead a decent, abiding life, the Council will consider your petition. Do you understand?"

Anan finally seemed to realize she had no recourse. "I understand."

Lady Nyirej stood. "I have one more thing, Lady Jarvai."

Milossa nodded. Lady Nyirej looked at Anan, her expression an odd combination of pity and disgust. "I disown you, Anan. You have shamed and dishonored us for the last time. You are no longer a Nyirej. You are no one and nothing to any of my Clan." She turned her back.

The Council, including Shiloh and Killian, followed her lead by standing and turning their backs. Killian shuddered as noises indicated Anan was being led from the room, holding tightly to Shiloh's hand, needing the warmth the contact gave him.

The Council returned to their seats after a couple of minutes. Milossa stared at Cheryl, Arnold, Amalie, and the other two for a long time before speaking.

"It was recommended to us that the indignity of being taken down by two young males, one of whom has never been trained to fight and, despite having an adult body, still has a child's mind, be sufficient punishment for the three of you," she said to Amalie and her friends.

"However, it is the consensus of the Council that it is not enough. You intended to kidnap a young male whose mental condition means he is not yet old enough to be marriageable, regardless of his physical age. You further harmed him by attempting to take him from his *Miisen* when both are still trying to recover from the harm done them in the first place. You also injured the *Miisen* in question during the attempt. You ignored an *Artris'* order to leave James Masrei in peace. You defied another *Artris'* order to leave his charges alone and report Mistress Cheryl to the Magistrate. These are very grave offenses and cannot be allowed to stand. They must be punished in such a way that no one will ever think it wise to follow in your footsteps.

"I ask the Council to consider a sentence of slavery for Amalie, Rada, and Sidi Nyirej. My suggestion is three years." At Milossa's statement, the Council began to confer where they sat.

Killian gasped. A slavery sentence? Although a traditionally and socially acceptable sentence, it was rarely used. It required a great deal of Council and community resources. On the other hand, he had no knowledge of such a punishment failing to rehabilitate. Some were even released early from their sentences because they learned quickly and honestly. With so many *Tii-su* paying such close attention, paying lip service to get out of trouble did not work. There were even a few who chose to remain in a collar lifelong, under the care of the family that sponsored them. He studied the women in question. All were young, in their late teens or early twenties, and all had been raised in the same branch of the Nyirej clan as Anan. He knew from talking to his peers that males from that part of the Clan often had trouble adjusting to how other families did things because it was so different from how they were raised. However, it didn't take long for them to improve. Could it prove true for these three also? If they were completely removed from anything that would reinforce their beliefs, it might.

Shiloh sat quietly for a moment, then walked over to Milossa. He knelt beside her chair so he could speak without being overheard. "My Lady, I do not have the training or experience to make such a decision. Is it possible for me to abstain from this vote?"

She leaned over to speak quietly to him. "You have a point, Shiloh," she replied gently. "However, we all must vote; no abstention is allowed unless you are a direct victim of the accused, or are too ill to attend. You know how the punishment works. You have to decide; are they likely candidates for it? Is it worth our time and effort in the hopes they never cause such harm again and raise their children to never cause such harm? Such a punishment isn't just about the offender, but the offender's daughters and sons. Parents teach their children what they believe. If they can be taught better, and come to believe it, what will they teach their children? You are deciding if they are worth our effort."

Shiloh looked at her for a minute then nodded his understanding of what she said. "Thank you, my Lady." He went back to his seat and studied them. They were angry. They looked as if they wanted to say that the Council had no right to do this. They could refuse to accept it, but the alternative was automatic banishment, sometimes even death, depending on the offense. He thought about what Milossa had said. They had been raised to think that, as females, they could do as they wished, and males had no choice but to submit. They'd been raised to think males were a convenience for females, with little or no value of their own. Most women in Rimalian society were raised to see males as less than themselves, but not like that. They were taught males were to be protected, sheltered, left to run the household and raise the children while the females went out and dealt with the rest of the universe. It was how males were expected to ensure continuation of the species, other than impregnation. It gave males an utterly vital role within their society. However, if these particular women could be taught men did have value, that they had feelings and opinions just as important as their own, could they be the start of changing that branch of their clan?

The Council began to move into groups, as discussion with immediate neighbors was no longer enough. Milossa stayed out of it, making her decision on the matter clear. Many approached her, and several even questioned the three women, making sure all could hear their answers. Shiloh remained silent, though, and he noticed that Killian did as well. He looked at his fiancé. "You've already decided?" he asked very softly.

"I have. You?" Killian asked curiously.

"I have," Shiloh replied. He continued to listen in the hopes of learning more about being an *Artris*. One of his new peers asked him what he asked Milossa and he shrugged. "I told her I didn't believe I had the training or experience to make such a decision properly, and asked if I might abstain. She told me that I couldn't, and gave me some points to consider."

The woman who had asked nodded approvingly, but didn't ask what he'd decided. Slowly everyone returned to their seats, indicating to Milossa they had all come to a decision. She called for the vote. Shiloh felt a little odd; this was his first vote as *Artris*, and he prayed he made the right call as he agreed to place the three in a collar. Lady Xeltrai stood and informed Milossa there had been some dissent about the length of time, and she suggested a compromise. Some thought two years was sufficient, and others believed five, so she suggested four; after all, a sentence could be shortened, but unless they managed to get into serious trouble, it could not be lengthened. Another quick vote was taken and Shiloh agreed with that, as well; Dana was right, if they truly changed, they could be released early, but their effort would be useless if the sentence was too short. Milossa ordered the arrangements be in place by the time they recovered sufficiently from their wounds.

Then Milossa turned to Cheryl and Arnold. Lady Masrei had already informed the Council of Cheryl's disownment; Arnold had been given the option to stay with the Clan and had chosen to go with his wife. "Mistress Cheryl, you have been disowned by your Clan. This Council also bans you from our communities for five years. You failed your duty as James' mother on several occasions, leading him to grievously harm his *Miisen* and be harmed grievously in turn. You acted in bad faith when you told Mistress Amalie that she may wed your son, knowing full well he is not yet mentally mature enough and that you no longer had custody of him. We also ban you from contact with James for five years.

"Master Arnold, you are also banned, for five years. You told Lady Ertrai that you couldn't warn anyone because Mistress Cheryl told you not to. We agree that a man has a duty to obey his wife. However, a man has a stronger duty to protect his children, even from their mother if necessary. You failed to do this." Milossa frowned at both of them.

Cheryl looked defiant but Arnold hung his head, looking shamed.

"If there is no further business?" Milossa asked.

Natalya stood up. "My Ladies, I have an issue that I believe we must address, as the situation arises from one of our decisions."

Milossa looked at her, then looked at Shiloh. "Go ahead, Lady Nedai."

"Regent *Artris* Larrestes has done me the honor of asking that I act as *Senki* for his upcoming wedding to Lady Zahirris. He requests a traditional ceremony here on the grounds, with you to officiate, as is his right. However, I submit that Lady Zahirris also has the right to claim such as his due, despite his divorce. I ask the Council how we might redress this," Natalya said.

Many of the Council began to murmur.

Richard, Lady Jonai, stood. "Can we not simply proclaim he has the right to a virgin's perks? We all know the marriage was not consummated. Indeed, we made sure it wouldn't be."

Many of the Council nodded in agreement, but a few looked as if they had reservations. One stood. "Excuse me, while I grant that both Lady Jonai and Lady Nedai are correct, there is some doubt as to whether either man in question is indeed a virgin."

Killian gritted his teeth. In his years as Regent, he'd found Andrea Jinn to be a nasty piece of work, one of those who, even when she knew the truth, still liked to spread malicious gossip. He stood. "If you wish to question my honor, you are free to deal with the consequences of it."

Shiloh also stood. "I agree, Lady Jinn. Please feel free to question my honor. I, however, will feel free to do the same for you."

There were more than a few who very carefully kept their faces passive, but of those Shiloh was close enough to see clearly, there were more than a few approving looks.

"You deny that you both share a bed?"

"We have shared a bed for more than three months now, due to the need to care for my brother and his *Miisen*. This is no secret," Killian answered.

"What about before that, while Lady Zahirris was in your care under Sanctuary?" Andrea asked with a snide smile.

Milossa made a rude noise. "Andrea, we addressed that when Anan made her accusations months ago. Surely you are old enough not to pay attention to gossip spread in an attempt to divert blame."

"Gossip isn't always untrue, Milossa, you know that," Andrea Jinn replied.

Shiloh turned to Kelia K'Arith. "My Lady, would you Verify that we are not lying when we state that we are virgins?"

Kelia smiled. "Go ahead."

"I am a virgin," Shiloh stated.

"I, too, am a virgin," Killian repeated.

Kelia studied them for a moment, then burst out laughing, drawing puzzled looks from everyone. Catan, who sat with Jaden and Jimmy, also began to laugh. Kelia drew a gasping breath, a huge grin on her face. "Neither one lies, my Ladies. They are virgins by our custom."

"What is so amusing?" Milossa asked with a slight hint of irritation in her voice as Kelia continued to chuckle quietly.

"My apologies, to you all, particularly you two, Lady Zahirris, Lady Larrestes. My Lady Jarvai, I'm sorry, but to explain what I find so amusing would breach their privacy in ways they do not allow," Kelia replied, trying unsuccessfully to stop chuckling.

Confused, Killian and Shiloh looked at each other. What in the worlds was she talking about? How more invasive could you get than questions about one's sex life?

"Is the Verification sufficient?" Milossa asked, looking around the chamber. Even Andrea wasn't going to insist the two weren't virgins; she wasn't stupid or contrary enough to risk an honor duel, especially if it would not only be with Killian and Shiloh, but Kelia, as well. "Very well, then. Let it be known then that Lady Zahirris, despite his Council-ordered marriage and divorce, is to be accorded the same privileges as any other virgin groom."

Shiloh was stunned. He stammered a thank you to all of them, and to Natalya in particular, blushing furiously. Knowing it came from the conversation Killian had had with Natalya the day before, Shiloh resolved to thank Killian more personally later. Milossa adjourned the Council meeting, and he and Killian were surrounded, congratulated, and asked their plans.

21

LATER THAT NIGHT, after they got the boys and Araminta to bed and asleep, surrounded by Shiloh's girls, Shiloh took Killian by the hand and led him to their private end suite bathroom. Killian had been quiet after they came back from the Council meeting. Their little family, including Jimmy, had spent a few hours in the den, cuddled together on the couch, which had been healing in its way, but now Killian needed something more. Shiloh could tell his fiancé was hurting and guessed the confrontation with Anan earlier that day had stirred everything up again, freshening still-healing wounds. He knew he was likely to be having his own nightmares that night, and he was glad Killian would be there to wake him from them. For now, though, he was going to see to Killian.

Killian remained passive as Shiloh slowly undressed him after running a hot bath for them both. Even his touch-sense was muted. It felt like he could sense Killian, but only through a fog. After getting them both naked, Shiloh wrapped his arms around Killian's waist. "I never realized how much your scars bother you, or where they came from."

Killian finally moved, embracing Shiloh tightly. "I hate them. I try very hard to just not think about them, especially since ..."

"Come on, love, into the bath and tell me while I hold you." Shiloh let Killian climb into the tub first, then sat behind him and draped himself over Killian's back. Killian hunched over, his arms around his knees. Shiloh rubbed Killian's arms and pressed a small kiss to the shoulder blade under his cheek. "Tell me."

"You know she tried to rape me. In the fight she slashed my shoulder, and ..." Killian drifted off again. He shuddered.

"And?" Shiloh asked softly. As bad as his experience with Anan had been, he knew he'd been lucky compared to Killian.

"The scars on my ... my groin are from her. She scratched me so badly I was still bleeding when I got home. You wouldn't believe the pain ... *Senka* put some ointment on for me, but three days without proper treatment, without even being able to take a bath because I was afraid to stop walking ... All of my wounds were infected. They were afraid I would end up losing ..." He stopped again, as another shudder racked his body. Shiloh gasped as Killian's touch-sense became a fiery pain, no longer muted, and held more tightly to him, trying to give him the love and acceptance he felt. "I did lose one. They replaced it with a matching prosthetic only a month before we met. Until then there was nothing there, because they knew I would grow. They figured it would be safe now, as I haven't grown in over a year. Waiting meant one surgery instead of several, unless for some reason ... They were worried such a bad infection would sterilize me, but other than losing a testicle, I'm fertile. They test me yearly, just in case, and I make donations that are frozen for me in case there are problems later. They say it's highly unlikely, but ..."

Shiloh could only imagine the issues Killian would have over that. Killian's father had told him masturbation was dirty, evil. And yet, to preserve his chances for children later, he'd had to do exactly that, at least once a year. It was a wonder Killian wasn't seriously fucked up about sex. Shiloh suspected Natalya's and Ignacio's hand, and Georges'.

Lost in his own thoughts, Killian shivered. Shiloh wrapped him closer in an attempt to warm him. He grabbed a mesh pouf and the shower gel and lathered it up, gently running it over

Killian's body, then his own, washing and rinsing them quickly. Then he stepped out and helped Killian out, drying them both.

When Killian reached for the clean sleep pants Shiloh had originally brought with them, Shiloh shook his head.

"No, come with me first." He led Killian over to the bathroom door, which held a full-length mirror. "Look at yourself." He traced a hand over the scar on Killian's shoulder as he stood behind Killian. He made sure to press his erection against Killian, graphically showing Killian how much he wanted him, no matter what. "This isn't ugly to me. It's a reminder of how strong you are." He smoothed his hands down Killian's stomach, feeling the indrawn breath, Killian's desire for Shiloh's touch, and the shame he wasn't perfect and unscarred like Shiloh.

Shiloh felt it all. He couldn't help it even if he'd wanted to. Shiloh kissed the strong spine in front of him even as he took hold of Killian's half-hard cock. With their height difference, he couldn't see in the mirror, but he didn't need to; he could feel Killian's emotions. Shiloh gently and lovingly fondled Killian, stroking him until he was hard, then slipped around and knelt at Killian's feet, looking at his face and then his groin. He licked each scar deliberately, with soft murmurs of how Killian was perfect, that the scars were a sign of strength. He paid equal attention to both balls, although he now knew why the left one always seemed more sensitive. The other was the prosthetic. and any sensitivity it had was purely due to the nerves in the skin covering it. He played with the prosthetic anyway, not knowing any other way to demonstrate how little it mattered.

Killian's hands fisted in his hair and he groaned. "Please, Sprite."

Shiloh sucked Killian's cock into his mouth, moaning as the hard shaft filled it, wrapping his hand around the length to help apply the right pressure. One of these days, Shiloh was going to deep throat that hard length, but until he learned how, Killian's pleasure in this was enough. Shiloh teased until he could sense the only thing Killian was feeling was pleasure and need for more of Shiloh. Then he stopped teasing and sucked harder, using one hand to squeeze and stroke Killian's cock and the other to play with his balls, rolling them carefully in his fingers.

"Shiloh!"

Shiloh swallowed everything greedily as Killian came, and came himself as Killian's pleasure slammed into him. He stroked and licked Killian's slowly softening cock, his head buzzing and dizzy from their orgasms.

Killian's knees buckled and he folded around Shiloh, holding tightly, kissing him, murmuring how much he loved Shiloh, thanking him for such pleasure. Gradually Shiloh's head cleared a little, and Killian tipped his head up and kissed him tenderly.

"Finally back with me?" he asked Shiloh softly, as he kissed him again.

Shiloh nodded a little as he teased Killian's tongue with his. *Oh, yeah. We've got to do that again.*

Killian drew back and stared at Shiloh, eyes wide. *Shiloh?*

Shiloh stared back, shocked, as he realized he had heard Killian's voice, but Killian hadn't spoken. "I heard you. In my head."

"I heard you say we had to do that again, while I was kissing you ..." He gave a choking laugh. "Our minds have linked," he said, amazed.

Shiloh was amazed, too. Then, "Does it bother you?"

Killian smiled. *No, why would it? Does it bother you?*

NO! Shiloh smiled back. *It will take some getting used to, though.*

I wonder what the limits are. Killian mused. "Is it only when we touch?"

They carefully separated, standing up. Shiloh flushed as he saw his cum drying on the floor. He grabbed some toilet paper and cleaned the mess up. *Killian?*

Hi, Sprite. They grinned. *Let's go to bed, love. I want to try this thing called a blowjob on you.*

By all means, love. I am more than willing to be your guinea pig.

They climbed into their bed and, nestling close, explored each other's minds more than their bodies, strengthening the link between them. Even as they fell asleep, the link remained, giving them a sense of peace and contentment neither had ever felt.

At least now we know what Kelia was laughing about. They laughed at the shared thought.

22

T HE DAY OF THE WEDDING, Killian woke up early. He smiled, touching Shiloh and finding he was still asleep. They had arrived three days earlier, the first time they'd seen each other in three months. They hadn't even had a chance to give each other a hug before every unmarried male on the island twelve years of age and older descended on the two of them, splitting into two groups and making off with them. The exception to that was Jaden, but no one said anything to stop him. The group that captured Killian just had to watch the things they said while teasing Killian, since Jaden was still too young for the normal, lascivious teasing that went on during a Promenade.

The groups of young males did have a great deal of fun putting aside the normal formality of dealing with *Artris* Shiloh and Regent Killian. That day, they were just two males like any others being captured for Promenade. Killian laughed to himself as he thought about that afternoon. His fellows had obviously planned it out, making sure that the two of them crossed paths but never giving them a chance to really speak. They'd barely been able to catch each other's hands for a quick squeeze before being dragged off in different directions. They'd all had a great time. He had seen a few things he really liked, and knew Shiloh had, also. The divorce had caused a few problems for Shiloh, despite the Council's proclamation, but before Shiloh could say anything, the young men, many of whom did a lot of the shopping for their households, reminded the offenders that they could boycott their shops if they liked ... These young men wielded a lot of economic power and were willing to use it, reminding the prickly shopkeepers it paid to be hospitable. That defense by his peers had nearly had Shiloh in tears.

Killian got up and made a light breakfast for everybody; Jaden, Jimmy, Araminta, William, and Carys were there with him in his house while Keith was with Shiloh at the Xeltrai House. William and the boys would help Killian get ready today while Keith, Valerian, Dana's eldest son, and probably her younger sons, would act as Shiloh's attendants. Milossa already had their rings and everything was set up for their honeymoon.

For the first ten days, they were just going to wander around the States, as Killian had never really gotten to see anything of the United States. Only Lucretia would know where they were, since she had agreed to ferry them about. After that, they were going to inspect their respective estates, first Shiloh's, and then Killian's, before joining Dana on her yearly inspections. This meant they would get to spend their first three months of marriage together. After that, they would have to start dealing with the first of their separations.

They had spent a lot of time working out how they were going to deal with their responsibilities, not only as *Artris* but also as spouses. It would be easier in five years, when Araminta was due to be confirmed as *Artris*. Until then, they would be doing a lot of traveling. Every other month, they would switch off visiting each other for a few days. The yearly inspections, they would do together, giving them nearly two solid months together.

Jaden and Jimmy were doing better, although still inseparable. They still slept in the guest bedroom of Shiloh's suite at Morgaine House and sometimes crawled into bed with Shiloh, looking for comfort, but they did continue to heal. They would stay with Lady Masrei for a couple of weeks while Shiloh and Killian were on their honeymoon. Then they would return to Morgaine House, where Keith and Sherry would look after them. Araminta would go to Natalya while Killian was gone. Having completed her initial training as a *Tii-su*, she would soon mentor with an experienced *Tii-su*, but, for now, she was on a break from training.

Amalie and her cousins were all fitted with collars, to show everyone they were slaves. No one could raise a hand to them or mistreat them. The penalty for abusing a slave was to join them in the collar or, in extreme circumstances, death, as slaves were not allowed to defend themselves. Several families had offered to sponsor each woman, which meant the *Tii-su* were able to closely match each woman to a family, improving their chances of being rehabilitated. Initial reports from the sponsors and *Tii-su* showed the women were resisting, but that wasn't unusual. As a matter of fact, everybody would have worried about their health if they were not defiant at first. Only if it continued after eighteen months would it indicate a lack of probable success. The *Tii-su* in charge did call both Shiloh and Killian and ask their permission for the three to attend the wedding festivities. They felt it would be a good way to show the women proper behavior and its benefits. Shiloh and Killian discussed it, first with each other and then with Jaden and Jimmy. In the end, all four agreed to allow the trio's attendance, on the condition that the women be kept away from Jaden and Jimmy.

The smell of breakfast brought everybody to the table, with William and the boys excitedly deciding how to fix Killian's hair for the wedding. Breakfast was eaten quickly, then, as Killian was going to wash up the dishes, Carys took him by the shoulders and gave him a gentle shove towards William, who took him by the hand. The boys fell in line as William began dragging Killian out of the kitchen.

"But—"

"Time for you to get ready," Carys said firmly. "You go on. I'll clean up in here."

Killian laughed as the boys began shoving him forward. He resisted just enough for them to play, making them laugh. They sent him to shower while they got his clothes ready. He quickly got washed head to toe, laughing as he felt Shiloh poke at him, asking if he was being ordered about as well. Over the past few months, both estates had gotten used to the fact Killian and Shiloh would suddenly laugh for no apparent reason. It had slowly dawned on the residents that their respective *Artris* had developed a bondlink, although no one asked and neither Shiloh nor Killian ever said; it was just too personal and private, too precious to share.

Two hours later, Killian was standing in front of Milossa with Shiloh at his side, he and Shiloh dressed in matching tuxedos. Both of them were grinning so widely their faces hurt, but neither of them could help it. He could feel Shiloh's happiness at getting married to him, and he knew Shiloh could feel his happiness, too. He was only vaguely aware of Milossa and everyone else. Natalya stood on his side, acting as his "*Senki*" and Dana stood on Shiloh's side, acting as Shiloh's "*Senki*."

Then Milossa was calling for any objections. When there were none, the words he'd been waiting for were said. "You may kiss your husband."

Killian felt Shiloh's shock as Milossa presented Lady and Lord Zahirris to the community. *Why?* Shiloh asked.

Killian smiled as he kissed Shiloh's knuckles. *Because I am Regent Artris Larrestes. When Araminta's confirmed, I step down. I'll always retain the rank of Regent, but I won't have to do the job. You will always be Artris, and my place will be with you, so I wished to take your name. That's okay isn't it?*

Oh, yes. I just never thought about it, I guess. Killian could feel Shiloh's pleasure. *Killian Larrestes Zahirris. Sounds good, love.*

Not as good as calling you my husband, Killian said. They both laughed as they were led over to the long table where their gifts had been placed. For more than an hour, they opened gifts while the food was brought out for the feast. Once they'd eaten, they danced in the square, first with each other and then with their "mothers": Natalya and Dana. Afterwards, it was less structured.

Throughout it all, they teased each other with mental images of the things they planned to do to each other when they were alone. Killian laughed and grabbed Shiloh, turning him to point out a young male, subtly "stalking" Jaden and Jimmy. He followed them about, helping during their turn at cleaning up the mess of the party. Shiloh grabbed Milossa's hand and pointed discreetly to the young man. "Who's that?"

Milossa looked and smiled. "That is Nikita Rosetai. He seems quite determined to gain their attention, doesn't he?"

The three watched for several moments. "Which one is he after?" Shiloh asked. "I assume he thinks Jaden must be of eligible age, since Jaden has been participating with Jimmy."

Killian nodded, thinking the same thing. The incident with them was widely known, but it didn't mean that everybody knew or recognized the two. Because of Jimmy, Jaden had been allowed to participate in things he was too young for, so as to not deprive Jimmy of activities he'd already been enjoying for several years. Milossa was quiet, watching.

Killian turned to her. "Tell us about him?"

"He's the youngest son of Lady Rosetai," Milossa answered. "He's about thirteen now, I believe. He's polite and quiet. And from his behavior, I would say he's willing to go for what he wants."

They watched a while longer. Jaden and Jimmy were polite but not exactly welcoming of the attention. Nikita didn't seem put off though.

"Which one is he after though?" Killian wondered.

Surprised, Shiloh said, "I think he's after both."

Milossa nodded. "I think you're right."

Catan snagged Nikita by the arm, pulling him away from the other two and bending down to whisper in Nikita's ear. They observed the stunned look Nikita gave the twosome as Catan continued to speak softly to him. They saw what could only be described as a pained look cross his face as he nodded to Catan. Catan gave him a quick hug and turned him loose, smiling as the young man made a beeline straight back to Jaden and Jimmy. There seemed to be less intensity coming off the young man as he continued to work with them.

"Hmm, you suppose Catan warned him off?" Killian asked.

"I'd say he made sure Nikita knows the deal with them," Milossa said. "He seems to be handling it well. Your young pair seems to be more accepting of him now."

"I guess we'll have to wait and see," Killian mused. He draped an arm around Shiloh and they shared another soft kiss, breaking apart when Milossa gave them both a playful push.

"Alright, you two, save that for bed." She looked around. "As a matter of fact, now would be a good time to make a break for it. Run, flee, scurry." She grinned.

They scurried.

23

K ILLIAN AND SHILOH walked home slowly, holding hands, knowing full well they would be stripping each other in seconds as soon as they were in the house. As they passed the Zahirris House, they saw Ewan in the front garden. He had been invited but had refused to come to the wedding.

Can we stop? Shiloh asked.

Of course, Sprite. Maybe he just didn't feel well enough to go to the party. Shiloh could tell Killian didn't think it was much of a possibility, but he appreciated that his new husband tried to make him feel better about his father's continued rejection.

They entered the garden, walking over to where Ewan sat.

"Hello, *Senka*, how are you today?" Shiloh asked softly.

Ewan glared at them. "What do you want now?" Looking unkempt, he sat in his pajamas. The hair he'd hacked off when Elizabeth died had grown out some, but it was uncombed and knotted now. Ewan was no longer even trying to care for himself.

"We married today, *Senka*. We hoped we'd see you at the wedding or the party, but I guess you weren't feeling up to it?" Shiloh hated what his father had done to him, but the man was still his father; he wanted to redevelop some kind of decent relationship with him.

"You say you married today, but you didn't invite me?" Ewan demanded. "Didn't ask my permission?"

Shiloh flinched back and Killian tucked him close protectively. He spoke up. "I brought you the invitation myself, Ewan. And Shiloh is *Artris*. He doesn't need your permission."

Ewan glared at them both. "You here to kick me out of my house, then?"

Shiloh sighed. His father was getting worse. The *Tii-su* had finally diagnosed his father with a paranoid psychosis; one they believed would worsen, although there was no telling when it would happen. They considered placing him in the Asylum on the Island, but no one wanted to do that until absolutely necessary. For whatever reason, he felt safest in the House on the Island and as long as he felt safe, he remained calm—if decidedly cranky—and no threat to anyone, or himself. The *Tii-su* kept a close eye on him, and Shiloh arranged for food and amenities to be taken to him. Shiloh had also hired two young Nameless males to live in Zahirris House to look after Ewan, and keep him company. To everyone's surprise, Ewan had accepted the young males into the household easily. "No, *Senka*, this is your home and I'm not going to kick you out of it. We just thought you might like to hear about the wedding."

"Then go away." Ewan folded his arms across his chest.

Shiloh nodded and turned away, Killian following closely. Once they were out of sight, Killian pulled Shiloh into his arms and held him as tears fell down Shiloh's face. They weren't the heartbroken tears of months ago, just the softer tears of continued hurt, but Killian still hated to see his Sprite cry.

I'm sorry, Sprite. I'd hoped this would be a sort of good day for him.

I just wish it would stop hurting.

He's your father, love. It doesn't matter what kind of asshole he's been, you still love him. It's not your fault he's like this. Hell, it's not even his fault. Remember what the Tii-su said, that your mother's death injured his mind and the wound became the psychosis that drives his behavior now. All you can do is make sure he's safe, comfortable, and taken care of; which you do admirably. He held his husband until he felt Shiloh relax, and then kissed him again. He felt Shiloh's resolve to enjoy his wedding day and not let even Ewan mar it. He took his husband's hand as they continued on their way home. *Let's go home and play.*

Play? Play what? Chess? I thought we were going home to make love.

Does this mean my Sprite is going to drag me off and have his wicked way with me?

Only if you promise to have your wicked way with me. Shiloh leered at Killian. *I want you to fuck me into the mattress.* He took off running as they drew close to the house.

With a laugh, Killian chased him, following him into their house and locking the door behind him. He was stunned when Shiloh began stripping even as he made his way up the stairs.

With a sultry look, Shiloh glanced over his shoulder at Killian. "You coming?"

Killian's heart stuttered as he watched Shiloh and followed him, undressing as he went. By the time they got to their bedroom, they were both naked. Killian pulled Shiloh into his arms, kissing him hungrily. *I want you, Sprite.*

Take me, Killian. Please take me. Shiloh gasped as Killian nipped his throat, sucking the bite hard and leaving a small, livid bruise.

Killian looked at the mark and felt satisfied by it, as if he wanted everyone to know they couldn't touch Shiloh. He hadn't realized he was so possessive. How did they miss learning this already?

Shiloh chuckled. *Because we were trying to be discreet. By all means, mark me anywhere you want.*

Really? You don't mind? Killian's cock hardened further as he pictured Shiloh with love bites all over.

Shiloh pressed himself closer. Killian shivered at the feel of that thick cock leaking on his skin. *I liked that one. Let's see if I like more. I want to mark you, too, though.*

Oh please, now. Killian pulled at Shiloh, as if he could bring Shiloh into his skin. He groaned, heat flashing through his body when Shiloh latched onto his throat, sucking up his own mark. He felt Shiloh's satisfaction. *I think we're both going to spend the rest of our lives covered in love bites, Sprite.*

I can enjoy that. Shiloh smoothed a hand down Killian's spine. They moved slowly towards the bed, then fell over on it, laughing as they rolled around. They touched each other everywhere, kissing and leaving small bites all over. And they shared the pleasure they felt between them, loving being able to feel the other's emotions. They laughed as they observed how hot it was to be able to talk and not have to stop kissing, biting, or sucking.

"Please, Killian, more." Shiloh arched underneath Killian, gasping as Killian latched onto a nipple again, pulling gently on the delicate gold ring that decorated it. Shiloh had gotten them done a few weeks ago as a surprise for Killian. The way Killian attacked his nipples, laving each one hungrily, flicking the delicate hoops, Shiloh had to believe Killian liked his surprise. He knew he liked Killian's response to them. He ran his hands over as much of Killian's back as he could reach, trailing fingers through Killian's loose hair as it fell around them, feeling like silk on his skin.

"I love these, Sprite. Love that you pierced these hard little nipples for me," Killian breathed against Shiloh's skin. His jaw had dropped when he'd realized Shiloh had gotten his nipples pierced. It was one of the hottest things he'd ever seen. He bit gently, knowing Shiloh seemed to be even more sensitive than before. Shiloh arched and cried out, and Killian chuckled before moving downward. He licked Shiloh's hard, leaking cock, wanting to hear his Sprite beg. Killian showed Shiloh what he intended to do through their bondlink, loving the way Shiloh's body tightened and then shuddered under him in reaction.

"Yes, please, Killian, don't tease …" Shiloh's begged, his hips moving restlessly. Impatient, Shiloh grabbed Killian's hair, dragging his husband up to him, kissing him fiercely, then looking him in the eyes. "Fuck me now, Killian, play later," he demanded, as he tilted his hips up into Killian's hard cock, their erections rubbing against each other. They both moaned at how good it felt. *Fuck me with this thick prick, husband mine.*

Killian lost it. He scrambled to find the lube, laughing as Shiloh grabbed his hand and gave him the bottle. Shiloh brought his legs up, opening himself up to his husband's touch, fire licking at his nerves as he thought about Killian being inside him, finally. Killian's hands shook as he lubed his fingers, then rimmed Shiloh's hole with more.

Up on your hands and knees, Sprite.

Shiloh met his eyes and shook his head. *No, I want to see you.*

I don't want to hurt you, Shiloh; it's supposed to be easiest the first time on hands and knees. They had waited so long for this and Killian didn't want anything to mar it.

Shiloh drew him back to him, kissing him tenderly. *It's you, Killian, it'll be perfect. I want to see you as you sink that huge cock into me.* He lifted his hips, seeking more pressure from the slick fingers teasing his hole.

Killian gave it to him, sliding one finger in, closing his eyes as the heat of Shiloh's body seared an imprint on Killian's mind. He opened them again to watch Shiloh closely, watching and feeling for any discomfort.

More, Killian, please. Feels so good.

Yes, you do feel good, so hot and tight. Killian slowly sank a second finger into Shiloh, leaning down to lick the leaking cock lying on Shiloh's belly, fondling his balls. Shiloh's hips moved more as he got used to two fingers, liking the slight burn and loving the sheer pleasure of the invasion. Killian finally gave him a third, gently stretching Shiloh, wanting to make sure Shiloh wouldn't be hurt by him.

You won't hurt me. Your fingers feel so good, Killian.

Yeah? What do you think of this? Killian twisted his fingers up, searching. He laughed when he felt the small gland and pressed, making Shiloh cry out. Good thing they were alone in the house; that cry would have woken everyone.

Shiloh didn't bother trying to talk. He just tried to remember how to breathe. *Fuckfuckfuck. Do that again, Killian.*

Killian obeyed, pressing gently as he thrust his fingers in that tight pink hole, watching Shiloh twist and shove himself down further. Killian found it hard to breathe as he watched Shiloh, and his balls drew up more as he watched his fingers sink easily into Shiloh's entrance. Shiloh cried out again, his hair fanned out on their pillows, head thrashing; Deity, his husband was so beautiful in his abandon, he held nothing back on any level.

Now, Killian, please, I want you inside me before I come.

Yes, Deity, yes. Slicking his cock, Killian made sure it was good and slippery. Then he pressed himself to Shiloh's hole, slowly, gritting his teeth as he struggled to give Shiloh the time he needed to adjust. He could feel it from both points of view, the heat and tight pressure of Shiloh's body, the burning pressure and pleasure of a thick cock driving slowly into him. Killian didn't bother trying to sort it out. He just kept on filling his lover, his husband. Finally, he was balls deep, both of them sighing in pleasure.

It's like home. They chuckled a little as they realized they had the same thought. The movement sent pleasure fracturing through their bodies.

Neither one moved for a minute; they just kissed tenderly, sinking deeper into each other's minds. Eventually, Killian gave in to the urge to move, thrusting slowly at first, then faster and harder as Shiloh demanded more, his hands holding him close and his body rising to meet Killian's thrusts. Shiloh made the most arousing, sweetest cries as Killian thrust harder and harder, pegging his gland repeatedly.

Moremoremoremorenowharderoh Deitymore.

Killian gave them what they both wanted, thrusting hard and fast. *Touch yourself, Sprite, I want to see you come for me.* Shiloh began to stroke himself, as he stared into Killian's eyes. Killian felt Shiloh's body tighten as cum spurted out of Shiloh's cock, Shiloh screaming as he came. Killian stared at Shiloh, loving the sight of his Sprite's ecstasy. He thrust once more, sinking as far into his husband as he could get, and let everything go. *Oh, Shiloh, you're beautiful,* he thought as he came, stars exploding behind his eyes.

Not as beautiful as you, Killian.

Killian collapsed, loving the way Shiloh's arms wrapped tightly around him, like he didn't want to let Killian go.

I don't want to let you go. I want you to just stay right here inside me.

Oh, man, I wish, Killian answered with a laugh, sleep licking at the edges of his mind; he could feel Shiloh was sleepy, too. But he didn't try to move. Neither of them even cared about the stickiness of Shiloh's cum between them. *You are so worth the wait, Sprite. I love you.*

I love you, too. You are worth everything.

Killian managed to stay inside Shiloh as he rolled them over so he didn't crush Shiloh. He loved the boneless way Shiloh draped over him, his hair falling softly around them. Killian wrapped some of it in his hand as he held Shiloh closer.

They fell asleep, smiling, content, needing nothing but each other.

24

WITH LUCRETIA'S HELP, Killian and Shiloh spent ten days exploring the States. Hand in hand, they walked around both trails at Devil's Tower, marveling at the columns of the monolith and laughing quietly as they spent half an hour watching a woodchuck scampering about. They even took video of the woodchuck with their phones, but the video didn't turn out well, much to their amusement. They spent a day in Yellowstone, marveling at the size of the herds of buffalo and elk, and even spotted some wolves. The tourist thing was done through Mount Rushmore, including stopping at something called the Cosmos Mystery Area. It had been a lot of fun, and they had a ton of strange-looking pictures from that little stop. Fascinated by the goldstone jewelry they found at both Rushmore and Devil's Tower, they bought some for themselves, Araminta, Jaden, and Jimmy.

They went whale watching in California, and wandering through the French Quarter in New Orleans. They thought about exploring Las Vegas, but decided to do that when they were both over twenty-one so they wouldn't be restricted in the places they could go. That discussion had also included a dissection of the humans' odd, and utterly inconsistent, notions of when adulthood began. Just for fun, they went shopping on Rodeo Drive, although they didn't buy much. They found a place in San Francisco where they could have dinner and go dancing. It didn't take them long to find they loved dancing together, and they didn't leave the floor until they were ready to go to their hotel. Even Niagara Falls made the list.

While their days were spent being tourists, they spent their nights exploring each other thoroughly. Their second night together, Shiloh topped Killian with explosive results. After that, they took turns topping, both of them loving how they made each other feel. As they explored each other's bodies, they further ventured into each other's minds, their bondlink growing deeper.

After their ten days alone, during which Shiloh blossomed back into his usual happy, bubbly self, they began the yearly inspections. Everything went well. and the few issues needing their attention were mostly due to the continued resentment of Gaili and Orlie toward Shiloh over the Council's decision.

By the time they were done with their inspections, it was time for the quarterly Council meeting, Shiloh's first real one. He was nervous, but things went well. What surprised Shiloh the most was the fact that several women approached him about being his surrogate, since as *Artris*, he was required to provide an heir. A few had been quite blunt about it, and there were one or two Shiloh and Killian both suspected were only offering because they thought they would be able to exert some control over the Zahirris clan as the mother of the heir. These women were rejected outright by both of them.

Amaliji, Lady Rosetai, contacted both of them about Nikita's interest in both Jimmy and Jaden. While they made it clear that Jimmy's developmental age was roughly on par with Jaden's chronological age, they agreed to foster a friendship between the three as long as Nikita did not court them until they were both older.

When questioned about Jaden, given Jaden's age and decidedly still childlike body, Nikita had shrugged, stating he knew Jimmy and Jaden were a package deal. It hadn't taken him long to realize he would get nowhere with Jimmy if he didn't accept Jaden. He liked the look of Jimmy and then quickly realized that Jaden was mentally attractive just as much as Jimmy was. When he found out Jaden was younger than he'd thought, he knew he'd have to wait longer to be able to court them. In his opinion, becoming friends was the first part of courting, so he was willing to wait to see if anything else would develop.

Reassured, Nikita and his mother were invited for a short visit. Jaden and Jimmy were a little standoffish at first, but the three quickly became good friends. One of the older women at Morgaine House observed them one day and poked Shiloh in the ribs, telling him that he and Killian would have lots of babies to spoil out of those three. When Shiloh mentioned it to Sherry and Keith, they both grinned and told him they'd better start planning the wedding, because the elder woman was the local matchmaker and her instincts had never been wrong.

Killian went back to his estate decidedly unhappy about being separated from Shiloh, but comforted himself with touching his husband several times through the day, being touched in return, and by reminding himself that five years wasn't so long compared to the decades they'd have together. They called each other frequently and even wrote letters to each other, something tangible they could hold when the loneliness became especially bad.

Since things were going so well with Morgaine House, now that Anan was no longer an issue, they'd arranged face-to-face visits every two months, alternating who traveled. In the meantime, they counted the days and worked their asses off so that when they did go to visit each other, they could spend as much time together as possible.

25

Two Months Later...

WHEN SHILOH FINALLY ARRIVED, Killian immediately dragged his husband upstairs to their bedroom, not caring about the fact it was still early morning. After all, they didn't have to worry about kids underfoot because they had the house to themselves. Araminta had begun her mentorship, and Jimmy and Jaden were visiting Lady Masrei again.

"I missed you, Sprite," Killian whispered, shutting the bedroom door and locking it before he kissed Shiloh hungrily. Shiloh's hands were everywhere as he pressed himself into Killian's arms.

"I missed you too, love." Shiloh tugged at Killian's shirt. "Get naked, now. I want in you."

Killian shivered at those words. Oh yeah, Shiloh's thick hard cock inside him sounded like heaven. He couldn't get undressed soon enough. He watched, laughing as Shiloh hurriedly got out of his own clothes. Once they were down to skin, they fell back on the bed and kissed each other like starving animals. They licked and bit, leaving livid marks everywhere.

"Oh, this isn't going to be long, Killian," Shiloh gasped as they came up for air.

"Good, because I need you in me, now." Killian rolled them so he was on the bottom, spreading his legs and pulling them up to his chest. "Fuck me now, foreplay later."

"You got it, baby." Shiloh reached into the nightstand and grabbed the lube he knew lived there now. Slicking his fingers, he began to push them into Killian's hole, gently but quickly stretching him until three of them were inside and Killian was pushing down on them, begging for more.

Shiloh finally began to push his cock into Killian. Both of them sighed.

This is perfect, Killian thought. When Shiloh was balls deep, Killian wrapped his legs around Shiloh's waist and his arms around Shiloh's shoulders, holding him close. *This is where I need you, Sprite, in my arms.*

Me, too, Kil. God, I've missed this, missed being inside you, the way you moan and beg.

Killian gasped as Shiloh moved, slowly at first, then faster, thrusting as deeply as possible into Killian.

So good, so hot. Shiloh pegged Killian's gland repeatedly, loving the way Killian cried out.

Killian met every thrust of Shiloh's hips with his own and, begging for more, stroked himself.

I want to see you come, now, Kil.

Killian exploded like the order was all he was waiting for. He saw stars, their mutual pleasure setting fire to his nerves even as he tried to keep his eyes open to watch Shiloh come. Despite how weak Killian felt, he managed to wrap his arms around Shiloh as his lover collapsed onto him. Breathing heavily, they were both unable to move.

For the first time in weeks, Killian felt content. His husband was where he belonged.

We both are, love, Shiloh replied to the thought, making Killian grin. Sometimes their bondlink was a pain because they couldn't really hide anything from each other, but at other times, like now, it was just perfect. Like Shiloh.

Killian had the vague notion they should clean up and get out and about—there was still work to do—but he felt so replete and content he didn't want to move, and he could feel that same peaceful, sleepy resistance to moving emanating from Shiloh. They fell asleep, smiling.

.   .   .

They did get some work done after their nap, taking the teasing in good part.

Killian was helping to take up the slack for Carys, who had been placed on bed rest for the last weeks of her pregnancy. She was driving William crazy because she didn't seem to grasp that the concept of "bed rest" meant you stayed in bed and rested. On more than a few occasions, William had been heard to remind her that bed rest did not mean you got up before dawn to gather eggs from the chicken coop or feed horses or the any of variety of things they'd all caught her trying to do.

In the end, Killian, William, Mary, and nearly every married male on the estate ganged up on her and told her the next time she tried to escape her bed, they would tie her to it with logging chains. Even so, Carys was not accepting her confinement well. Each of the residents of the estate visited regularly to cheer her up and keep her company, which allowed William to finish up the baby projects. When Killian got a clue as to Carys' ill temper, he had a quiet word with William, asking him if bed rest meant no sex at all, too. He'd had quite the laugh the next morning when he went to visit and William answered the door in his robe, grinned, flipped him off, and shut the door in his face, not to be seen the rest of the day. Apparently, sex was still on the menu. Carys was a little more sociable after that, and so was William.

One evening, Shiloh and Killian visited the expectant pair for a nice evening of talking and playing cards. Afterwards, they walked home slowly, enjoying the cool, crisp evening. Harvest was coming soon, and they would be working almost from sunup to sundown to get everything done. This was the calm before the yearly storm, so to speak, and they were making the most of it while they could. Although Shiloh was looking forward to being able to see the fruits of his labor, as it were.

Killian puttered around in the kitchen with Shiloh, cooking a late dinner together, and then sat close at the table to eat. They washed up together, made some hot chocolate, and then cuddled on their couch in the den. Relaxed, they watched a little TV and quietly discussed their plans for the next day.

"Shiloh?"

"Hmm?"

"I heard from Kelia this morning." Shiloh looked at him curiously. "She says she knows a young woman that might be an appropriate surrogate, if we would like to talk to her."

Shiloh was silent for a moment. Killian felt Shiloh's initial rejection of the idea, which surprised Killian. He knew Shiloh wanted children.

"I don't want either of us having to be single parents. Well, not any more than we already are, with the boys and Araminta," Shiloh answered. "With the way things are right now, that's effectively what we'd be. Whether the baby was with you or me, most of the time, we're apart. I would rather wait and raise our children together."

Killian thought about it. Shiloh was right. It just hadn't been something he'd considered. He'd been a single parent since he was thirteen, so he hadn't perceived their separations as an issue for childrearing. And with the needs of Jaden and Jimmy both, Shiloh had been thrown into the deep end of single parenthood, even if he hadn't complained once, something that made Killian love him even more. "Okay I can see that. I'm sorry, I just never thought of it as a problem."

"Because you've been there, done that," Shiloh replied with an affectionate smile. He kissed Killian's cheek. "Is it a problem that I'd rather wait to raise more children?"

Killian shook his head. "No, Sprite, I get what you're saying and it doesn't bother me. It's not like we can't change our minds later, if circumstances change."

"It would be nice to have some time to ourselves too, before we have babies underfoot." Shiloh leered theatrically.

Killian looked at him, then gently pushed Shiloh down on his back on the couch. He moved so he covered his husband, dropping kisses on that lithe little body as he moved up, until he finally reached Shiloh's lips. He kissed his Sprite, savoring the taste of him.

Shiloh laughed as they came up for air. "We've got time to ourselves right now, Sprite," Killian said with grin. He groaned as Shiloh undulated under him, and leaned back down to kiss his Sprite again hungrily.

They were slowly removing each other's clothes, kissing as they did, when Killian's phone rang.

"Fuck!" Fumbling to find the dratted thing in the dark, he fell off the couch.

Shiloh finally found the phone and handed it to Killian with a rueful smile.

"Killian?" William sounded scared. Then he groaned like he was in pain. "Carys' water broke and there's a lot of blood in it."

"Fuck! Alright, William, hang on, I'll call Lucretia. She'll help."

"Please hurry, Carys has passed out."

"Don't move her, William. We don't know what's wrong. Help's coming." Killian turned to see Shiloh was already talking to Lucretia on his own phone, telling her what was going on, having listened to what William said through his bondlink with Killian.

Shiloh nodded to Killian to show things were under control.

And then William's voice was replaced by a "call dropped" tone. Thankfully, it rang again almost immediately.

"We're at the hospital on the island, Killian. Thank you." William sounded relieved.

"Go with Carys, William, we'll deal with things here."

William hung up without even saying goodbye.

Catan and Kelia both appeared in the den, concern on their faces.

"Deity!" Shiloh gasped.

"Sorry," Catan said, "but time is of the essence, I believe. Who's going?"

"I'll call Mary, and William's parents," Killian said, slightly more accustomed to the fact that *Sennrojai* did not stand on ceremony during an emergency.

"Don't bother," Catan replied. "We've met them before, so we'll grab them, too. We'll take you to the hospital before we fetch the boys,"

Kelia reached out to Killian and Shiloh. "Carys may not make it, Killian," she said as gently as possible. "That's nothing William needs to hear because he needs hope, but right now it doesn't look good."

Oh, Deity, please. Killian shared the thought with Shiloh. Surely Deity would not be that cruel.

"Have hope. She could pull through. But you need to be prepared, just in case." Kelia looked at Shiloh sadly. "This is one of the heavier parts of being an *Artris*: picking up the pieces."

Shiloh nodded. "At least we're still dressed, I suppose. Let's go."

Suddenly they were in the brightly lit Arrival Room of the Hospital on Rimalia. They quickly left, because the room was exactly what its name implied—a safe place to teleport in and out of—so it needed to be clear at all times to avoid possible collisions. Lucretia would have sent Carys and William to this room.

The two *Artris* went up to the maternity ward, where they found William and Araminta in the waiting room. When William saw Killian, he ran and threw himself into Killian's arms, crying in fear for his wife and child.

Holding his best friend tightly, Killian reminded William that Carys was young and strong and told him to have faith that both she and the baby would be okay. Shiloh stroked William's back, asking him if he had the logging chains for Carys, because it was a fair bet she'd need a day or two to recover and he didn't think she'd take that well. She'd expect to just walk out and go harvest everything by herself, in a day, just like any typical stubborn female.

Reassured somewhat, William gave a hiccupy laugh and they all settled down to wait.

Two hours later, a pair of *Tii-su* came out of the surgery ward looking both grim and pleased at the same time. One of them carried a small bundle. Killian braced himself for bad news, feeling Shiloh do the same.

"Carys is alive, William, but she's lost a lot of blood," one *Tii-su* said as the other handed the small bundle to its father. William's knees gave out and Killian and Shiloh caught him, supporting him and the baby. "Your daughter, however, is healthy, beautiful, and has some hellacious lungs on her."

William tried to speak, but didn't seem able to.

Knowing what he wanted, one of the *Tii-su* spoke. "We've given her several units of blood and we've repaired the rupture that caused the hemorrhage. She's very weak, but she's alive and her mind is intact. We expect her to recover, in time."

"What caused the rupture?" Killian asked as they stood holding William and the baby.

"It looks like the fetus implanted on a weaker section of the uterus. Carys will need some tests done to determine the risks of such a thing happening if she gets pregnant again." She waggled a finger at William. "No more babies for four years. Carys needs time to heal completely, and it gives you time to get your little princess there potty-trained."

William nodded obediently. "Can I see her?"

"Of course. Although, right now she's unconscious," the other *Tii-su* answered.

William straightened and brushed a kiss over his daughter's face as she lay content in his arms. "Come on, Lucretia, let's go see *Senki*," he said softly, naming the girl. William looked around until he saw Lucretia sitting with Catan and Kelia. "She and Carys would be dead if you hadn't acted so quickly. Thank you."

The *Sennrojai* nodded. "You're very welcome, child. Go on, go see your wife." She smiled, a few happy tears sliding down her face.

Killian drew Shiloh close, hugging him in sheer relief. The three new grandparents joined the hug, dragging the *Tii-su* and *Sennrojai* into it as well, all of them crying with sheer relief. Jaden, Jimmy, and Araminta all wiggled into the hug as well.

•   •   •

After inviting Lucretia and the new grandparents to stay with them, Killian and Shiloh spent the night on the Island. Lucretia accepted, apparently so she could fawn over her new namesake, who was soon nicknamed Tia. As a new father, William was just grateful for the help. Killian took care of informing the appropriate people of William's parents' whereabouts. Carys awakened late the next day, demanding to see her daughter. She was awake for about an hour, long enough for everyone to see her and for the new family to spend some time together, alone. After that, the *Tii-su* were much more confident of Carys' recovery.

Kelia and Catan returned the boys to Lady Masrei, and Lucretia returned Killian and Shiloh to Killian's estate, where the tenants swarmed the three of them. It took a little time to reassure everyone that Carys would be okay, and William and the baby were well. During the chaos, Killian caught Shiloh's amused thought that it was a good thing they had pictures of the baby on their phones, or they'd be in danger of the crowd stringing them up.

26

THE LAST THREE DAYS of Shiloh's visit passed by without incident. As well as helping to prepare for the harvest, Killian and Shiloh joined the other men on the estate in rearranging William and Carys' house so that when, she was allowed to come home, it would be as easy as possible for William to look after both his wife and his daughter. One of the young unmarried males, Gregorio, also volunteered to move in with the couple to help until Carys was on her feet again. Killian spoke with the young man's father, who vouched for his son's ability to manage a household, so Killian agreed on William's behalf.

After doing so, Killian had a niggling feeling that wouldn't go away, and he called Kelia. She was very curious when he asked her to bring the young woman she'd mentioned as a possible surrogate, as was Shiloh.

"What's up?" Shiloh asked, walking into the study. "I thought we agreed to wait?"

Killian shook his head, rubbing his neck. "I don't know. I just have this feeling that she needs to be here, now."

"So you haven't changed your mind?" Shiloh asked, confused.

"I wouldn't make that decision without you, Shiloh," Killian said softly. "This is something different, I think. Maybe it has something to do with why Kelia suggested her, because I didn't ask Kelia to find us a surrogate."

Shiloh walked around the desk and Killian turned in his chair, so Shiloh could sit in his lap. They sat quietly, cuddling. It was nice, comforting at a time when both were upset about Shiloh needing to return to Morgaine House.

Kelia called out from the front hall and Killian and Shiloh went out to meet them. The young Rimalian woman with Kelia was tall, broad-shouldered, and about sixteen or seventeen, Killian guessed. She had an odd kind of timidity, though, one that puzzled Killian; Rimalian women were usually extremely bold and confidant. Maybe it was the circumstances.

Kelia introduced her as Rylie Vallamei.

Rylie bowed slightly after a gentle nudge from Kelia. Giving Kelia a puzzled look, Killian and Shiloh led them to the study.

"I must apologize to you both, Killian, Shiloh," Kelia said as they sat down.

"Why?" Shiloh had quickly learned Kelia could be very prickly, but didn't necessarily stand on ceremony. She rarely apologized for anything, and with the power to back that attitude up, seldom needed to.

"I've brought Rylie under false pretenses." She patted Rylie's hand as if to reassure her. It was a gesture they often used with Jimmy, and Killian had the suspicion it was for the same reason. Kelia nodded, clearly catching the thought. "You're correct, however, Rylie isn't delayed in development, she's brain-damaged. Her mother contacted me about your need for a surrogate. I arrived to speak to her and found Rylie being treated in a way I consider abusive. I decided the easiest way to get Rylie out of there was to agree she would make an excellent surrogate candidate and convinced her mother to allow the girl to come with me."

Killian grinned. "Let me guess, you might have gently influenced that decision."

Kelia grinned back. "I might have. No one deserves to be treated like that. I'm hoping Rylie might find a safe home with one or the other of you."

Before she could say anything further, there was a knock on the door. Killian bid whoever it was to come in and William and Carys' helper, Gregorio, walked in carrying a handful of receipts. "Sorry, my Lady, but you asked that I bring you the receipts for the baby supplies and stuff, as well as—" He stopped, staring at Rylie as though dumbstruck.

Kelia, Killian, and Shiloh watched as he dropped the receipts in his hand and moved towards Rylie. She flinched back a little and he knelt in front of her.

"Shh, Rylie, I would never hurt you. No one will hurt you anymore, *Miisen*."

"What about *Senki*, Gregorio?" she asked haltingly.

Gregorio pointed first at Killian, then at Kelia and Shiloh. "He is my *Artris*, and they are *Artris* as well. They are powerful people, more powerful than your *Senki*. You are my *Miisen*, and if you wish to stay with me here, your *Senki* can't force you to leave."

When Rylie reached out slowly, Killian noticed a fine tremor in her hand; he wondered if it was normal for her or from the shock of bonding with her lifemate. She touched Gregorio lightly, and the most brilliant smile Killian had ever seen graced her face, matching Gregorio's.

Kelia, Killian, and Shiloh couldn't help but smile as well, basking in the sheer joy the two broadcast, happy tears in their eyes. This was how it should be when lifemates met.

Killian stood and walked over to the pair, drawing them to their feet and ushering them to the door. "Go on, Gregorio, take the rest of the day. Rylie is welcome to live here as long as she wishes. Go get to know each other."

"But my Lady, what about—"

"Don't worry, I've got the receipts, and William and Carys don't come home with the baby for a few more days yet," Killian said with a smile. "There's time yet. Go on."

"What exactly happened to her?" Shiloh asked after the other two left, hand in hand, glowing. "And how was she being abused?"

"The abuse is subjective, I'm afraid. Just constant belittlement and teasing with a very cruel edge to it. Most people wouldn't think twice but she takes everything to heart, believes all of it. As for what happened to her, she survived a cattle stampede, of all things."

"A cattle stampede?" Killian asked. "How old was she?"

"She was about ten years old and doesn't remember a thing of it, but she suffered several blows to the head as well as other severe injuries," Kelia told them. "Needless to say, the head injuries addled her wits. It was three years before she was declared as healed as she was going to get. She had to re-learn to walk, feed herself, all of it. She starts shaking when she's overtired, and she gets frustrated when she doesn't understand things. Something told me to go ahead and call you about her— I guess now I know why. I had planned to ask Catan to take her in if you weren't interested."

Killian laughed. "I was going to tell you we weren't looking for a surrogate right now, but I had a conversation with Gregorio and his father this morning and I just had this funny feeling."

Shiloh shook his head. "You know what they say; Deity works in mysterious ways."

"Well, I think Deity definitely had Gregorio in mind for her," Kelia said softly, chuckling. "He's exactly what she needs."

"How old is she?" Killian asked.

"Chronologically, she's nineteen. Developmentally, it is harder to pin down. I would suggest you have a complete assessment done. I already made arrangements for one. All you have to do is see that she keeps the appointment." Kelia shook her head. "I think she would develop more with the right environment and care, but I'm not qualified to make that assessment. I don't have that kind of training."

"Who am I dealing with for that?" Killian asked.

"Michaela," Kelia answered.

"How much trouble is her mother going to be?" Killian asked. "Will I need to formally petition for custody of her?"

"Given the woman thinks Rylie's only useful as a brood mare, who knows? However, the woman is avaricious, so if she planned on selling Rylie as a surrogate ... It could go either way." Kelia answered. Her cell phone rang. "Speaking of." She answered the phone. "Hello, Jackie." Kelia put her finger to her lips and put the phone on speaker.

"Have you introduced Rylie to Lady Larrestes and Lady Zahirris?" Jackie asked, without much in the way of courtesy.

"As a matter of fact I have," Kelia replied blandly.

"Good, tell them that the cost of her services is two hundred thousand per pregnancy and they pay her upkeep during pregnancy. I believe that's quite fair."

"And if they decide to go elsewhere, Jackie?" Kelia asked.

"Well I'm sure there are others around that will pay appropriately for her services. After all, that's about all that works on her and she needs to do her part to earn her keep, same as everyone else in this family," Jackie answered. "Bring her back here if they don't want her."

"You just crossed the line, Jackie," Kelia told the heartless woman with a pleased smile for Killian and Shiloh.

"What do you mean, 'crossed the line'?" Jackie asked. "I'm her mother. It's my job to make sure she's provided for. Since she's incapable of making money in any other fashion, this will support her well, as well as help support us, since we've been paying for her for so many years. You think she's cheap to look after?"

"You are correct in that it is your job to provide for her until she can provide for herself, but given her condition, that may be the rest of her life," Kelia said. "There's no time limit on maternal duty, Jackie. You may not, however, sell her like a brood mare. Such a thing is specifically banned by the Council. I had hoped you wouldn't do something like this but since you have, please present yourself to Council at the quarterly meeting after harvest. As Lady Larrestes has already offered Rylie a home on his estate for as long as she wishes, I am assigning guardianship of Rylie to him until Council decides her placement."

"You can't do that!" Jackie sputtered.

"Yes, I can," Kelia retorted. "I will be contacting your *Artris* and I will tell her what I've done and why. Since Rylie is not capable of looking after herself at the present time, any *Artris* may act on her behalf. I do not believe that returning Rylie to you serves her best interests. You may make your arguments to Council."

"And if Council sides with me?"

"Then Rylie will return to you with her *Miisen*," Kelia said.

"*Miisen*?" Jackie asked, a puzzled tone to her voice. "She doesn't have a *Miisen*."

"She does now. They have just met, and it is the reason Lady Larrestes offered her a home if she wished. Rylie had not yet made a decision, but that is now out of her hands. Good day, Jackie." Kelia hung up and sighed heavily. "Americans have many good qualities, but sometimes they influence those of us who live among them far too much."

"In what way?" Shiloh asked. He'd grown up in the States and didn't think he'd been unduly influenced.

"The belief that anything and anyone that doesn't make money every minute is worthless," Kelia replied, frowning. Killian rose to pour three small glasses of brandy, handing one to Kelia and one to Shiloh, sipping his as he sat back down beside his husband. Kelia sipped hers, and tipped her head back, rolling her neck to relax the muscles. "Stupid bitch."

"Now, my Lady," Shiloh said, "that's an insult to the real bitches—she's not smart enough to be one."

Kelia chuckled. "You're right, little one." She winked at Killian. "You've got quite a smart male there."

"Am I supposed to do anything but agree with that?" Killian asked as Shiloh elbowed him. "Are you trying to get me in trouble, lady?"

They all shared a laugh. Killian offered Kelia a room for the night and she accepted. "I'll take you back to Morgaine House in the morning, Shiloh."

Shiloh's jaw dropped. "You can do that?"

"Yup, but don't discuss it," Kelia replied. "Very few know I'm that strong already. The theory is, since one of my lifemates is capable of it, my mind caught on to the trick sooner."

Killian and Shiloh both were surprised, but they just nodded. *Sennrojai*, being so powerful and developing such scary abilities as they grew older, tended to keep low profiles. It wasn't unheard of, after all, for a group of scared people to get together and try to kill a *Sennrojai*. Such a thing was mostly attempted when the *Sennrojai* was quite young and as vulnerable as anyone else was.

Killian offered Kelia his study so she could make the appropriate calls about Rylie. He and Shiloh went out to check the day's progress and spend a little time alone.

•   •   •

Killian closed the bedroom door behind him, smiling as he watched Shiloh. They went to bed early, after Kelia assured them she didn't need to be entertained and that they should go on. She understood they were newly married and rarely saw each other.

Shiloh sat on the bed cross-legged, brushing his hair. Killian climbed up behind him and took the brush, slowly brushing out Shiloh's hair, savoring the feel of the heavy black silk. He had noticed when they woke up in the morning that their long hair, flung out above their heads, often piled up on the pillows so that you couldn't tell his from Shiloh's. Somehow, it never tangled together, though, which Killian found interesting.

When he was done with Shiloh's hair, Shiloh took the brush and started in on Killian's. Killian hummed in pleasure. He loved this time of night. They were slowly developing intimate routines for themselves, things like brushing each other's hair before bed. Shiloh laid the brush aside and began to knead Killian's shoulders, leaning forward and pressing a kiss on the nape of Killian's neck.

Shiloh's hands slipped under Killian's shirt, sliding forward to tease Killian's nipples. Killian leaned back against his husband, letting him play.

"Too many clothes, love," Shiloh whispered as he kissed Killian's throat.

They slowly undressed, and Killian gently pushed Shiloh onto his back. Kissing his way over Shiloh's body, he hummed against Shiloh's skin, knowing he loved the way it felt. Shiloh sighed, relaxing underneath him. They moved slowly, languidly touching.

Killian drew Shiloh up on his knees and then turned him, drawing Shiloh's back to his chest, encouraging Shiloh to rest his weight on him. He played with the delicate little gold hoops that decorated Shiloh's nipples, smiling as Shiloh moaned for him, enjoying the echo of pleasure in his own nipples. Shiloh felt so perfect in his arms and he moaned as Killian continued to play and tease, gently biting the nape of Shiloh's neck.

Then he slowly pushed Shiloh forward, licking his spine, kissing it, until Shiloh was on all fours. He followed Shiloh's spine, down into his crease, licking and nuzzling, until he reached that tight little hole. He licked at it, smiling as Shiloh cried out softly. His husband tasted tangy, a little sweaty, good. He feasted as it relaxed, then began to press his fingers in. Shiloh managed to reach for the lube on the nightstand and passed it back to Killian, who kissed his hole in thanks, giving it another lick. Shiloh shivered and moaned, making Killian smile more. They shared the pleasure they were both experiencing back and forth, but instead of igniting a blaze that consumed them before they could think, it was a slow burn where every touch was heightened. Killian took his time stretching Shiloh, kissing and biting the round cheeks in front of him, playing with Shiloh's balls gently.

Finally, he sank into Shiloh, using his hold in Shiloh's hair to gently pull his husband back to sit on his thighs, impaling him. Shiloh's breath caught as Killian bit his neck again, sucking up a deep mark, one that would be there for days. They began to move in tandem, Shiloh's head resting on Killian's shoulder as Killian fucked him, slowly beginning to move faster. He played with those delicate hoops again, then slid his hand down Shiloh's stomach to grasp that beautiful prick, gently brushing Shiloh's hand away. He stroked in rhythm with his thrusts, still playing with Shiloh's nipples with his other hand, wanting nothing more than to drive him out of his mind with pleasure. Shiloh's soft moans became mewling cries as one of his hands reached up to sink into Killian's hair, holding his head to Shiloh's neck as the other gripped Killian's hip. They moved together, coming together as Shiloh's body threw itself over the cliff, flying, drawing Killian after him.

They knelt, still connected, breathing heavily, ecstasy echoing through their minds as Killian wrapped his arms around Shiloh, tears slipping down his cheeks as he buried his face in Shiloh's hair. Shiloh's hand stayed in his hair as the other arm held Killian's arms tight to his chest, not wanting to be loosed any more than Killian wanted to let him go. Killian carefully laid them on their sides, somehow managing to stay inside Shiloh, drawing the blanket over them. They spoke of their love as they fell asleep. Throughout the night, they woke up and made love again and again.

27

A WEEK LATER, Killian was tired as he walked home from visiting William and his family. Carys was recovering well, but Shiloh had called it when he said she wouldn't take being bedridden well. The two doted on little Tia, who had everyone wrapped around her fingers. Gregorio and Rylie both moved in with the couple and it turned out that Rylie was a natural nanny; Killian kept that in mind. Right now, childcare on the estate was shared between those males old enough to be responsible and the fathers, depending on their duties on the estate. He wondered if it would be less stressful for his families if he set up a little daycare. Nobody seemed to mind sharing the babysitting—in fact, he himself often helped, either going over to the tenants' homes or they dropped the children off with him, depending on needs. However, if he had a tenant naturally inclined to babysitting, then it might be a good way to allow her to feel useful without overburdening her. Michaela was coming to assess Rylie next week. He would wait and see how that turned out, maybe he would discuss it with Michaela. The whole estate was planning to throw a party, not only to celebrate little Lucretia's arrival and

Carys' well-being, but the harvest, and Killian's marriage as well. Since there was so much to celebrate this year, they were planning to have a blowout party, with the whole village and neighboring estates invited.

Killian had laughed when he called to tell Natalya that apparently it was his "turn" this year. It was a fact of life in their little enclave that every year, one estate or another threw a huge shindig, inviting everybody, yet not one of the estate owners ever said, "Let's have a party." The estate owners and managers all suspected a conspiracy among the tenants, but they just looked the other way and paid for the party. It was fun and their people enjoyed the opportunity to mix and mingle in ways they didn't normally have time for. There was often a rash of Hunts after the harvest parties, since they gave the young, unmarried members of their community a chance to hang out under the watchful eyes of their elders, without quite so many restrictions.

This year was going to be a masquerade, and all of his tenants were quite excited about it. Killian decided he needed to go to the village tomorrow to see what there was to find for costumes. It would be fun to tell Shiloh about the masquerade tonight when he called his husband.

Killian absently fingered the slowly fading love bite on his throat, just at the collar of his shirt. Shiloh had left that one the morning he'd returned home. He grinned as he thought of their lovemaking in the shower that morning. They had been shocked when they finally made it downstairs and found Kelia had cooked breakfast. She'd laughed at them and said that just because she was a female, it didn't mean she couldn't cook.

He walked inside and sighed. It was so lonely in the house these days, and he missed having his siblings with him and Shiloh next to him every night. The first week away from Shiloh was always the hardest. At least Araminta was coming home for a few months in two weeks' time. And at the end of next summer, Jaden and Jimmy would be spending a year with him on his estate, so he would have them underfoot and Shiloh would be the one suffering with an empty house.

Killian sighed; it wasn't what he or Shiloh wanted, but it was the best solution they could devise. They just kept reminding each other it wasn't forever. That brought his thoughts back around to Rylie and Gregorio as he went upstairs.

Lady Vallamei had called, asking to visit and meet with him about Rylie. It had been a pleasant enough visit yesterday; Rylie had been happy to see her grand aunt, who had always treated her kindly, if very much as a child. Rylie didn't seem to mind but Gregorio had become upset.

Gregorio had informed Lady Vallamei that if she'd bothered to spend a little more time with Rylie, she'd realize Rylie wasn't a child, regardless of her injuries. Apparently, Lady Vallamei had been told that because of her injuries, Rylie would forever be at the mental capacity of about a six- or seven-year-old. Killian spoke up at that point, telling her that in the limited time he'd spent with Rylie, he'd place her at about ten years of age. Lady Vallamei had been very surprised and asked if Killian would forward a copy of Rylie's assessment to her. Happy that someone in her Clan cared, he'd agreed to authorize Michaela to also make reports to Lady Vallamei. Upon finding out Gregorio would reach fourteen in four months, Lady Vallamei suggested that it might be best to give Gregorio custody of Rylie in the long run. Killian smiled to himself as he recalled the stunned look on Gregorio's face at her comment. It was really nice to know that Rylie and Gregorio would have Lady Vallamei's support.

Killian walked into the bathroom, stripping, then turning on the water. A good hot shower, call Shiloh, then sleep for a while. He and Shiloh both slept very little when they were separated, waking up searching for each other in the bed several times a night. The searches often led to oddly timed phone calls. The exciting life of an *Artris* didn't help, he thought with a rueful smile. Stepping into the water, he sighed as the hot water began to ease the tension in his shoulders. He washed quickly, then reached down within himself and touched Shiloh while stroking his erection, grinning as Shiloh responded in kind. Whatever his gorgeous husband was doing, he must be alone. He quickly stroked himself, not needing much to bring himself off when he could feel Shiloh doing the same thing and sharing between them how good it felt. Memories of Shiloh's mouth on him, sucking and licking, sent him over the edge. He came hard, calling Shiloh's name, then slid down the wall of the shower, breathing hard.

He felt Shiloh's tender touch and smiled to himself, sending Shiloh back his intention to call in a few minutes. He rinsed off and climbed out of the shower, drying off. He thought about putting his sleep pants on, but decided not to bother and wrapped a towel around his hips instead. If this call was like most made between them at night, phone sex was happening and he'd need another shower anyway.

Humming to himself, he walked back to his bedroom. Killian had just bent down to retrieve his cell phone from his pants when he heard an odd sound. Turning, he flinched back instinctively, mentally shouting *"ANAN!"* in horror as he saw a bat swinging at his head.

28

WHEN KILLIAN CAME TO, he was freezing cold, and naked. His wrists were bound and attached to some kind of hook in the ceiling. His feet were chained tightly to the floor. Looking around as much as he could, he concluded that he seemed to be in some kind of dungeon. There were chains on the walls and there was an odd, fusty scent in the room.

Laughter sounded behind him.

"Oh good, you're finally awake," a horribly familiar voice said. Killian struggled not to flinch as Anan ran her hand over his back, pinching his bare ass. She walked around to face him.

"I didn't think you were suicidal, Anan," he said calmly. He couldn't panic or think about what Anan might have seen in the shower, since she'd apparently been lying in wait for him. "You know the penalty for ignoring the ban is death." He had to stay calm or he wouldn't survive. The lack of clothes made it a little more difficult, though.

Anan smirked. "Only if I'm caught, and since no one even knows you're gone ... Well, I have plenty of time to teach you a lesson or two before I kill you." She smiled as she slapped his face, hard. "They might eventually find your body, but they'll never know what happened." This time she punched him in the stomach.

He wanted to throw up when he saw her pick up a flogging whip. "Your first lesson will be how it feels to be whipped. You know, you really should lock your doors. Of course, for you it's a moot point, but still. It was so easy for me to slip in during the day and just wait." She struck at his legs with the whip. It was all he could do not to scream as it bit into his skin. Then she ran the handle of the whip down his chest and stomach, brushing it over his groin. "I watched you in the shower ... you're actually quite something when you touch yourself." Anan walked around him as she gloated. "Maybe if you do it for me in a little while, I'll just cut your throat instead whipping you bloody and leaving you to hang there until you die. Although, bleeding to death might take you a couple of days, even if it is hastened by dehydration." Anan struck him again, this time squarely on his back. Blood begin to trickle down his spine, but he didn't cry out.

He reached down within himself to find Shiloh. Panicked relief spread through their link. He tried to calm Shiloh's babble, but Anan struck him with the whip again, this time over his abdomen. Apparently, this hit was not quite as hard since he didn't feel blood seep down his skin. Shiloh felt his pain, though, and pleaded for information on where he was. But he didn't know where he was, he just knew who took him.

"You know, if you hadn't acted like such a prude five years ago, we wouldn't be here right now," Anan said conversationally. "But no, you didn't know how to behave, despite what Janet assured my mother and I. You cost me everything, so I'm going to take everything from you."

Anan struck his legs hard with the whip again, and then took a dagger and sliced his cheek deeply enough to bleed freely. "Once I'm done teaching you a lesson, I'm going to capture that little slut you married and teach him his place, as well."

Killian struggled to concentrate on what Anan was saying and pass the information to Shiloh. He pulled against the chains.

Anan laughed. "Maybe I should do it before you die. It would be good for him to see what's going to happen to him."

She struck him with the whip again; this time the leather wrapped around his lower back, the tip digging into his skin right above his flaccid cock.

Refusing to give her the satisfaction, Killian bit his lip to keep from crying out. He knew she wanted him to break before she killed him, he could feel it even with his limited senses. Her eyes revealed nothing but rage and hatred.

Anan caressed his cheek, and then ran her hand down his body, cupping his genitals, giving them a squeeze. She laughed at the shudder he couldn't completely repress.

"Oh, a new game to play." She gave him a few strokes, trying to get him hard, frowning when he remained flaccid.

Did she really expect him to get hard for her? He hadn't when he was thirteen and untouched, what made her think she could get that result now?

Screeching, Anan punched him in the stomach before she picked up the whip again. "You'd better do better than that, Killian. You're my toy now, and you'll learn your place and how to behave before you die. The longer your lesson takes, the more you suffer." She struck him several more times with the whip, on his back and his legs, drawing blood again. "You might as well scream, no one will hear you, but it might make you feel better."

"How do you know no one will hear?" he managed to ask. If he could get her to tell him where they were, he could tell Shiloh who would undoubtedly tell the *Sennrojai*.

"You're all alone, Killian. Poor thing, your slutty husband not at home—probably fucking that pretty twink of a housekeeper—your freak siblings are gone, and you don't even have friends to come visit you." After one more strike with the whip, Anan began to touch him again, even reaching between his legs to fondle his hole. The caresses were worse than the whip and it was all he could do not to vomit. But if he retched in his current position, he might choke. He struggled against the chains again. "No one will even miss you for a day or two; after all, at this time of month, you're often doing paperwork just like every other *Artris*. Plenty of time for me to do what I want." With her fingernails, Anan scratched his penis, hard enough to make him want to scream at the pain but not draw blood. He fought not to black out. He knew he'd never wake up if he lost consciousness or retreated from reality. Deprived of her "fun," Anan would just beat him to death and go after Shiloh.

Which reminded him ... Killian warned Shiloh of her plan and felt him wanting to know where they were.

Pain seared him again as she struck him several more times with the whip to get his attention and then went back to fondling him.

Killian struggled to keep his voice steady as he spoke. "I know I was alone in the house but that still doesn't tell me why you think you won't get caught."

Picking up her dagger again, Anan sliced his other cheek with a smug laugh.

"How do you know you weren't seen taking me from the house?"

"Oh, but that's the beauty of it. We haven't left the house." She struck him again with the whip then pushed the handle between his butt cheeks. "Maybe I should fuck you with this. Could be interesting." She drew the blade down his back and he could feel blood flowing more freely now.

Struggling to draw enough breath, Killian pushed for more information. "What do you mean 'we haven't left the house?' There's no place like this in my house."

Anan stalked around Killian almost constantly, making it hard to watch her; he assumed her movements were so he wouldn't know where she'd hit next, or with what.

Anan punched him in the stomach again. When she went back to fondling him, dragging her nails over his sac, he promised himself a bleach scrub when he got out of this. *If* he got out of this.

Distancing himself from Anan's groping, he told Shiloh Anan claimed they hadn't left his house. Shiloh told him to hang on as Anan struck him with the whip several times in succession. Then he felt her carve something on the small of his back, just above his ass. He flinched when she caressed his butt possessively; her touch made him feel her insanity, her rage, and worst of all, her lust. "You look good with my name on your ass," she said before taking the whip to him again. "As for there not being a place like this in your house, I assure you there is—your mother's old playroom. She used to invite my mother and I to play with her toys in here. How did you think these chains and hooks got here all nice and convenient?"

"You lie," he said to provoke the woman. Her reaction would probably be painful, but it might tell him something too.

He was right about her response being painful. She scratched his penis again, this time bringing blood to the surface. She watched him greedily as he fought not to scream.

"I told you, you might as well scream. No one will hear you and the more you please me, the better off you'll be." Anan's backhand landed across his cheekbone and eyes, driving his head back. "As for this room, your mother converted it from a cell in the dungeon. If someone was home, they might hear your screams faintly, but you're all alone."

Anan slashed his chest with her dagger as he told Shiloh what she'd said. Killian clung to his husband's promises of immediate rescue as Anan continued to pour her insanity into her blows. Between the dagger and the whip, he was covered in so much blood he couldn't feel how much the new strikes bled.

What happened next took less than a minute but felt like a century. Shiloh, Kelia, Catan, Lucretia, and another woman he didn't know but assumed was a *Sennrojai* appeared behind Anan. Before Anan could strike him again or even realize they were no longer alone, Kelia stepped forward, grasped Anan's head, and gave it a quick, violent twist. Killian heard her neck snap.

Shiloh stepped up to him, touching his face gently. *I love you, Killian.* He chanted those four words over and over through their bondlink as the women took action.

The strange woman, who had eyes just like his, reached up and snapped the chains that bound him to the hook in the ceiling with her bare hands, much to Killian's and Shiloh's shock. As Shiloh steadied him, still repeating those four words, she knelt and did the same with the chains binding his feet.

Suddenly, everything began to spin. Killian grasped at Shiloh as he blacked out.

29

KILLIAN WAS IN AND OUT of consciousness for several days. Shiloh was with him every time he surfaced, refusing to let Killian withdraw into himself in pain and shame. He touched Killian constantly, even though he could feel that while on one hand, Killian craved the tender touch of his husband, on the other, Killian was repulsed by the thought of anyone touching him for any reason. He waited patiently in Killian's mind, repeating over and over that he loved Killian, that he wanted Killian, that it would be okay.

This time, when Killian awoke, Shiloh was scrunched alongside him on the bed, holding his hand, asleep. They had Killian propped up on his side, so as to put the least amount of pressure on his wounds. Killian studied Shiloh's beautiful face. He felt dirty, unworthy of this wonderful man.

"Bullshit," said a soft, accented, unfamiliar voice.

Killian looked beyond Shiloh and saw the strange woman who had helped rescue him. "Who ..." he swallowed around his dry throat. "You?"

"Daeanara Larrestes," she answered softly. She stood up from the chair she'd sat in.

He gasped in shock.

Shiloh began to shift, waking up in response to Killian's reaction. Daeanara touched Shiloh tenderly and he settled back to sleep, snuggling a little closer to Killian, breathing out a sigh that sounded like Killian's name.

"You're still alive?" he asked stupidly. Obviously, she was. The woman was right there, touching his face.

"Very few people know I'm still alive, child mine." As she touched him, the lingering pain in his head faded. He stared up at this woman, the only *Sennrojai* the Larrestes had ever produced. If memory served, Daeanara was over three thousand years old, yet she looked as if she might be only in her early seventies. A strong, healthy, active seventy-something. "Kelia is one of them. When your Shiloh told Kelia of the dungeon, which neither she nor Lucretia had any clue about, Kelia appealed to me. I knew exactly where to look."

He couldn't speak, so he thought loudly, *Thank you.*

You're welcome, child mine. She stroked his face affectionately. *I've watched you a long time, Killian. At every turn, you have acted with honor and courage, unlike your mother, who was a disgrace.*

You know what I've been through? Anger began to burn inside him. All he'd been through, and she did nothing? What about Jaden and Araminta? All they had suffered.

I would be angry if I were you, too, child mine. Unfortunately, as a Sennrojai, just because I see something happening, doesn't mean I'm able to do anything about it. Thankfully, sometimes I can reduce the damage a little, maybe even save a life. For instance, when Janet killed your father, Lucretia could hear your sister but didn't know who she was or where to look for her and your brother. Janet would have killed them by the time Lucretia could have found them. So I grabbed Lucretia and plopped her right in the middle.

Which saved their lives, Killian said. His anger drained away as he felt what she didn't express: the painful knowledge born of experience that sometimes preventing one tragedy led to a greater one; her belief that things—even horrible things—did have purpose, even if it was completely beyond human or Rimalian comprehension; that Deity had plans for all of Her children, plans that changed according to their choices. Some choices would lead them down to ruin and others would be their salvation, and there was no telling which way each person would go. Deity had given Her children free will, and She had to abide by it as well, which meant watching Her children hurt each other terribly, so She offered the only comfort She could: Love, in all its varied forms. *You really believe that?*

Yes, I talk to Deity a lot. After all, She's oftentimes my only company. She doesn't really answer me, per se, but sometimes I ask questions. Sometimes, when the answer is no, I sense the most crushing pain I've ever encountered, and sometimes, when the answer is yes, I feel incredibly warm, safe, and loved.

Do you always get an answer?

Oh, no. Most of the time, I get no discernible response at all. I don't think Deity ignores me; it just may mean I'm not ready for an answer. When I begged Deity for a reason to allow Hitler to live, after I'd seen what he and his cohorts would do, I was given a vision I still have nightmares about, a vision so terrible I think I nearly lost my sanity. I think only Deity's grace preserved my sanity. Many of my fellow Sennrojai experienced the same. Then She gave me other visions, of children born, of happy families, but to reach that good, Europe had to make it through the bad.

One of those children is your child, Killian. Your daughter. A daughter like me. You and your Sprite must guard her carefully because she will be strong-willed and powerful if she survives.

A daughter? Killian was stunned. A *Sennrojai* daughter? Deity help him. It wasn't unheard of for a *Sennrojai* infant to be murdered, along with the parents, in the belief that if the parents produced one such child, they could produce another.

Laughter greeted that thought. *I'm sure She will, if you let Her. Some of your help lies beside you, I believe.*

Killian looked at Shiloh. Even sleeping peacefully, he could see the signs of stress and fear in his husband's face.

He shuddered as he thought of Anan, glad she was dead, that she would never terrorize anyone again, but wished he didn't feel so violated.

It's only been a week, child mine, and you've been sleeping or drugged for and from surgery for much of it. Give yourself time, little one. You will heal, inside and out.

Surgery?

Plastic surgery, to remove some of the scarring that would have occurred if not attended to immediately. The doctor is brilliant, really. But he couldn't fix everything, so Shiloh made the decisions about what to remove. Anan's name from your skin was the first priority. The cuts to your face were quite easy to fix, according to the doctor, and some of the marks on your back were easily repaired. You will still be scarred, but you do not bear your tormentor's name, and your face won't show your ordeal. Shiloh knew you wouldn't care about your face, and neither did he, but there was no sense to leave them when they were, in the doctor's words, 'An easy fix.' In addition to that, I have worked to heal some of the worst injuries without scarring.

Since I can sense your fear about other things, because of what happened last time, there is no infection. The new scratches on your groin are almost gone already. You still have all the bits you had before. Physically, you are healing very well. The question is, are you going to let that creature destroy you emotionally?

I feel so ashamed. I didn't even mange to defend myself…

And when were you supposed to do that? Daeanara chided. *When you were unconscious? When you were chained hand and foot? You did the best you could, Killian. It was a sneak attack intended to make sure you couldn't fight back this time. The strength you displayed was more than impressive. Many would have broken, would have screamed, would have retreated within themselves until it was over, and they were dead. You stayed conscious and fighting as best you could until it was safe, and the threat gone. You not only managed to get Anan to give you the information you needed to save yourself and your husband, you warned him. That is something to be proud of.*

As for your very understandable sense of violation, I suggest you give yourself a little time and many hot baths with Shiloh to help you feel clean, and then you two should make new memories to exorcise that sense of violation. You are not the only one who suffered through the assault. Shiloh will need to heal every bit as much as you.

Something else occurred to Killian. Didn't she realize I could get help? That I have a bond with Shiloh?

Daeanara sighed and shook her head.

None of us have a clear answer for that. Some people are blinded by their anger and hatred, and Ana was very much such a person. But it is also possible that being psi-null herself, such bonds are just not something she ever considered in any of her behavior. Perhaps she thought that even if you had a bond, it wouldn't enable you to get help, since she'd taken such care to keep you ignorant. You really were quite clever in managing to manipulate her into giving you more information.

Daeanara leaned down and kissed Shiloh's head, and then kissed Killian's forehead. "I love you, child mine. And I've come to love your little Sprite. You have a lot of happiness ahead of you, if you're willing to work for it." She touched his temple, and he could feel her encourage his body to sleep. "I'll visit again later, child mine."

As Shiloh snuggled closer, Killian's eyes closed. He touched Shiloh's face, breathed in the sweet scent of his husband, and let sleep take him.

30

W HILE KILLIAN REMAINED in the hospital on Rimalia, Shiloh ordered the dungeon be thoroughly searched and then sealed. One of the tenants, an archaeology student, had objected and requested that it be studied before being closed away. Shiloh decided it could be studied after Killian's death. Until then, it was to be sealed and remain that way. He understood it was important to know the full history of the house, which had sat on the same piece of land in one form or another for over fifteen hundred years, but Killian's well-being was far more important.

Shiloh stayed with Killian, taking care of his husband while he healed. During Killian's hospital stay, he fed and bathed him, ensuring Killian's modesty was protected as much as possible. When Killian had to let the doctor and *Tii-su* do their thing, Shiloh held Killian's hand through it all, never leaving Killian alone for the procedures. Every night, he slept beside Killian, holding his hand against the nightmares.

Killian had learned the cosmetic surgeon was an outsider—a human—but he was also one of the most respected and brilliant people in his field on the planet. He was also a very forgiving man, and even tried to refuse the reparations the Council assigned him for their semi-kidnapping of him. When he'd seen the damage done to Killian, he had quite understood that time had been of the essence, and he was quite willing to keep silent about Rimalia and its people. After all, it involved a patient's confidentiality. His understanding meant he now had a whole new pool of patients. Quite a few Rimalians were impressed with his work on Killian and had already made appointments via his office to get consultations about their own scars. A few of the *Tii-su* trainees had even become interested in reconstructive surgery, a specialty that Rimalians had not actually thought to offer training for, since Rimalians tended to consider scars as just part of life. Any other kind of reconstructive work was simply arranged for on an as needed basis. Dr. Flynn agreed to help those trainees find the right schools, when they completed their training on Rimalia.

After three weeks, Killian was allowed to go home to his estate, Shiloh going with him. Whenever Killian began to feel dirty and unclean again, Shiloh would draw a bath and help Killian into it, either sitting beside the tub and helping Killian scrub every bit of skin, or climbing in and holding Killian, washing them both tenderly.

Lady Masrei brought Jaden and Jimmy home to them. Araminta and the boys frequently crawled into bed with Shiloh and Killian, this time to comfort the two adults. Shiloh managed the harvest for Killian, since he wasn't recovered enough to do so, and frequently called Sherry to make sure things were going well at Morgaine House in the US.

By the time the harvest party came around, Killian was feeling much more himself. Intense therapy with *Tii-su* helped him begin to move past the trauma, and Shiloh's unwavering love and acceptance was a balm for his spirit he didn't know how he'd live without. Daeanara visited twice more, but only when they were alone. Killian discovered his ancestress was a funny woman, and he and Shiloh enjoyed her visits, although they understood why Daeanara hid herself away. Too much contact with people caused her pain, because she saw too much about them and the things they might go through.

The masquerade had been put off until the next year; his tenants insisted there wasn't enough time for people to find or make the perfect costumes, but Killian was fairly certain it was so he would be more comfortable this year, knowing for certain who was who. He said nothing, though. He just went along with the story, grateful his tenants cared so much about him. They truly were wonderful people. Two days before the party, the men stormed the house, sending Killian and Shiloh to William and Carys to stay while they cleaned the house from top to bottom; for those who came to the party and wouldn't be in any condition to leave and many of the rooms hadn't been used in over a year.

The harvest party was the huge blowout it was promised to be, with everybody in the enclave coming. Children ran amok, chasing each other everywhere; young adults flirted under amused, watchful, older eyes; and full adults indulged in a little excess, knowing their children were safe. Everyone ate, drank, and were very merry. Friendships were created or renewed, and life celebrated.

Never far from each other, Killian and Shiloh danced most of the night.

Showering together later that night—or early the next morning—Killian watched Shiloh. They hadn't made love since the attack. Killian would have assumed Shiloh didn't want him anymore, but he caught too many instances of frustrated, suppressed lust, images of the things they had done in the past and that Shiloh wanted to do again. As his body responded to Shiloh's unsuccessfully suppressed interest, he knew he could finally give his husband what they both needed. He gently turned Shiloh around after washing his back for him and tipped Shiloh's face up, tenderly kissing his Sprite.

Surprise, then need, poured through their bondlink as Shiloh kissed him back hungrily. *Please.*

Oh yes, Sprite, I want, too, Killian replied.

Shiloh turned the shower off, grabbed towels for both of them, quickly drying Killian, then himself. Then he took Killian's hand and led him to bed.

Killian climbed up on the bed, as Shiloh rummaged around in the nightstand for the lube. Shiloh crawled up beside Killian, drawing him closer until he was on top, kissing him thoroughly.

When they came up for air, Shiloh looked into Killian's blue eyes. "Trust me, love?"

"Always, Sprite," Killian replied softly. He kissed Shiloh again, needing the taste of his husband.

"Then lay on your stomach," Shiloh said softly. Killian hesitated, knowing what Shiloh was going to do. He was still self-conscious about the scars on his back. All of his scars, actually, but most of the worst ones were on his back. Shiloh had used a smartphone and taken a picture of his back to reassure Killian that Anan's name had been removed. Until then, Killian hadn't been able to really accept it, despite the fact he knew you couldn't lie when speaking mind-to-mind. Dr. Flynn assured him most of the scars would fade in time. However, some of them would be permanent.

Shiloh watched him, waiting patiently. Killian could refuse or he could agree, it was up to him. As Killian lay down on his stomach, he heard Shiloh's sigh of relief and felt the emotion in his mind.

What Shiloh did first surprised him. He moved so he covered as much of Killian's body as possible, laying his head between Killian's shoulder blades to drop a soft kiss on the skin and caressing Killian's arms and shoulders, encouraging Killian to relax, to let everything go. Killian could feel Shiloh's erection against his legs but Shiloh did nothing about it. He just lay there, slowly massaging Killian's arms and shoulders, leaving his head pillowed between Killian's shoulder blades. Killian gradually relaxed, enjoying the feel of Shiloh's weight and warmth at his back. He could also feel Shiloh's relief at being so close to Killian: Shiloh had needed to touch his husband for so long, and finally he could. Killian tried to apologize but Shiloh shushed him, telling him it was okay, Killian was worth any wait, worth everything.

Slowly, Shiloh began to rub his cheek over Killian's back, gradually lifting himself in order to move, gently nudging Killian to spread his legs to give Shiloh room to kneel between them. Feeling exposed, Killian held still as Shiloh leaned over him, dragging his loose hair over Killian's skin, drawing a shiver from him. Shiloh inched down so he could start at Killian's feet, slowly working his way up, covering every inch of Killian's body with kisses—even between his butt cheeks, taking a quick swipe with his tongue at Killian's hole—before moving farther upwards.

Killian began to moan and move restlessly. Pleasure fogged his mind, until all that existed was Shiloh and the pleasure he gave so generously. Shiloh nudged him over onto his back, and began at his feet again, kissing everywhere. Killian reached for his husband only to have his hands kissed and returned to the bed. *Shhh, just feel, love. That's what I want you to do, just enjoy.*

Sprite ...

Shhh, Killian, I love you, love this, love exploring you head to toe. Shiloh slowly sucked Killian's cock into his mouth, giving that aching length a few teasing sucks before moving lower to nuzzle the heavy balls hanging beneath, licking them, sucking first the right one, then the left, reveling in the small cries Killian made, the helpless movements. Then he reached for the lube, slicking his fingers.

Killian's mind was a haze of pleasure as a slim, callused finger pressed gently into him. He moaned and moved his hips, wanting more. Which he got when a second finger began to thrust inside him, grazing his gland, zinging him with electric bolts of lightning. Killian began to beg, vocally and through their bondlink, for more.

Please Sprite, I need you inside me. That plea earned him a third finger and Shiloh licking his rock hard cock with the same maddeningly slow deliberation he'd displayed all night. Killian reached down to flick Shiloh's nipple rings, knowing how good it felt to Shiloh. *Now. Shiloh, please, love, husband. Please ...*

Oh, yes, husband mine, now. Shiloh slicked his cock and pressed it into Killian slowly, never stopping until he was balls deep. They stared into each other's eyes as they kissed tenderly.

Yess... The ecstatic thought was shared as they moved together slowly, Killian's hips meeting Shiloh's, Killian groaning as every thrust pegged his gland. He ran his hands over Shiloh's back, his ass, into his hair, down his chest, flicking the hard nubs of his nipples. Everywhere he could reach, he touched. Killian was rewarded by Shiloh's hips moving faster, driving him higher and higher, closer and closer to the cliff.

Harder, more, Sprite. Please, harder. Killian begged and pleaded, mewling as Shiloh obeyed, moving faster until he was slamming into Killian's ass. Killian began to cry out with every thrust and reached for himself with Shiloh's encouragement. He stroked in time to Shiloh's thrusts and his whole body convulsed as he came, shooting hot seed between them. He was so lost in his pleasure, and Shiloh's as Shiloh came, he completely lost touch with reality, floating in a haze where nothing existed but the two of them. He could have stayed floating forever, and felt Shiloh's agreement that this was the only way to be.

A cold, damp object on his foot brought him abruptly back to reality, making him yelp as he yanked his foot back from the wet, inquisitive nose of one of Shiloh's girls. Shiloh began to laugh as all three dogs, who had been lying quietly on the floor, jumped up on the bed, wriggling, snuffling, and licking both Killian and Shiloh. Killian stared up into Shiloh's beautiful face and joined in his laughter.

Thank Deity for his Sprite.

And for snuffly puppies.

EPILOGUE

TWENTY-SIX-YEAR-OLD KILLIAN Larrestes Zahirris walked into his study to find his husband of eight years asleep in his favorite chair, their tiny, year-old daughter on his chest. Genetically, little Daeanara was Shiloh's daughter because they chose to fulfill the Zahirris Clan's need for an heir first, but in reality, it didn't matter to them. She was perfect. Shiloh had announced that next time, they should see what Killian came up with, and after that, if they wanted more children, just leave it up to nature. Killian had repeated Daeanara's prediction to Shiloh, and while they were scared for the child, they were determined to protect her.

Killian smiled as he looked down at his family. They had decided to go with an egg donor and a separate surrogate for the pregnancy, just to avoid any attempted claims on the child by another Family.

Jaden and Jimmy were quite settled, fully healed from their initial ordeal, although they were still inseparable. They had reached a point where they were trying to learn to at least be in different rooms. Jimmy had blossomed in Jaden's care and his ability to function increased, improving his diagnosis. He would always be slow, but he was happy.

Rylie had been found to be severely brain-damaged, which they already knew, but more than capable of learning, given the proper training and support. Gregorio, as her *Miisen*, had been given guardianship of her when he turned fourteen, it being unheard of for lifemates to abuse one another. Killian made sure Rylie received the help she needed, which Lady Vallamei insisted on helping to arrange, and Rylie had grown by leaps and bounds. She and Gregorio lived happily together, and Gregorio's fiancée got along quite well with Rylie, much to his relief, since he was madly in love with his fiancée. If Rylie hadn't liked the woman, there would have been problems.

Killian knelt in front of Shiloh, and ran his hand up the inside of Shiloh's leg. *Hey, Sprite, what'cha got there?*

A Spritelet, was Shiloh's sleepy response. Spritelet was Killian's pet name for their daughter, a happy, winsome baby with Shiloh's green eyes and thick, bright red curls that had to have come from the egg donor. Shiloh opened his eyes as Killian tenderly lifted their sleeping daughter into his arms, cradling her close.

"Come with me, Sprite, I have a surprise for you," Killian said softly with a smile. He kissed his daughter as he led the way out of the study. The years had taken their toll on Shiloh's girls. One had been hit in the head several years ago while defending Jaden and Jimmy, and had been so badly hurt Shiloh had decided it was best to put her down rather than make her suffer. Less than a year later, another had died of cancer. Then, three months ago, Jenny, had gone to sleep with them one night and never woke up. The girls lived good, happy lives, but each loss had torn at Shiloh, and he refused to get another dog. Thanks to their bondlink, Killian knew it was fear making that decision. He and Shiloh both missed playing with the girls and spending evenings petting them while cuddling on the couch.

Killian led Shiloh out of the house to where Keith, his wife, and his husband—a *Miisen* pair—and a very pregnant Sherry stood, holding wriggling puppies. Shiloh gasped when he saw the pups and Killian smiled as he felt Shiloh's pleasure. The pups were set down as Shiloh knelt, and they swarmed him, as dogs everywhere did. There was just something about Shiloh dogs were drawn to. Rescues from the local pound, only Deity knew what they were because no one else had a clue, but they had already been declared healthy, happy pups by the vet. Then Sherry's husband stepped forward with two kittens in his arms.

Shiloh laughed. "Pups and kittens?"

"Well," Killian said with an embarrassed shrug, "the kittens were on their last week of death row. I couldn't leave them there, could I?"

"You're such a soft touch," Shiloh said with a smile. He stood and reached for the kittens, who were quite happy to go to him, and weren't in the least concerned about the happy, yappy pups swirling around them. He drew Killian in for a kiss. "Thank you, love. You're right. It'll be good to have pups again."

Killian smiled. "Don't forget our little kitties. How much do you want to bet the cats rule the house within a week?"

Shiloh laughed and they all began to play with the new animals. When Daeanara woke, she was carefully introduced, then set down on the front lawn to play.

Shiloh snuggled under Killian's arm as they watched the menagerie. *I love you, husband mine.*

I love you too, Sprite.

About the Author

TN Tarrant is a hard-working single mom living in the wilds of Wyoming, who enjoys embarrassing her child with bright red lipstick prints to the forehead. When she isn't embarrassing her child, or hunting, killing, and dragging groceries home through the snow, she loves to write romantic stories with hot lovers. She suffers from a love of extremely bad jokes and has a tendency to inflict them on innocent bystanders.